The Asuras

A Dreamworld Odyssey

By

Neil Perry Gordon

Contents

Chapter 1 First Night 1

Chapter 2 Professor Dawson 5

Chapter 3 Monica Taylor 10

Chapter 4 The Vanguard of Purity 14

Chapter 5 Nightmare 21

Chapter 6 Going Lucid 27

Chapter 7 Coffee with Gus 31

Chapter 8 Flying Lucid 34

Chapter 9 The Rally 41

Chapter 10 Gateway 45

Chapter 11 First Contact 50

Chapter 12 Washington, DC 56

Chapter 13 Covenant of Freedom 60

Chapter 14 Dream Lab 67

Chapter 15 Past Lives 74

Chapter 16 The Vanguard Rally 80

Chapter 17 Fighting Back 85

Chapter 18 Riot 89

Chapter 19 Searching for Anand 96

Chapter 20 Gus's Tug of Conscience 100

Chapter 21 Gus Visits Monica 104

Chapter 22 Reunited 108

Chapter 23 A Shared Awakening 112

Chapter 24 The Akashic Records 115

Chapter 25 A Change in Gus 120

Chapter 26 Emma in Trouble 124

Chapter 27 The Gates 128

Chapter 28 Emma is Trapped 135

Chapter 29 An Audacious Plan 139

Chapter 30 Return to The Covenant 145

Chapter 31 Who is Gus Williams? 152

Chapter 32 A Pact 157

Chapter 33 Gus at The Vanguard 161

Chapter 34 Gus Is Taken 165

Chapter 35 Dreams for Humanity 172

Chapter 36 Day One 176

Chapter 37 A Fractured Sleep 180

Chapter 38 Searching for the President 184

Chapter 39 A Spiritual Strategy 189

Chapter 40 Prophecy Revealed 193

Chapter 41 Strategy Revealed 198

Chapter 42 The Three Loci 203

Chapter 43 Trek through Afghanistan 211

Chapter 44 Taliban 215

Chapter 45 Prison 220

Chapter 46 Dreams of Mahbouba 226

Chapter 47 Mullah Miracle 230

Chapter 48 A Detour 235

Chapter 49 Emma Returns 238

Chapter 50 Removed 241

Chapter 51 Put Under 245

Chapter 52 The Three Rivers 252

Chapter 53 The Sun Demon 259

Chapter 54 Emma's Soul 264

Chapter 55 Mother 269

Chapter 56 Searching for Gus 274

About the Novelist 277

Chapter 1
First Night

I stood in the heart of a moonlit forest. The air was thick with an otherworldly stillness, and the trees loomed like silent sentinels. In the distance, a pale glow emanated from a clearing, drawing me closer with an irresistible pull. With every step, the sensation of being watched intensified, as if unseen eyes bore into me.

I emerged into the clearing, and there, bathed in an eerie radiance, was a figure that froze my heart. It was Mother, her form almost translucent, as though caught between the realms of the living and the ethereal. She stood before a strange being, a creature that defied comprehension. Its form was a fusion of the grotesque and the alien, its presence sending a shiver down my spine.

Mother's voice, always a soothing balm in times of uncertainty, trembled as she spoke to the creature. Her words were a plea, a desperate attempt to understand the entity that loomed over her. But her voice was met with an eerie silence, as though the air around her had been robbed of sound.

As I watched, paralyzed by fear and disbelief, the being extended its hand, a hand adorned with appendages resembling elongated fingers. A sense of dread hung heavy in the air, and as Mother's eyes met mine, I saw a mixture of sadness, resolve, and an unspoken plea for me to understand.

And then, as if the fabric of the dream itself was woven with cruelty, the creature's appendages enveloped my mother's form. A brilliant light, blinding in its intensity, surrounded them both. I watched in helpless horror as her voice was silenced, her form dissolving into the luminous embrace of the alien being.

A scream welled within me, but no sound emerged. I tried to rush forward, to break through the barrier between us, but an invisible force held me in place. Mother's eyes remained fixed on mine until they, too, were consumed by the blinding light; and then, as suddenly as it had begun, the dream shattered.

I jolted awake, my body drenched in a cold sweat. My heart raced, and tears blurred my vision as I grappled with the relentless grip of lingering emotions. This was not unlike the countless nightmarish dreams that had haunted me throughout my life, though now I was without Mother to call upon and comfort me. Tonight marked my first night in the unfamiliar apartment on the campus of Harvard University, and Monica, my new roommate, slept soundly in the twin-size bed a few feet away. I briefly considered waking her, but the thought of revealing my inner turmoil to someone I had just met earlier that day gave me pause.

With a sigh, I swung my feet off the bed and sat up momentarily, gathering my resolve. The unsettling dreams had been a constant companion, infiltrating my nights with sinister tales. But Mother had always been there to soothe my fears, allowing me to seek refuge between her and Father in their comforting embrace when I was a child. Then, after Father's untimely passing due to a sudden heart attack, I never again found solace in her bed.

Standing up, I padded softly over to the window, my gaze fixated on the desolate courtyard of the sprawling apartment complex. Lamps cast a warm amber glow over the grassy expanse. Memories of the previous day flooded my thoughts—the farewell, the tears, and the unspoken worry exchanged between Mother and me.

"Oh, Emmashka." Mother's voice echoed in my mind, pulling me back to that emotional moment.

"I'll be fine, Mamashka," I assured her, my voice wavering with determination and uncertainty. Her embrace lingered as her tears fell onto my shoulder.

"There's nothing more I can say," she choked out, her voice heavy with emotion. "You'll be fine."

A ping from my phone interrupted our farewell, and I glanced down to see a message from Kyle. "You'd better get going; it's a long drive," she said, releasing me.

I sighed, trying to hide my nervousness. "Now, don't start. Harvard's only three hours away."

"Three and a half," Mother corrected, her eyes fixed on me with love and concern.

A smile tugged at my lips. "There's always Facetime," I reminded her, reaching for my bag.

"I'll walk out with you," Mother suggested, guiding me onto the front porch. The crisp air carried a bittersweet tinge.

As we waited, Kyle's voice broke the silence. "Oh, hi, Mrs. Zigler," he said, approaching us.

Mother's grip on my hand tightened. With her free hand, she raised two fingers to her eyes and pointed them toward the road—a silent reminder to my boyfriend to remain focused while driving.

"I promise," Kyle assured her with a chuckle, flashing his charismatic dimpled smile.

She patted his stubbled cheek affectionately. "You are the charmer."

I couldn't help but roll my eyes. "Stop it, Mother," I insisted, kissing her cheek one last time before hurrying toward the waiting silver Ford Edge parked at the curb. Pausing, I turned back to give her a last, lingering look. With a pained smile, I managed to say, "Love you, Mamashka."

"Love you, Emmashka," Mother replied, carrying pride and longing.

"Let's go, Emmashka," Kyle chimed in, his playful tone teasing our endearing terms of affection.

*

After settling me into my room, Kyle bid me farewell and returned to New Paltz. We had been a couple since our junior year at SUNY New Paltz. When I secured a full academic scholarship to Harvard, we mutually decided to pause our relationship while navigating our respective paths. Not that I intended to date anyone else—my focus was firmly fixed on my life's mission: countering the surging wave of fascism threatening world order.

Between the two options of pursuing a Master's degree in either political science or law, I found myself in a contemplative dilemma. A law degree would give me a profound grasp of legal frameworks, human rights intricacies, and social justice. Armed with such expertise, I could adeptly challenge and confront the ideologies and actions of the fascists through the channels of law. Becoming a human rights advocate or joining organizations dedicated to social justice would be within my reach. The prospect of instigating policy changes that counteracted the insidious influences of fascism also beckoned. My proficiency in navigating intricate legal difficulties would be a powerful tool to safeguard individual rights against the oppressive undertow.

On the other hand, a Master's in Political Science held its significance. It would provide me with a broader comprehension of political systems and ideologies—a panoramic insight into the structures fascism sought to manipulate. While it might not give the laser-focused legal acumen that law did, it had the potential to illuminate the broader spectrum of political undercurrents. Either path demanded years of devoted study, leaving me with little room for romantic entanglements. Besides, my tumultuous sleep patterns, disrupted by persistent nightmares, rendered the idea of sharing a night with a lover far beyond my realm of possibility.

Chapter 2
Professor Dawson

Sitting in my first class on modern politics, I listened intently as Professor Dawson, a tall, thin man wearing a worn, wrinkled linen coat that hung off his bony shoulders, paced back and forth at the front of the lecture hall. His passionate voice filled the air, carrying a sense of urgency that made it clear this was no ordinary academic discourse. He spoke of a world on the precipice, shifting tides, and mounting dangers that threatened to engulf us all.

A chill ran down my spine as he spoke of the autocrats who had risen to power with a calculated disregard for human rights. The names of the world's authoritarians seemed to reverberate with an ominous resonance, like the thunderous footsteps of a coming storm. Professor Dawson dissected their methods, their agendas, and the chaotic wake they left behind. He painted a stark picture of the fragile state of our global order, a tapestry fraying at its edges, where alliances strained and ideological divisions deepened.

"Look around you," he implored, his gaze sweeping across the room, seemingly locking eyes with each of us. "We're living in a time where the specter of fascism looms large, casting its shadow over our democracies. It's not a distant threat—it's here, right now," he said, pressing a finger downward.

He spoke of propaganda, misinformation, and manipulating public sentiment—a playbook of tactics wielded by autocrats to tighten their grip on power. His words resonated with a disquieting familiarity, echoing my fears and convictions. I clenched my pen, my knuckles turning white. This was why I was here: to arm myself with knowledge, to understand the intricate mechanisms of power and control so I could stand against them.

"Fellow scholars," he continued. "I implore you to cast aside any notions of detached academia. The topic transcends the confines of theoretical debate; it strikes at the heart of our existence, freedoms, and shared future. Today, we confront the rising tide of fascism—a force that, if left unchecked, threatens to dismantle the very foundations upon which our societies were built.

"Take notice. Fascism is not a relic of history relegated to dusty textbooks and black-and-white images. It is not a distant threat confined to far-off lands. It is a specter that haunts our present, weaving its tendrils into the fabric of our lives, institutions, and collective consciousness. Autocrats rise to power through a calculated manipulation of our fears, exploiting the fault lines of division, sowing chaos, and dismantling the institutions that once safeguarded our freedoms.

"We've seen the consequences in the pages of history—the devastation, the suffering, the loss of human potential. But we must not fall into the trap of assuming that we are immune, that our democratic ideals are invulnerable. The very nature of fascism is to corrode, erode, and subjugate. Even America, once a nation that proudly stood as a beacon of freedom, is now under the dangerous grip of a growing virus of autocracy," he said and paused to take a sip of whatever was in his thermos.

"Imagine, if you will, a world where dissent is silenced, media is controlled, and truth is a commodity bartered for power. Imagine a world where minorities, the marginalized, and the vulnerable are trampled underfoot, their voices stifled by a regime that thrives on division and hatred. Imagine a world where the principles of justice, equality, and democracy echo a bygone era.

"But, my students, imagination alone is not enough. We stand at a crossroads where complacency and inaction are tantamount to complicity. To defeat fascism, we must arm ourselves with knowledge that can dissect its mechanisms, expose its tactics, and lay bare its insidious propaganda. We must recognize that the battle is not fought on distant shores alone; it is waged within our communities, institutions, and within the chambers of power.

"Let me be clear: the stakes are dire," he said with an outstretched arm that swept across the lecture hall. "If we fail to rise to this challenge, if we succumb to the allure of apathy or the paralysis of indifference, we risk an unrecognizable future: a future where the ideals of democracy, justice, and human rights are nothing but distant echoes. A future where the flames of fascism consume the progress we've fought so hard to achieve.

"Our responsibility, as scholars, thinkers, and citizens, is to refuse the descent into darkness. We must be vigilant, courageous, and unwavering in our commitment to the values that define us. It's incumbent upon us to hold the line against the tide of fascism, to defend the principles that have shaped our societies, and to ensure that the legacy we leave behind is one of progress, freedom, and unity.

"So, my dear students, let this be a call to action, a rallying cry to stand against the encroaching storm. This battle against fascism is not for the faint of heart; it requires dedication, sacrifice, and an unyielding resolve. But know this—as you leave this lecture hall today, you carry the power to shape the course of history. The choice is yours. Will you be a passive observer or an agent of change? The future of humanity hangs in the balance, and we must ensure that the light of freedom, justice, and compassion continues to shine in even the darkest of times."

Professor Dawson's lecture, dissecting the rise and reign of these strongmen, reignited an unyielding resolve that already existed within me. The path I had chosen was affirmed in the most profound way possible. With every word, I felt the weight of responsibility deepen, and the cause's urgency magnified.

I glanced out the large classroom windows where the sun's warm glow over the sprawling campus starkly contrasted the dark narratives unfolding within these walls. And yet, there was a strange sense of alignment—a reminder that even in the brightest of times, shadows existed, lurking beneath the surface. Professor Dawson's lecture was a call to action, an urgent plea to confront the looming specter of fascism and the fragility of our shared humanity.

As the lecture concluded and my classmates began to file out, I remained in my seat momentarily, lost in thought. This was just the beginning, I realized. The battle against the rising tide of fascism would require more than just knowledge; it would demand courage, strategy, and an unwavering commitment to protecting the values we held dear.

As I gathered my belongings, my name was called out. When I looked up, Professor Dawson stared at me from the podium.

Surprised he knew me by name, I stood up.

"Ms. Zigler," he said again and, with a flick of his hand, summoned me to approach.

I smiled and walked down the steps. "How do you know my name, Professor?"

He looked over his glasses and said, "I've read your file and have been looking forward to having you in my class."

"You've read my transcript?" I said, wide-eyed.

"You have quite the reputation. It's not easy getting yourself noticed at a state college."

I couldn't help but feel a sense of surprise mixed with a hint of pride. My activism and writing had garnered local attention, but having a Harvard professor acknowledge it was a different level altogether.

"Thank you, Professor," I said, my nervousness giving way to genuine gratitude.

"Your insights are astute, and your passion is evident," he continued. "We need more voices like yours in today's world. Fascism is a dire threat that must be confronted head-on."

I nodded, his words resonating deeply with my convictions. "I believe that, too. It's a fight we can't afford to lose."

The professor leaned on the podium, studying me for a moment. "You have a real potential to make a difference, Ms. Zigler. Harvard has a history of nurturing leaders who shape the course of history. I have a proposition for you."

My heart quickened at his words. A proposition? From a Harvard professor?

"I'm teaching a course called *Global Resilience and the Fight Against Authoritarianism.* It's a select class with few students, but I believe your insights would be invaluable."

I sat there, almost unable to believe what I was hearing. A course focused on precisely what I was deeply passionate about. And he wanted me to be a part of it.

"I'm honored, Professor Dawson. Truly honored," I managed to say, with a hand over my heart.

He smiled, his eyes reflecting a genuine enthusiasm. "Good. I believe you'll find it an enriching experience. It's a platform to hone your understanding, engage in deep discussions, and forge connections with like-minded students."

"I'm in," I said without hesitation. "I'm ready to contribute and learn."

He extended his hand, and I shook it with purpose. "Welcome aboard," he said. "Let's work together to make a real impact against the tide of authoritarianism before it's too late."

I nodded and said, "Yes, I want that too."

Chapter 3
Monica Taylor

Walking across the storied grounds of Harvard's campus with Monica felt like stepping into a realm of intellectual wonder. The sun bathed the red-brick buildings in a golden glow, infusing the air with an aura of academic brilliance. Monica's animated chatter about her upbringing in New York City and her parents' psychology careers was a captivating introduction to the person who would become my roommate and, unexpectedly, my confidante.

Monica's eyes lit up as she shared her passion for the intricacies of the human psyche. Her enthusiasm was infectious, making me hang onto her every word. As I listened, I was drawn into her world, eager to learn more about the subject that deeply intrigued her.

In exchange, I shared my life's mission of opposing autocratic regimes and the spread of fascism.

The vulnerability in my voice was met with Monica's understanding nods and encouraging smiles. It was as if she saw the fire within me, the determination to fight against the looming darkness. Her unwavering support felt like a comforting embrace on this new journey.

As we walked beneath the canopy of trees, our laughter danced in the breeze, creating an atmosphere of shared camaraderie. The stories we swapped and the easy banter we exchanged felt like the building blocks of a genuine friendship. With every step, the walls of formality crumbled, replaced by a bond that transcended the surface level.

Stopping at John Harvard's iconic statue, a symbol of the university's legacy, Monica and I exchanged knowing looks. The statue stood as a testament to the knowledge and purpose cultivated here for centuries, and in that moment, it seemed to acknowledge our aspirations.

As we returned to our apartment, I felt a sense of belonging. Monica and I had ventured beyond small talk and shared anecdotes; we had glimpsed each other's passions and vulnerabilities. I felt a profound anticipation for the friendship that was taking root, for the connection that would shape not only our time at Harvard but also the trajectory of our lives.

Monica hailed from the Upper East Side streets of New York City. Her upbringing was deeply entwined with the world of psychology, thanks to her parents, both esteemed professors in the field at Columbia University. Growing up surrounded by discussions of the mind and behavior, it was almost inevitable that Monica would follow in her parents' footsteps. "They seemed to be okay with Harvard," she quipped.

But it wasn't until a few days later that I learned something about Monica that would directly affect my life.

"Emma, can I talk to you about something?" Monica's voice was concerned and curious as we sat at our kitchen table.

I looked up from my jumbled notes, my fatigue probably evident. "Sure, Monica. What's up?"

She hesitated for a moment, as if gathering her thoughts. "I've been noticing your sleep patterns, and it seems you've been having a tough time. Restless nights, right?"

I sighed, realizing that my struggles hadn't gone unnoticed. "Yeah, it's been that way my entire life."

"Are you serious?" she asked, wide-eyed.

"I have nightmares," I said with a shrug. "All the time."

"About what?" Monica asked, turning around from her desk chair.

I shrugged and said, "Monsters, mostly."

Monica stared at me, her blue eyes seeming to sparkle. "You know I'm studying for a Ph.D. in psychology specializing in the study of dreams."

I jerked my head back and said, "That's interesting. Maybe you can tell me what my dreams mean."

"Maybe I can do more than that," Monica offered.

"How so?"

"Have you heard about lucid dreaming?" Monica asked with a tilt of her head.

I raised an eyebrow, intrigued despite my weariness. "Lucid dreaming? What's that?"

Monica leaned forward, her eyes bright with excitement. "It's when you become aware that you're dreaming while still in the dream. You can take control, change the dream's direction, confront your fears—basically, you're the boss of your dream world."

My interest was piqued. "Wait, are you saying I could do something about my nightmares?"

She nodded, a small smile playing on her lips. "Exactly. Lucid dreaming could give you the power to stand up to those nightmares and even turn the tables on them."

I couldn't help but be skeptical. "Sounds almost too good to be true."

Monica leaned back, her enthusiasm tempered by understanding. "It might sound far-fetched, but it's grounded in science. I've been researching and practicing it myself, and I think it could be beneficial for you, Emma."

I crossed my arms, considering her words. "So, where do I even start with something like this?"

Monica's smile widened, sensing my curiosity. "That's where I come in. I can teach you techniques to realize when you're in a dream, to question the dream's reality, and eventually take charge. It's like discovering a hidden world within your mind."

A hint of interest stirred within me. "You're serious about this?"

She nodded eagerly. "Absolutely. I want to make a positive impact with what I'm studying. I'm all in if I can help you overcome those nightmares."

Gratitude swelled within me. "Thanks, Monica. I genuinely appreciate that, but I don't know."

"Emma, I've been studying lucid dreaming for a while now. I've even practiced it and seen how it can empower people to confront their fears and anxieties. I want to help you if you can give it a shot."

I looked into Monica's eyes, seeing the genuine compassion and determination. It was an offer of support I hadn't expected but one I yearned for. With a nod, I said, "Okay, Monica. I'm willing to give it a try."

A smile of satisfaction spread across Monica's face. "Great! But it won't be easy, and it'll take practice. I truly believe you can harness your dreams' power to fight back against your nightmares."

I tried to return a genuine smile and said, "Thank you."

She reached out to squeeze my hand reassuringly. "No need to thank me. We'll be good friends, and I genuinely want to help. We can work together to tackle those nightmares and give you some control of your life."

Monica's dedication and optimism were infectious. As she spoke about psychology and lucid dreaming, I felt a glimmer of hope. The idea of finally confronting my nightmares and regaining some agency in my dreams was daunting and exhilarating. With Monica's guidance, I felt ready to embark on a journey toward better sleep and a newfound sense of empowerment.

"Now," Monica said, reaching over to push back a lock of my stringy brown hair, "you need a bit of grooming."

I ran a finger over my bushy eyebrows and smiled. "I never have time for—"

"Nonsense," Monica interrupted. "You're gorgeous, and it's a shame to let it go to waste."

I chuckled. "Whatever you say."

Chapter 4
The Vanguard of Purity

Gently, I glided my open palm down the length of my dress, smoothing out a few stubborn wrinkles with a hint of satisfaction. Meeting my gaze in the mirror, I took a moment to appreciate the transformation. With Monica's unwavering guidance and a rejuvenating salon visit, I was elevated to a newfound radiance.

The persistent shadows that once lurked beneath my eyes had miraculously diminished, a feat I largely credited to the adept application of concealer, a skill Monica had generously shared. With a mixture of artful makeup techniques and insightful advice, I stood before the mirror, a testament to my newfound self-assurance and readiness to embrace the challenges ahead. Armed with these small and previously unused potent tools, I was ready to seize the world and its opportunities. However, where I was planning to venture out to was hardly a place where looks alone would be required.

Determined to understand the enemy firsthand, I had decided to attend the gathering of a fascist-leaning group calling themselves The Vanguard of Purity. This faction convened under the façade of academic exploration, cloaking their extremism in scholarly discourse.

I imagined the organization's name carried a dual meaning that resonated with the group's ideology. "Vanguard" signifies being at the forefront, leading the way, and acting as a pioneer for its purpose. In this context, it would imply that the members consider themselves champions of their perceived cause, which, in this case, was the propagation of their fascist and white supremacist beliefs.

"Purity" is a loaded term often associated with ethnocentrism and racial supremacy. It reflects the group's desire for a supposedly pure and homogeneous society, where they believe their race and cultural identity are preserved and dominant. The term is often used to mask discriminatory and exclusionary ideologies, as it suggests that anything outside a particular group's narrow definition of purity is impure or undesirable.

Thus, The Vanguard of Purity combined these elements to present the group as an elite and avant-garde force dedicated to preserving their perceived racial and cultural purity, even though such ideas are rooted in harmful and exclusionary beliefs.

A heavy sense of foreboding hung in the air as I stepped into the dimly lit room adorned with austere symbols that resonated with their toxic beliefs. The walls bore the weight of unsettling images, each a stark representation of the ideology that had drawn these individuals together. A banner at the front of the room displayed an emblem I didn't recognize—a sinister fusion of angular shapes and dark colors, clearly embodying the group's intent. It loomed ominously, casting a chilling shadow over the proceedings.

Intricate patterns, etched in deep crimson and obsidian shades, adorned these surrounding banners. They seemed to writhe and contort, mirroring the very ideas they symbolized, ideas rooted in discord, prejudice, and a drive to assert dominance. The Nazi-like symbols held a macabre allure, drawing the gaze in fascination even as they sent a shiver down my spine.

A wooden podium stood at the center of the room, its surface marred with carvings that resembled an amalgamation of ancient sigils. Though unfamiliar, these symbols exuded an air of mysticism, tainted by the group's obvious despicable intentions. The flickering candles that lined the room cast eerie shadows, amplifying their mystique while further heightening the sense of my unease.

The meeting attendees formed an unsettling tableau—a congregation united by their allegiance to a cause that left a bitter taste in the air. Poised at the podium was a white man with a short haircut and a groomed beard, both in a warm chestnut color; he held court with an air of authority, his demeanor rigid and unwavering.

"Ladies and gentlemen, we've gathered here today because we share a common concern—the fabric of our great nation is unraveling," the leader said. His words were delivered with calculated precision, and each sentence was punctuated with a sense of urgency and enthusiasm. "We're standing on the precipice, teetering dangerously. If we don't act now, we'll no longer recognize the America we once knew and loved."

He exuded a self-assured confidence stemming from beliefs as if he held the keys to an alternate reality that only he could comprehend. "We must return to the principles that made this country great. Principles like individual liberty, hard work, and a sense of community," he added. "My friends, these are not outdated notions; they are instead timeless values that are more relevant today than ever."

The speaker's eyes held a steely resolve that resonated with those who hung on his every word, seeking validation for their convictions. "But let's be clear, we don't have the luxury of time. Every day, decisions are being made that push us further away from these core values. We need to rally, and we must do it now."

In the sea of seats that stretched before them, the attendees listened intently, their expressions a mix of allegiance and agreement. Most were white men, their faces etched with anger and perceived victimhood. They seemed to be searching for a purpose to cling to, a scapegoat for their discontent. Some wore business suits that hinted at serious professional lives outside this dimly lit room, while others appeared rougher around the edges, their demeanor reflecting a hardened disposition, more blue-collar.

"We all have lives outside this room—jobs, families, responsibilities," the speaker concluded. "But this... this is about safeguarding the world we will leave for our children. And that's why The Vanguard of Purity must be the vanguard of change, of a return to true American values. We can't wait for someone else to take up this mantle. The urgency begs for action now."

Nodding of heads accompanied by exclamations of encouragement urged the speaker on.

"Let's take this message to the streets, workplaces, and homes," the speaker said, a final rallying cry. "Let's work to rebuild the America we know is possible before it becomes a land unrecognizable to us all."

Amidst the crowd, a few tough-looking women caught my eye. Their presence was a testament to the extent of this group's ideological grip. They bore the same grim expressions, their determination mirroring their male counterparts. However, despite their stern faces, something about them hinted at inner turmoil, as if their involvement in this gathering was not without internal conflicts.

As I observed from the edges, I felt detached—an innate aversion to the toxic energy that permeated the room. None of these individuals drew me in; their beliefs and convictions seemed like foreign entities, distant and uninviting. Instead, I felt a growing urgency to challenge their notions, to disrupt the very foundation on which they stood, and to stand as a bulwark against the wave of darkness that threatened to engulf both the physical and spiritual realms.

As I sat in the meeting, my thoughts whirled around the topic of discussion—a planned rally in downtown Boston to support the president's proposal of withdrawing from NATO—a campaign promise he made and planned to see through during his second term. The idea was to emphasize a focus on America's interests at home and to avoid entanglement in matters deemed beyond our borders. As I glanced around the room, I could see the divided opinions etched on the faces. Some appeared enthusiastic, nodding in agreement with the proposed stance, while others wore expressions of concern and skepticism.

As the speaker left the podium, my eyes drifted to his name tag, revealing "Gus Williams." He stood tall, his slender frame accentuated by piercing blue eyes. Strangely, his presence felt oddly familiar. As he descended the aisle, Gus passionately presented the case for NATO withdrawal. He echoed the president's perspective that reallocating resources and focusing on domestic concerns would benefit our nation economically. The discussion grew more profound, and I pondered the far-reaching implications of such a decision. The stability of international relations and the security of nations hung in the balance, and the notion of abandoning long-standing alliances left me with a sense of unease.

My mind flickered to images of news headlines and geopolitical tensions. I realized that this rally wasn't merely a casual gathering of ideas but a reflection of the broader currents shaping the world around us. As the debate continued, I leaned forward, intent on absorbing every viewpoint shared in the room. Many other supporters shared the decisions being made here.

While my focus remained on the discussions, my thoughts inevitably strayed to the urgency of my purpose in a world increasingly defined by complex political dynamics. The rise of divisive ideologies and the potential for misguided decisions only solidified my commitment to stand against forces that threatened the very fabric of humanity's interconnectedness. As I sat in that meeting, surrounded by passionate voices, I silently vowed to use my voice, however small, to challenge the course that led us away from unity and into isolation.

The room's intensity gave way to a collective sense of anticipation as the meeting wound down. The attendees began to disperse, mingling in clusters of whispered conversations. I stayed on the fringe, observing the dynamics at play, while my eyes occasionally met those of Gus, the charismatic leader whose presence seemed to command attention effortlessly.

Gus was not, in my opinion, your stereotypical fascist leader, at least not in appearance. He exuded a certain charm that was hard to deny. With his sharp features and disarming smile, he cut a striking figure. Yet, beneath the allure, a calculated determination betrayed a deeper purpose. I watched him engage in conversations, his body language confident and assured.

Moments later, our paths converged. Gus approached me with a subtle grin, his blue eyes locking onto mine as if trying to unravel the mystery behind them. "I don't think I've seen you around before," he remarked, his voice smooth and inviting.

I offered a tentative smile, my nerves surfacing as I met his gaze. "No, I'm new," I admitted, my tone betraying a hint of hesitation.

Gus looked at my hand-written name badge. "Hello, Emma. I'm Gus. President of The Vanguard," he said, offering his hand.

I gripped it and said, "Nice to meet you."

Gus leaned casually against a nearby wall, his posture relaxed yet attentive. "So, Emma, what brings you here?" he inquired, his curiosity genuine but laced with a hint of scrutiny.

I felt my heart race, my mind trying to formulate a response to deflect suspicion while keeping my true intentions concealed. "I suppose I'm just trying to understand different perspectives," I answered, my words carefully chosen.

Gus raised an eyebrow, his expression thoughtful. "Different perspectives, huh? You don't strike me as someone who's merely curious," he said, leaning in slightly, his gaze searching my face for any signs of vulnerability. "Are you a supporter of our cause?" he asked pointedly.

My pulse quickened, and I hesitated, racing for a plausible answer. "I wouldn't say I'm a supporter, per se," I replied cautiously. "I'm more interested in delving into the ideologies that motivate people."

Gus seemed intrigued by my response, his lips curling into a half-smile. "Ah, you're a deep thinker, then." His eyes bore into mine as if trying to decipher the thoughts swirling beneath the surface.

"Mmm, I suppose you could say that," I said, my voice steadier now, though the nervous flutter in my chest remained.

"Are you a graduate student?"

"Yes, I'm studying law with an emphasis in political science," I said.

"Another lawyer. Just what the world needs."

I smiled and said, "But who knows, I may change my mind and become a college professor."

He leaned closer, his tone lowering to a conspiratorial level. "Well, I'm always open to conversations with curious minds. Maybe we can continue this discussion over coffee sometime."

A mix of emotions swirled within me—caution, curiosity, and a subtle undercurrent of danger. But as I met Gus's gaze, I realized this encounter could be an opportunity. An opportunity to engage, challenge, and perhaps sow the seeds of doubt in his convictions. With a nod, I replied, "I'd like that."

Gus's smile widened, and he pulled out his phone, his fingers dancing across the screen as he added my number.

"Until then," he said, his gaze lingering on mine before he turned and walked away, leaving me with a mixture of unease and a newfound sense of purpose.

As I watched him go, I couldn't help but wonder if I was treading on dangerous ground or if this encounter would become the catalyst for a deeper exploration into the hearts and minds of those entangled in the web of divisive ideologies. Only time would reveal the path this encounter had set me on.

Chapter 5
Nightmare

In the shrouded confines of my bedroom, darkness hung heavy, wrapping around the edges of my vision like a suffocating veil. Moonlight filtered through the window, casting an eerie glow that revealed distorted shadows dancing across the walls. My pulse quickened as an unmistakable sense of foreboding seeped into my consciousness, setting my nerves on edge.

In the dim corner, a figure materialized: Gus. But this was no longer the Gus I had just met, the charismatic, handsome young man and leader of The Vanguard. His features contorted and morphed, twisting into a nightmarish visage that bore no resemblance to humanity. A sickly grin stretched across his face, lips curling in a sinister mockery of his once-charming smile.

I tried to move away from the grotesque spectacle before me, but an invisible force held me in place. Panic surged through my veins as I realized I was trapped, a helpless spectator in my unrelenting terror theater. The air grew thick with an oppressive weight, and every sound—the rustling of the drapes, the faint creaking of the floorboards—seemed magnified to an unbearable intensity.

Gus's voice cut through the silence, a chilling echo that emanated from all directions simultaneously. His words were incomprehensible, a cacophony of syllables that sent a shiver down my spine. As his voice filled the air, an unnatural pressure seemed to bear down, as though the very atmosphere was constricting around me.

I watched in horror as his form contorted further, his limbs elongating and twisting in unnatural ways. Once warm and inviting, his eyes were now windows to an evil that chilled me to the core. The glint in his eyes held a promise of torment, a maleficent intent that seeped into my very soul.

A guttural scream clawed its way up my throat, but the sound was distorted and inhuman, a haunting cry that sent tremors through the air. I tried to summon my voice, to call out for help, but the words were snatched away by an unseen force, leaving me trapped in silence.

And then, as if responding to a hidden command, the room seemed to twist and writhe, its dimensions warping into a nightmarish landscape. Reality fractured around me, plunging me deeper into the abyss of terror. The walls pulsed and shifted, a vortex of color and form that defied all logic.

As the nightmare's grip tightened, a primal fear surged within me. I fought against the invisible bonds that held me captive, my heart racing as I struggled to escape this nightmare. "Mother!" I cried out, my voice carrying a desperate plea for salvation.

But it wasn't my mother who answered. Monica, her concerned eyes searching mine, gently shook me awake. The room snapped back into focus, the moonlight casting gentle patterns on the walls. With a gasp, I realized I was safe, back in my bed.

"Emma, are you okay?" Monica's voice was a soothing balm after the nightmarish vision.

I nodded, my heart slowly steadying its pace. "Yeah, I'm okay. It was just… so vivid. I could feel every detail, every emotion."

Monica's brows furrowed, her expression a mix of empathy and determination. "Emma, you can't keep letting these nightmares consume you like this. You need to take control. You must learn lucid dreaming."

I was skeptical. "But is such a thing even possible?"

Monica's smile was gentle yet persistent. "Absolutely. It takes practice, but it's a powerful tool."

The idea of taking charge of my dreams was intriguing, even enticing. But the doubt still lingered. "Monica, I don't know… It sounds almost too good to be true."

She reached out, placing a reassuring hand on mine. "Emma, I've seen it work for others. And I believe it can work for you, too. You're not alone in this. I'll be with you every step of the way, guiding you through the process."

I looked into her eyes, seeing a genuine sincerity that resonated deep within me. Maybe it was time to stop being a passive observer in my nightmares. Perhaps it was time to face those demons, even if it meant entering a realm of dreams that had haunted me for so long.

"Okay," I finally said, my voice determined. "Okay, Monica. Teach me."

*

In the softly lit room of Harvard's Sleep and Dream Research Center, I settled onto the comfortable reclining chair, my heart fluttering with anticipation and nervousness. Wires and sensors were attached to various parts of my body, the modern machinery forming an intricate web around me. Monica's reassuring smile eased some of my tension as she adjusted the monitors.

"Comfortable, Emma?" Monica asked, her voice soothing.

I nodded, ignoring the odd sensation of electrodes on my scalp and chest. "Yeah, I think so."

Monica's fingers danced across the controls, adjusting the settings. "All right, I'll monitor your brain activity, eye movements, and muscle tone while you sleep. This will give me insight into the different phases of your sleep cycle, particularly the REM stage where dreams are most vivid."

I took a deep breath, trying to relax. "And this will help me understand my nightmares better?"

Monica nodded, her gaze warm. "Exactly. The data collected will provide a comprehensive picture of your sleep patterns and the moments when your nightmares occur. With this information, we can tailor techniques to help you become lucid within those dreams."

As Monica finished the preparations, she dimmed the lights in the room. "All right, Emma, I will lower the lights and play soothing sounds to help you relax, and when you're ready, close your eyes and drift off to sleep naturally."

Already exhausted from my lack of restful sleep, I closed my eyes, allowing the gentle hum of the machines and the soft sounds of a babbling brook in my earbuds to lull me into a state of relaxation. The room faded away as I focused on my breath, letting go of the worries that had plagued me for so long.

Time lost meaning as I slipped into sleep's embrace, my mind gradually surrendering to the darkness. Unfamiliar sensations fluttered around me, a mix of calm and curiosity. I wasn't sure how much time had passed when I felt a gentle touch on my shoulder.

"Emma, wake up." Monica's voice reached me from afar.

Slowly, I opened my eyes to find Monica standing over me, her expression both concerned and intrigued. "How are you feeling?"

I stretched, the wires and sensors momentarily forgotten. "It was strange, like I was aware of falling asleep, and then I started dreaming."

Monica looked interested. "Do you remember what it was about?"

I hesitated momentarily, the images still fresh and haunting in my mind. "It was something from my past, something I hadn't thought about in years," I began, my voice trembling as the memory returned with vivid clarity.

The dream had taken me back to my teen years when innocence still shielded me from the harsh realities of life. I was walking home from school, filled with adolescent concerns, when a cruel scene unfolded.

A Mexican man was diligently working in my neighbor's yard, his hands calloused and dirty from the soil. He was planting flowers, his movements gentle and precise, a look of concentration on his face. But what had captured my attention was my neighbor Mr. Allen, his face twisted with rage and contempt.

He was yelling at the worker, his voice filled with malice. "Can't you do anything right? You're worthless! Just like the rest of your kind!" he spat, his words like venom.

I watched, paralyzed with shock and fear, as Mr. Allen raised his hand and struck the Mexican worker across the face. The cruelty of the act was staggering, the humiliation and pain evident in the worker's eyes.

Yet he said nothing, merely bowing his head and continuing his work, his body trembling with suppressed emotion.

The scene played out with an unrelenting clarity that left me breathless and horrified. I could feel the sun's heat on my skin, hear the birds in the trees, and smell the freshly turned earth. It was like I was there again, a helpless witness to an act of unspeakable cruelty.

And then, just as suddenly as it had begun, the dream ended, leaving me with a profound sense of sadness and a realization of the injustices still permeating our society.

I looked at Monica, tears welling in my eyes as the impact of the dream hit me. "It was something frightening," I said, my voice barely above a whisper.

Monica reached out and squeezed my hand, her eyes filled with understanding. "It must have been very unsettling, but remember, dreams can be a window to our subconscious, a way to process things we may not even realize we're holding onto."

I nodded, knowing that she was right. The dream had brought to the surface a memory that had been buried for years, a reminder of the darker aspects of humanity that I had tried to forget. It was a lesson, perhaps a call to action and a challenge never to turn a blind eye to injustice, no matter how painful it may be to confront.

Monica patted my arm. "The good news is that your brain activity showed a shift consistent with entering the REM stage. Let's take a look at the data."

Monitors flickered to life, displaying intricate graphs and patterns. Monica's brows furrowed as she studied the information, her excitement palpable. "Your dream patterns are fascinating, Emma. I've never seen anything like it. I'll need to analyze this further, but you'll do fine."

A sense of accomplishment surged within me. The technology and Monica's expertise were helping to unravel the mysteries of my nightmares. As we delved deeper into the data, I felt a newfound sense of hope blossoming within me. With each monitor and each line of data, I had the confidence that I was one step closer to reclaiming control over my dreams.

Chapter 6
Going Lucid

Over the next few days, Monica guided me through the intricacies of lucid dreaming using the cutting-edge sleep and dream research facilities at Harvard. The room was equipped with various advanced equipment, from brainwave monitors to eye-movement trackers, all designed to analyze and enhance the dream experience.

Monica explained that the key to achieving lucidity was cultivating a heightened self-awareness, even within the dream state. She helped me create a dream journal, encouraging me to jot down any fragments of dreams I could remember upon waking. This practice, she explained, would help me recognize patterns and recurring themes in my dreams, ultimately increasing my chances of recognizing when I was dreaming.

We began with relaxation exercises, focusing on deep breathing and calming visualizations. Monica's soothing voice guided me into a state of relaxation, allowing me to disconnect from the annoying concerns of the waking world. As I lay on a comfortable recliner, the room's soft lighting and serene ambiance created an atmosphere conducive to entering the dream realm.

Monica then introduced me to "binaural beats," a technique that uses specific audio frequencies to influence brainwave activity. She fitted me with earbuds, and as I listened, the binaural beats began to synchronize my brainwaves, mimicking the patterns that occur during REM sleep—the stage where dreams are most vivid. This synchronization, Monica explained, could facilitate a smoother transition into a dream state and increase the likelihood of lucidity.

As the binaural beats played, Monica encouraged me to imagine a familiar place where I felt safe and empowered. She explained that, in the dream world, this location could serve as a trigger to help me recognize when I was dreaming. With her guidance, I visualized my happy place outside New Paltz at a serene forest clearing surrounded by towering trees and dappled sunlight.

The next step was reality checks. Monica taught me to question my surroundings multiple times throughout the day, asking myself whether I was awake or dreaming. The habit of questioning reality, she said, would eventually carry over into my dreams, where inconsistencies and impossibilities would become evident.

With each session, I grew more adept at recognizing the subtle shifts between wakefulness and dreaming. I started to notice the inconsistencies—the way colors seemed to bleed together in dreams, the way light didn't behave as it should. These cues became my allies, helping me pierce the veil between the waking world and the realm of dreams.

Then, I had my first lucid dream.

I ran, my breath in ragged gasps as I stumbled through a twisting, shadowy maze. My heart pounded as strange, distorted figures chased me, their faces shifting and morphing just beyond my sight.

Fear drove me forward, the haunting whispers of the figures filling me with terror. I felt their cold hands nearly brushing against my back as the dark corridor closed around me. Panic surged, but then something stirred—a flicker of realization.

The walls, the figures, and the panic were all too familiar. I'd been here before. Only this time, something was different. A knowing took root deep within me.

"I'm dreaming," I whispered, and the very fabric of the dream trembled at my realization.

The walls seemed to shiver, and the air grew thick with palpable energy as if the dream had awakened my consciousness. Shadows danced and swirled; the once-menacing figures that haunted me paused in their relentless pursuit, their faces contorting in confusion.

I stopped running, turning to face the strange figures. My fear was replaced by determination as I focused my will on the dream. A newfound clarity washed over me, and I understood that I held the reins of my fate.

The figures faltered, and I raised my hand, feeling a sudden power to change everything.

The corridor shifted, the walls brightened, and the shadows retreated. I swept my arm, banishing the figures and transforming the maze into a lush garden filled with vibrant colors and sweet fragrances.

My heart swelled with triumph, and I reveled in the beauty of my creation. The fear was gone, replaced by a profound sense of empowerment. I'd conquered the terror, discovering a hidden strength within myself.

I woke with a smile, the memory of my victory a beacon of light in the darkness. The dream had changed, and so had I. This realization that I could control my dreams and turn a nightmare into something beautiful was nothing short of liberating. Lucid dreaming had set me free, releasing me from the prison of my subconscious fears. I would no longer feel the crushing weight of dread when I closed my eyes at night. The nightmares that had haunted me were now under my control, subject to my will.

I owed so much to Monica for this freedom. She had introduced me to the concept of lucid dreaming, patiently guiding me through the techniques and encouraging me to confront my fears. Her wisdom and unwavering support were my lighthouses in the dark, leading me to discover a strength I never knew I possessed.

I planned to use this ability and learn from it. The world of my dreams was no longer a place of terror but a canvas on which I could paint, explore, and grow. I saw endless possibilities and opportunities to face my innermost fears, explore hidden corners of my psyche, and create landscapes filled with wonder.

With each passing night, I delved deeper, unlocking secrets and gaining insights that not only enriched my dreams but began to shape my waking life. I found courage, creativity, and a sense of peace transcending the boundary between dream and reality.

Monica's gift freed me from my nightmares and gave me a tool to enrich my life, learn, and evolve. I knew this was just the beginning of my journey into the depths of my mind. Lucid dreaming had become more than a way to conquer fear; it was a pathway to self-discovery, a key to unlocking my potential.

I no longer feared the dark; I had learned to wield the light.

Chapter 7
Coffee with Gus

I settled into my seat at the bustling corner of the café, my heart beating a little faster as anticipation mixed with nervousness. My research on The Vanguard had been extensive, and the deeper I delved, the more intrigued I became. On top of that, I was about to see Gus again, this time outside the group meeting.

He arrived, his confident smile and magnetic presence immediately striking me. The connection was instant, and I felt an unexpected pull of attraction that excited and alarmed me. I was here for answers, not feelings, I reminded myself.

Our handshake was firm, and pleasantries were exchanged. "Emma, it's been too long," he said, his eyes sparkling.

"Yes, it has," I replied, a little breathless.

Gus nodded. "I've been looking forward to our conversation."

"So, Gus," I continued, my voice firm but edged with curiosity, "tell me about The Vanguard. What's the philosophy behind it?"

He leaned closer, his gaze never leaving mine. "Emma, it's about empowering the true spirit of our nation, ensuring everyone's potential is realized. Regardless of what many think, it's not about exclusion, but embracing what makes all of us strong."

His words were persuasive, and I was caught in his charisma, fighting back an attraction that confused and exhilarated me. "But how do you reconcile the allegations of racism and white supremacy?" I pressed, leaning forward, our conversation intensifying.

Gus shook his head, his voice passionate. "It's not that at all," he insisted. "It's about lifting everyone up, Emma, not suppressing them. Those who criticize us don't see the bigger picture."

"What about the people who feel threatened by your organization's views?" I asked, my voice tinged with challenge.

Gus smiled, unruffled. "Their fears are based on a misunderstanding. Trust me, our principles are about uniting, not dividing."

Our debate continued, each question probing deeper, each answer revealing more complexity. And with each word, I felt a growing desire to know him more intimately, a longing I knew I had to resist.

"You know, I've even been invited to the White House, where I advised the president," he revealed, his eyes dancing excitedly.

"You're advising the president?" I asked, stunned.

He nodded, a satisfied smile on his face. "Yes, it's an incredible opportunity to bring about real change."

The news about Gus and the president added a new dimension to our conversation and my conflicting feelings. His influence was more significant than I'd realized, and the stakes were higher. The afternoon wore on; our dialogue was rich and engaging, filled with ideology, influence, ambiguity, and contradictions. The romantic tension between us built, weaving through our conversation, becoming an unspoken challenge I struggled to suppress.

Gus suddenly leaned back in his chair, studying me thoughtfully as we lingered over coffee. "You know, Emma, I value your perspective. Have you ever considered joining us at The Vanguard? Your voice could bring fresh insight to our organization."

His question caught me off guard, and I could feel my heart racing. Was this an opportunity or a trap? My mind buzzed with conflicting thoughts, not least of which was my growing attraction to Gus. I couldn't deny the allure of being close to him.

"Joining you?" I stammered, trying to hide my surprise. "That's… unexpected."

"I think it would benefit both sides," Gus insisted, his eyes locked on mine. "You'll be able to voice your opposing opinions from within, and perhaps we can learn from each other."

I considered his words, my mind torn. Was this an opportunity to influence change from the inside, or was my judgment clouded by my feelings for Gus? "I'll need some time to think about it," I finally said, my voice filled with uncertainty.

"Of course," Gus replied, his smile warm and encouraging. "Take all the time you need. Just remember, sometimes, being on the inside can make a real difference. Think of it as a direct line to the president."

I left the café, my head spinning. Gus's offer was tempting because of the influence and power it could bring and because of him. I had to admit to myself that my attraction affected my considerations. But there were more significant questions at play. Was it better to fight from within or maintain my distance? Could I trust Gus, or was I being manipulated? And most concerning of all, could I trust myself, knowing how I felt about him?

The allure of Gus, the enigma of The Vanguard, the proximity to the White House, and my unexpected, burgeoning feelings had become an intertwined reality. I knew that my journey into his realm was far from over, and I was determined to navigate it with courage and caution, no matter how seductive the path might be.

My mind was a whirlwind of thoughts and emotions. Gus had shown me a world of complexity and power, and I had found myself drawn to him in a way I hadn't anticipated.

Chapter 8
Flying Lucid

I'd been practicing lucid dreaming under Monica's guidance for several weeks, and the surreal realm had become more comfortable, more real. My nights, no longer haunted by bad dreams, were filled with vivid encounters, each more enthralling than the last. Remembering my roommate's instructions, I explored my deepest desires and fears.

One night, as I stood at the edge of a cliff, the ground fell beneath me, revealing a fantastic landscape that took my breath away. Towering mountains kissed the sky, lush forests whispered secrets, sparkling rivers danced, and majestic cities gleamed. I took a deep breath and, recalling Monica's words, spread my arms and leaped.

The sensation of flying was like nothing else. The wind embraced me, lifting me higher and higher, carrying me through clouds and beyond. I soared over valleys filled with blossoming bright pink flowers, past mountains with snow-covered peaks that sparkled like diamonds, and over vast plains where mythical creatures of my creation roamed carefree. I felt a release I had never known, an exhilaration that stirred my very soul.

In another dream, I found myself on a familiar porch, my deceased grandmother sitting in a rocking chair, smiling as always. We talked, our words carrying the weight of love and memory. "Babushka, I've missed you so much," I said, my eyes brimming with tears.

"I've been watching over you, dear. I'm so proud of the woman you've become," my grandmother replied, holding my hand. We talked for hours, laughing, sharing, and remembering. But then, as the dream continued, my grandmother's expression became more serious and contemplative. She looked into my eyes with a mix of concern and wisdom. "Emmashka," she said, her voice trembling with an unspoken fear, "do not venture beyond the safe confines of your dreams. You have a gift, my dear, a rare ability to pierce the spirit world, but you mustn't try."

Her words sent a chill down my spine, and I could feel my heart pounding in my chest. "What do you mean the spirit world?" I asked, my voice barely a whisper.

"There are beings, entities, that might not have your best interests at heart. Some of them seek to harm you, twisting your gift for their dark purposes," she explained, her eyes filled with concern.

Her words rocked me, a storm of confusion and fear whirling inside me. Was this real? Why would my grandmother warn me about dangers in the spirit world?

My grandmother must have sensed my doubt because she squeezed my hand reassuringly. "I know it's hard to comprehend, Emmashka, but please heed my warning. Be careful with this gift. It can be a blessing, but misused or misunderstood, it can lead you into darkness."

Her words lingered in my mind long after I woke, a haunting reminder of a world I had only begun to explore. The comfort and joy of reconnecting with my grandmother were now tinged with a newfound awareness of the unknown and possibly dangerous realms I'd been navigating. Her warning became a pivotal moment in my journey, a crossroads that challenged me to question the nature of my dreams and the notion of the existence of a spirit world.

But most dreams were less ethereal because they were about Gus, a compelling and sometimes confusing figure. One night, I allowed myself to explore my feelings for him, seeing him as a political enigma and a man. In that dream, we were together in a room lit only by the soft glow of candles. He looked into my eyes, his gaze filled with desire and understanding.

"Emma, there's so much more to me than what you see," he whispered, his lips close to mine. "Can I show you?"

The candles flickered, casting dancing shadows across the walls, and the air between us was charged with an electric current of anticipation. Gus's breath was warm on my cheek; each exhale an invitation to venture deeper into the uncharted territory of our connection. The room, with its ambient glow, seemed to shrink until it was just the two of us, alone in a universe of our own making.

His hands, strong yet gentle, traced the contours of my face, a silent promise to honor the vulnerability we both felt. "There are layers to this soul of mine," he murmured, drawing me closer until the space between us became a whisper. "Let me share them with you; let me reveal the man behind the cause."

In the muted light, every touch was a word, every kiss a sentence, and every embrace a chapter in the story we were writing. The world outside faded into insignificance as we surrendered to the moment, our spirits soaring on the wings of newfound intimacy. In the aftermath, wrapped in a cocoon of warmth and affection, I understood that with Gus, love was a revolution all its own.

Monica's teachings showed me that my dreams were not an escape but a path to understanding, a journey into my soul and perhaps further, as my grandmother suggested and warned. Through it all, this mystery of Gus lingered as a question, a challenge, something I knew I would have to confront. My nights of soaring over fantastic landscapes, connecting with lost loved ones, and exploring my hidden desires prepared me for the complex reality of my waking life.

One night, something shifted. A chill wind blew through my dreamscape, and shadows gathered at the corners of my mind. As I soared above a landscape that had always been enchanting, I caught sight of something unsettling in the distance. Like a storm cloud, the darkness seemed to move and pulse with virulent energy. I felt a pull, a curiosity that overcame my fear, and I flew closer.

The darkness took shape as I approached. Ethereal beings, twisted and grotesque, lurked within, their eyes glowing with a wicked gleam. They whispered in a language I couldn't understand, their voices a discordant melody that filled me with dread. Could this be what my grandmother had warned me about?

At the center of this gathering, I saw Gus. His eyes were blank, and his face contorted into agony and longing. He seemed trapped, ensnared by these beings, their tendrils reaching into his very soul. "Emma!" he called out, his voice a desperate plea. "Help me!"

I tried to reach him, but the beings were too strong. They pushed me back with a force that sent me spiraling into darkness. A shiver ran down my spine as I recalled my grandmother's warning. Her voice echoed in my mind: "Some of them seek to harm you, twisting your gift for their dark purposes." Her cautionary words had become a chilling reality.

I woke with a start, my heart pounding, the echo of Gus's cry still ringing in my ears. Realizing that these entities were real was terrifying and compelling. My grandmother's warning resonated with new meaning, guiding me as I ventured deeper into this unknown realm.

My journey into the world of dreams had taken a new turn filled with danger and uncertainty, but I was determined to face it, unravel the mystery, understand the influence on Gus, and find a way to fight it. I sighed, knowing the stakes were higher now, the path more treacherous, but my courage and determination were unwavering, bolstered by the loving concern of my grandmother.

I knew that I had only scratched the surface of a truth far greater and more complex than I could have ever imagined. Could it be that my dreams were no longer just a path to self-discovery? Perhaps they were a battlefield, a realm where the struggle for the soul of humanity was being waged. *How else could the overwhelming tide of fascism be infecting the world?* If this was so, I was no longer just a dreamer but a witness to some infiltration into humanity.

My mind was reeling with questions and disbelief. The images of Gus, trapped and in agony, haunted my waking thoughts. *Could evil beings indeed have influenced him in the dream world?* It seemed possible after what I'd seen. My lucid dreams began as a gateway to exploration and self-discovery, but now they had taken a dark and dangerous turn.

"Monica, I saw something terrible," I shared, my voice trembling. "Gus was there in my dreams while these terrible entities had ensnared him. Can such things truly happen? Can dreams have such power?"

"Entities?" Monica's eyes widened, a look of concern crossing her face. She took my hand, her touch both calming and reassuring.

"Yes, hideous ones, similar to the ones in my nightmares before I learned to be lucid," I said and continued to share the details of my dream.

"Emma, what you're describing is profound and deeply unsettling, but I believe it's not your imagination. There are beliefs that dreams can bridge the physical and spiritual realms, providing insights into higher truths often inaccessible in our waking consciousness."

"But how can I know what's real?" I asked, desperation creeping into my voice. "And how can I help Gus if this is more than just a dream?"

Monica nodded contemplatively and then said, "Have you heard about Rudolf Steiner?"

"Rudolf Steiner?" I repeated, my curiosity piqued by the unfamiliar name.

Monica's eyes lit up, and she leaned forward, her interest evident. "Yes, Emma, Rudolf Steiner is someone I've studied extensively, particularly because of his interest in the dream world," she said, her voice filled with both authority and enthusiasm. "He was an Austrian philosopher, social reformer, architect, and esotericist, born in 1861. He founded Anthroposophy, a spiritual movement deeply exploring the connection between the physical and spiritual realms."

She paused, her eyes reflecting her passion for the subject. "Steiner believed that dreams bridge our waking world with the spiritual world, providing insights into higher truths that may be inaccessible otherwise. His thoughts on dreams have always fascinated me."

Her words flowed confidently, a testament to her deep understanding of Steiner's philosophy. "He saw dreams as more than random thoughts or images. To Steiner, dreams are gateways, paths to explore realms beyond our everyday consciousness. Through dreams, we can traverse different spiritual planes and even encounter beings of various natures."

She looked at me intently, her eyes probing. "His ideas might illuminate what you've been experiencing, Emma. According to Steiner, dreams can be profound spiritual experiences connecting the soul with a broader spiritual universe. What you're describing resonates strongly with his teachings."

Her words sent a chill down my spine. Monica's dedicated study of Steiner, driven by her interest in the dream world, had opened the door to a new world waiting to be explored. The path I had set upon, filled with dreams and mysteries, had turned toward something vast and uncharted. The dream world was no longer just a curiosity but a realm filled with possibility and danger, beckoning me to delve deeper.

I felt a spark of hope. If there was someone who could help me understand these complex and terrifying dreams, I could find a way to help Gus, and maybe even more than that. "Thank you, Monica," I said, determination strengthening my voice. "If these dreams are indeed a connection to something greater than might influence not just Gus but humanity, I must explore it further."

Monica's eyes met mine, a complex blend of understanding and concern dancing in her gaze. She nodded gravely, her voice laden with caution. "Emma, such a path will be veiled in shadows and uncertainty. The consequences of delving into the unknown could be far-reaching and perilous."

I felt a chill at her words. "Are you suggesting that what's unfolding in the dream world might be dangerous?"

Monica swallowed hard, her face pale. "It's possible. This is uncharted territory. We've never delved this deeply into the dream realm before."

"What should I do?" The question escaped my lips, a plea for guidance in a situation that seemed to spiral further out of control with each passing moment.

Monica shrugged, her expression troubled. "The choice is yours, Emma. You have the option to end this now."

I exhaled heavily, my mind racing. "I could," I admitted, the words in a whisper.

"You must decide," Monica urged, her voice gentle yet firm.

Her words hung in the air, heavy with the weight of a decision that could change the course of my life. The allure of an easier path called to me, tempting me with the promise of simplicity and safety. A job without risks, a life with my mother, and embracing comfort and normality.

Monica's following words sliced through my indecision like a knife. "I don't believe you chose Harvard just to retreat when confronted with your first significant challenge," she suggested. Her observation resonated deep within me, igniting a spark of determination that had been smoldering all along. I had come here with a purpose, a mission to explore the unknown. I couldn't simply turn my back on the mysteries unfolding in my dreams. I had a unique ability to lucid dream, a skill that was now more urgent and necessary than ever. The answers were waiting, hidden in the shadows, and I was committed to uncovering them.

With newfound clarity and resolve, I looked at Monica, my decision made. "I'm going to continue. I must understand what I've seen, no matter the risk."

Monica nodded, her expression a mix of pride and worry. "I'll support you, Emma. But remember, be cautious. We don't know what awaits us in the depths of the dream world."

Her words were a reminder, a warning, and a promise, all wrapped into one. And with that, I decided to continue my journey into the unknown, driven by curiosity and courage and mindful of the potential dangers ahead.

Chapter 9
The Rally

The Vanguard of Purity rally was an unnerving spectacle designed precisely to cloak its true nature. Flags and banners fluttered in the air, symbols reminiscent of a dark era, though carefully toned down. People clapped and cheered, drawn into the web of a charismatic speaker who spoke of unity, strength, and tradition. Yet, behind those polished words, hidden messages sent a chill down my spine. The atmosphere was filled with tension that hinted at something sinister.

Gus's invitation to this event left me feeling both upset and humiliated. I was struggling with my emotions as he guided me to his table. "Gus, I never expected this from you," I said, my voice choked with emotion. "How could you think I'd want to be part of this?"

He looked at me, confused. "I thought you were interested, Emma. You've attended meetings and even had coffee with me. I thought you wanted to understand."

"To understand what? This?" I gestured around, feeling the heat of anger rising within me. "This display is everything I'm fighting against!"

Gus's face tightened, and he became defensive. "You came to the meetings. You listened. I thought you were open to learning about our cause."

"Learning?" I shot back, tears stinging my eyes. "I came to those meetings to try to understand you, not to be swept up in this madness!"

He frowned, his voice rising. "Madness? So, you've been playing me all this time? Pretending to care, to gather information. Is that it?"

"No, Gus, that's not it at all," I pleaded, realizing I might be shutting the door between us. "I care about you. I wanted to understand you, but this…" I looked around, unable to find the words.

The speaker's voice boomed through the hall, touting purity, strength, and a return to traditional values. It all sounded so appealing, yet so twisted. I glanced at Gus, his face a turmoil of emotions, and my heart ached.

"Listen to me," I said softly, touching his arm. "I like you, that I can't deny. But more than that, I believe that maybe, just maybe, I can help you see through all of this. My dreams and visions may hold the key to saving you."

He looked at me, his eyes wide, anger and confusion battling in his expression. "Saving me? Emma, what are you talking about?"

I took a deep breath, knowing what I was about to say would sound strange. "Gus, I've been having dreams. They're not just regular dreams; I'm conscious within them, able to control and explore. In lucid dreams, I've seen and felt things that feel real. I believe that if I can go deeper into this dream world, I might be able to glimpse something within you, find a way to reach you, and help you see beyond these beliefs," I said, waving my hand.

He stared at me, his face displaying a mix of disbelief and curiosity. "Lucid dreams? You mean you're awake in your dreams? Emma, that sounds like fantasy."

"It's not fantasy; it's a real phenomenon," I explained, my voice filled with earnestness. "Some people can become aware that they're dreaming and even control what happens in the dream. It's like having a foot in two worlds. I've been experiencing it; my roommate Monica has taught me how. I've seen things that I can't ignore. I have to try to understand it, Gus. For you, for us, for everyone."

His uncertainty turned to ridicule as he stood up, preparing to leave for the stage. "Emma, I appreciate that you care, but this... lucid dreaming? It's absurd. Are you sure you're not losing touch with reality?" he asked, his voice filled with concern.

His words stung, but I held my ground, my eyes fixed on his. "I know what I've experienced, Gus. And I believe in what I'm doing. I'm not crazy, and I'm not deluded."

He shook his head, a sad smile on his face. "I have to go. I'm speaking next." He looked at me, his eyes softening for a brief moment.

"I hope you find what you're looking for, Emma. But I think you're chasing shadows."

With that, he turned and walked away, leaving me feeling a mixture of anger, confusion, and determination. The rally's noise crescendoed as Gus took the stage, his voice clear and confident as he addressed the crowd. I couldn't help but listen to his words, which I knew were laced with hidden meanings and veiled threats.

"Vanguardians," Gus began, his voice resonating through the hall, "we gather here today as a testament to our unity, our shared vision for a brighter and purer future. We believe in the power of heritage, community strength, and tradition's wisdom." There was applause, but I could hear the underlying message, the not-so-subtle hints at exclusion and superiority.

"Our society is being eroded by forces that seek to undermine our values, that push us away from our roots," he continued, his tone becoming more impassioned. "But we, The Vanguard, stand firm, unyielding in our commitment to protect and preserve what is rightfully ours."

His words were carefully chosen, his message skillfully veiled, but I knew what he was saying. I could see the symbols and insignias around the room, the subtle nods to a dark and dangerous ideology. The parallels with the haunting images of Nazi Germany were all too clear.

I felt a chill run down my spine as I realized the true nature of what I was witnessing, the depths of Gus's involvement, and the challenges ahead. The rally continued, but I was lost in my thoughts, torn between my feelings for Gus and my horror at what he was becoming.

I knew that my quest to understand my dreams, to delve into the dream world, and to reach Gus was becoming increasingly important. I could see his path and the darkness he was being drawn into. Despite his dismissal of my beliefs, I knew I had to try to save him.

I left the rally that day with a heavy heart but a clear purpose. The battle had only just begun, and I was determined to fight. Gus might not understand, and he might think of me as unstable, but I knew what to do.

The dream world had shown me a path, and I was ready to follow it, even into the lion's den, no matter where it led.

Chapter 10
Gateway

Monica's eyes were sharp and attentive as she observed the monitors, her hand making careful notes. The soft hum of machinery filled the room as I settled onto the bed, my heart pounding with anticipation and anxiety.

"Remember," Monica said, her voice steady and calming, "what we're attempting here is based on one man's philosophy. There are no scientific facts. Steiner proposed that the dream world is a bridge, a gateway that may allow us to pierce into the spiritual realm, but we must be cautious. There are, without doubt, unknown variables and potential hazards."

I nodded, taking a deep breath as I considered her words. "I understand. I'm ready to explore, but I'll heed your warnings."

Monica's hand rested on my shoulder, her touch reassuring. "You're venturing into a place that may be filled with wonder and enlightenment but could harbor dark entities. Steiner mentioned beings known as the 'Asuras.' They are considered the opposing forces to spiritual development, often associated with darkness, materialism, and selfish desires. Imagine them as beings trying to cut us off from our higher spiritual nature, working to make our thinking and feeling more rigid and dense."

"So they want to pull us toward materialistic desires? Away from spiritual growth?" I inquired.

"Exactly," Monica agreed. "The Asuras work at the level of the human ego, trying to anchor it in the physical world, preventing us from evolving toward a higher understanding. They want to create a barrier between our souls and the spiritual world, making it difficult for us to grow and reach enlightenment."

"That sounds terrifying. So they're essentially the enemies of human spiritual progress?" I said, while considering if the Asuras were responsible for the surge of fascism.

"Yes, you could say that. Steiner's lectures present a continuous struggle between the forces of light and darkness, good and evil," Monica said, her eyes filled with the subject's weight. "In Steiner's spiritual cosmology, the Asuras are considered the nemesis of the Archangels. They are beings of incredible power and malice, always striving to create chaos and hinder human spiritual growth. As forces of light and guidance, the Archangels battle to keep these evil entities subdued. It's a complex interplay, a cosmic struggle beyond our ordinary understanding. The Asuras should not be taken lightly, especially if you consider venturing into the spiritual world through your dreams. Their influence can be subtle, seductive, and destructive, all at once."

"Archangels?" I repeated, the name capturing my attention.

Monica's eyes narrowed as she considered my question. "Yes, Archangels," she began, choosing her words carefully. "These beings occupy a unique position in the spiritual hierarchy. Not merely symbolic, Archangels exist as spiritual entities, each with distinct attributes and missions."

My eyes widened, my curiosity piqued. "And they really exist?"

"They certainly do exist," Monica replied, calm and measured. "They are considered higher spiritual beings, two levels above humans in the spiritual hierarchy. Their purpose is manifold, working on the level of cultures and guiding entire epochs of human development."

"Two levels? What's the first level?" I asked, curious.

Monica leaned in, her expression taking on a hint of seriousness mixed with a reverence for the topic. "The first level above humans is often considered to be that of angels. These entities are more individualized, focusing on personal spiritual growth and protection," she explained. "Archangels, however, operate on a broader spectrum. They're wise and ancient, guiding not just individuals but entire nations and epochs."

"Would you say they're the decision-makers of the spiritual realm?" I probed, fascinated by the depth of her knowledge.

Monica chuckled softly. "Decision-makers might be too human a term for them, but they certainly are influencers, shaping the flow of spiritual energies on a grand scale. They are the emissaries of divine will, you might say."

"What's their purpose, specifically? How do they interact with us?" I asked, my mind racing with the implications of what Monica was sharing.

Monica looked at me, her eyes severe but also filled with a kind of warmth. "The Archangels guide and inspire humanity. They help to shape our cultural evolution, working behind the scenes to influence thoughts, feelings, and even historical events. They are guardians of spiritual truths and wisdom, intervening in ways that might be subtle or even invisible to our ordinary senses. As Steiner described, their battle with the Asuras is part of a greater cosmic drama, where the Archangels strive to lead humanity toward spiritual enlightenment, while the Asuras seek to pull us away from it."

I listened, absorbing the information, feeling fascinated and somewhat overwhelmed. The idea that spiritual beings were engaged in a battle for humanity's very soul was intriguing and terrifying. It opened the door to a world of complexity I had never considered. My dreams and explorations were not just about my journey, but were connected to something more significant. "Yet how would I know if what I see in my dreams is real or just a product of my imagination?" I asked, my voice tinged with doubt. "How could I possibly find an actual portal to the spirit world?"

Monica nodded, her face thoughtful. "Emma, that's a question many seekers have asked. I truly believe dreams are not just figments of our imagination; they can be pathways to deeper truths. But differentiating between mere fantasy and genuine spiritual insight requires discernment."

"So, how do I develop that discernment?" I pressed.

"Through practice, reflection, and guidance," Monica answered. "But you must remember that the spiritual realm doesn't conform to our ordinary logic and expectations. Finding a 'portal,' as you put it, might not be a matter of simply locating a door or gateway."

I furrowed my brows, struggling to grasp the concept. "Then how do I enter the spirit world through my dreams?"

Monica sighed. "The spiritual world is interwoven with our physical existence. It's not necessarily a separate place to enter but a different state of consciousness to attune to. The journey inward might lead you there, but there's no specific roadmap."

"But what if I get lost? What if I become trapped in that realm?" The questions tumbled out of me, driven by curiosity and fear.

Monica reached over and took my hand, her grip firm and reassuring. "That's a real concern, and I won't downplay the risks. Venturing into the spiritual realm through lucid dreaming can be like navigating uncharted waters. There may be currents and whirlpools that could pull you off course. That's why you must approach this with humility, caution, and clear intention."

Monica released my hand and stood, moving toward the central monitoring system. "We're going to be systematic about this, Emma. I'll monitor your vital signs throughout the process to ensure your safety. If I see anything that indicates extreme stress or other unusual reactions, I'll wake you immediately."

I watched as she assembled the devices, her hands deftly connecting wires and calibrating sensors. A slight sense of trepidation rose within me, but I pushed it aside. I needed to do this, something that called to me deeply and fundamentally.

Monica returned to my side, holding a set of electrodes and a heart rate monitor. "This will help me keep track of your heart rate, brain waves, and other important indicators," she explained, attaching the sensors to my skin with gentle care. "I'll be here with you every step of the way, watching over you as you explore."

I met her eyes, gratitude and trust mingling with the fear and excitement that churned within me. Her presence was a comfort, a solid anchor in this daring journey I was about to embark on.

"Are you ready?" she asked, her voice soft but filled with a steely determination.

I nodded, feeling a sense of resolve settle over me. "I'm ready."

"Then let's begin," she said, dimming the lights and guiding me to a reclined position. "Remember to keep your intention clear and trust yourself. You have the strength and wisdom to navigate this path. I'll be watching, ready to step in if needed."

With those words, she started the equipment. I closed my eyes, took a deep breath, and allowed myself to drift into the dream world, guided by my inner compass and driven by a desire to uncover the truths hidden beyond the veil of ordinary perception.

Chapter 11
First Contact

I stood in a tranquil garden, a haven of beauty and peace. The soft rustling of leaves, the murmur of a distant brook, and the gentle fragrance of blooming flowers filled the air. I looked around, taking in the surroundings, and recognized the sensation of lucidity. "I'm dreaming," I told myself.

Addressing the dream with a deep breath and purpose, I declared, "I wish to find the gateway into the spirit world." My voice was steady and filled with determination.

The garden seemed to respond, the trees swaying and the air growing still as if the very fabric of the dream were listening to my request. There was a pause when time seemed to stretch, and the landscape before me held its breath. The soft rustling of the leaves ceased, and even the distant murmur of the brook fell silent.

Slowly, an archway of intertwining vines began to take shape before me. They writhed and twisted, growing and interlocking, as if guided by an invisible hand. A shiver ran down my spine as I watched the spectacle, mesmerized by the power and mystery of the dream.

A soft and ethereal voice broke the silence, its tone filled with caution and concern. "Why do you wish to pass into the spirit world, child of Earth?" it asked, echoing through the garden. "This is not a place for the living. Their notions often mislead those who dare to enter and become trapped by their desires."

I turned, searching for the source of the voice, but finding none. It seemed to come from everywhere and nowhere, a whisper in the wind. I gathered my thoughts and replied, "I must find the source of humankind's troubles. I need to understand the darkness that plagues us. I believe the answers lie beyond."

The voice sighed, a sound like the rustle of autumn leaves. "Your quest is noble but fraught with danger. The spirit world is not what you imagine. It is complex, deceptive, and indifferent to human whims."

"I understand the risks," I insisted, my resolve unwavering, "but I must do this. I must try."

The voice fell silent, and the garden seemed to shudder, acknowledging my determination. The archway of vines completed its formation, and within its frame, a shimmering opening appeared. The portal pulsed and swirled, an everchanging dance of colors and lights. It was mesmerizing, terrifying, and beautiful all at once.

Through this gateway, I glimpsed a landscape so alien I assumed it could only be the spirit world. It was barren and lunar, with towering cliffs of black rock and vast, empty plains. A chill ran through me as I realized I was standing on the threshold of the unknown.

The voice spoke once more, its tone tinged with resignation. "Then go, child of Earth, with courage and wisdom. May you find what you seek."

With a final look at the beautiful garden, I approached the gateway, my heart pounding but my mind clear. The mysteries of the spirit world awaited, though I had no idea what they were or if I was ready to face them.

With courage summoned from deep within, I approached the gateway and stepped through. The garden vanished, replaced by the stark and desolate terrain of what I assumed was the spiritual realm. The ground was hard beneath my feet, the air thin and void of scent.

Determined, I called out to the distance, echoing through the emptiness. "Asuras, show yourselves!"

From the towering cliffs, shimmering forms began to emerge. At first, they were indistinct, mere mirages in the distance. But as they approached, they took on a more human appearance. Ordinary people, I thought as they drew near. They looked just like ordinary people.

I stood my ground, my heart pounding but my resolve unwavering. "Are you the Asuras?" I asked, my voice carrying across the desolate landscape.

In a collective voice, they answered, "We are the Asuras." Their eyes were watchful, curious, and wary. They did not seem to understand why a living being had entered their realm. They could not seem to understand my intention. "What could you possibly want?" they asked, their voices mingling into one.

I looked at them, the so-called evil beings, and realized the complexity of my task. I was here to understand, connect, and find a way to heal a rift that had endured for eons. "I've come to learn," I replied, my voice firm. "I've come to understand."

The Asuras regarded me with eyes that were ancient and knowing, eyes that had seen civilizations rise and fall. "You seek to challenge us, human?" one of them asked, their collective voice echoing through the barren landscape.

"I seek to understand," I corrected, my voice firm. "I need to know why you torment humanity. Why you bring suffering and chaos."

A murmur went through the gathering of Asuras, their expressions shifting, becoming more contemplative. One of them, who appeared to be an elder, stepped forward, his face etched with ancient wisdom. "We do not torment," he said, voice resonating with authority. "We challenge. We test. We also embody destruction and chaos, a necessary part of the Divine's cosmic design."

I frowned, trying to understand. "But why? Why is this necessary? Why must there be so much pain, so much suffering?"

The elder Asura's eyes softened, and he reached out, his hand hovering just above my shoulder. "Life is not meant to be easy or without strife," the being explained. "Growth can only occur from struggle. Enlightenment comes from understanding both the light and the dark. We are part of that balance."

"But the pain, the destruction," I protested, tears stinging my eyes. "It's too much. There must be another way."

"This is our purpose," another Asura said. "We were created to be the challenge humanity must face and overcome."

"So, it's not you I need to fight?" I said, the words coming to me as if from a deep well of understanding. "It's the weak souls of earthly beings, the fear, the greed, the hatred? Is that what's tearing humanity apart?"

The Asuras fell into a thoughtful silence, their eyes locked on me, considering my words.

"You are right, child of Earth," the wise Asurian said, its voice gentle yet firm. "The battle is not here in the spiritual realm. It is on Earth, within the hearts and minds of your fellow earthly beings."

"You must take your fight there," another added, her eyes dark and piercing. "You must be the light in the darkness, the strength in the weakness. You must be the one to bring balance."

I looked around at the barren landscape, feeling the weight of their words and the task's enormity before me. It was daunting and overwhelming, but I knew it was my path if this were true. "I understand," I said, my voice filled with resolve. "I will do what I must. I will take the fight to Earth."

The Asurians nodded, their faces filled with respect and sorrow. "Go then, Emma," the elder Asura said, his voice filled with warmth. "Go with our blessing, our hope. May you find the strength and wisdom to heal your world."

I shook my head. "But why would you want me to succeed against your purpose?"

The wise Asura's face crinkled into a smile that held centuries of understanding. "Child, our purpose is not what you think. We do not exist to destroy but to challenge. We are not the enemy of humankind but a reflection of its inner turmoil. We exist to make your people confront what they are and what they can become."

"But your nature is chaos and destruction," I insisted, still struggling to reconcile what I'd learned.

"That is the form but not the essence," the Asurian replied, its voice a soothing melody that seemed to resonate in the very air around us. "Suffering is not our wish. It's a reflection of your collective souls. You battle with us, but what you're fighting is within yourselves. Weakness, greed, hatred, fear—those are the real foes. Conquer them, and you conquer us. You see us as invaders and corrupters, but our existence is tied to the very nature of humanity's struggles."

"But it's you," I said, sweeping an arm, my voice trembling with confusion and growing realization, "who infect those souls."

As I spoke, there was a sudden hush. The barren landscape seemed to hold its breath, the wind ceasing its mournful howl. Then a singular voice, soft and haunting, asked, "What do you mean when you say 'who infect those souls'?"

"I mean those on Earth," I added and hesitated, a chilling thought crossing my mind. "But maybe you thought I meant the souls yet to be born. Is that what you do?" The question hung in the air like a shadow, dark and foreboding.

The Asuras exchanged knowing glances, their eyes reflecting a complexity beyond my understanding. After what felt like an eternity, the wise Asurian, who had been guiding the conversation, spoke again, his voice tinged with a sadness that echoed in the depths of my soul.

"O, child of Earth, consider this: What seems an affliction is merely the reflection of what resides within. We are not the architects of humanity's flaws or desires; we are but their mirror. The souls waiting to be born bear the imprints of their fate, shaped by the legacy of those who walked before them. It is not our purpose to taint but to pose the challenge, to scrutinize the resolve of humankind. Recognize that your struggle with us is, in truth, a struggle with the core of human nature itself."

These words struck me like a bolt of lightning, illuminating truths that were at once profound and terrifying. I was beginning to understand that the battle I sought was not against some external evil but against the darkness within, the shadows that lurked in the corners of the human soul.

The Asuras were not the enemy but a reflection, a manifestation of our inner demons. The realization was both humbling and empowering, and I knew then that my path was clear. The fight must be taken to Earth, to the hearts and minds of my fellow beings, where the real battle lay.

Chapter 12
Washington, DC

Early that morning, we arrived at the Mall in Washington, DC, along with a diverse group of students led by Professor Dawson from his various courses at Harvard. As we gathered around the Lincoln Memorial, the day was charged with electric energy, hopeful and tinged with fear. We contemplated the eerie parallels to our own time in the shadow of a president who had faced the unimaginable horrors of a civil war. Such a war now seemed a distant nightmare, but the rumblings of discontent that separated the extremists of the Right and Left suggested that it was not out of the question.

Thousands joined us, like-minded people from all over the country. The force of white supremacists brandishing fascist-inspired flags and banners glared from afar; they crept closer, their faces twisted with rage, and the tension in the air grew thick and palpable.

The confrontations began with harsh words and stares, like sparks threatening to ignite a wildfire. Calm and resolute, Professor Dawson tried to engage some of them in conversation. "Why are you here?" he asked one man, his voice steady. "Can't we talk peacefully about our differences?"

The man spat and sneered, his eyes wild. "There's nothing to talk about with traitors like you."

I watched, my heart pounding, as more of their group joined the fray, taunting us with slurs and threats. Violence erupted suddenly, a fist thrown, a scream, and then it was chaos.

I watched in horror as Professor Dawson was attacked by an assailant with a folding chair, his face smeared with blood as he collapsed to the floor. Panic and anger surged within, but I pushed it down, focusing on what needed to be done. I yanked a young girl to safety, guided an elderly man away from the throng, and shielded a fellow student as the violence raged around us. There were shouts and cries, the air thick with fear and aggression. I found myself face to face with a woman with hatred in her eyes. "You think you can change anything?" she screamed at me. "You're just a child, playing at revolution."

"I'm standing for what's right," I replied, my voice firm but calm. "Aren't you tired of all this hatred?"

Her face twisted further, but there was a momentary flicker of doubt in her eyes before she turned away.

The clash intensified as the police arrived, trying to restore order but often escalating the violence themselves. Through it all, I continued to help where I could, my actions a blur of determination and courage. When the dust finally settled, and the cameras from the cable news channels encircled us, a reporter pulled me aside, my heart still racing from the turmoil.

Facing the camera, the weight of the moment upon me, I found my resolve. "Today was a vivid display of humanity's dual nature," I declared, my voice resonating with conviction. "We witnessed the depths of animosity but also the heights of bravery and kindness. This isn't merely a clash of political factions or beliefs—it's a crucial struggle for our nation's very spirit, the essence of our shared humanity."

The reporter leaned in, her gaze intent. "What message do you hope to convey?"

I took a breath, my eyes never leaving the lens, reaching out to unseen millions. "I want everyone watching to understand that we are not isolated in this challenge. We're the beacon in the murk, the resolve in the uncertainty. In unity, we must repudiate the dread and division that fray our bonds. Let's be galvanized by the words of President Lincoln"—I gestured to the memorial behind us—"and labor for a harmonious and empathetic future."

After the interview, I was immediately swept up in the collective embrace of my peers, their faces alight with a mix of elation and a shared sense of purpose. They clapped me on the back, their eyes gleaming—a mirror of the hope I'd just voiced into the camera.

"Emma, that was incredible," Professor Dawson exclaimed, holding a bloody rag to the wound on the back of his head. "You stepped up and spoke the truth at such a challenging moment. Your words will make a difference!"

"Are you all right?" I asked, touching his shoulder. "We should get you to a hospital."

"No, I'm fine," the professor said. "It's not deep."

*

Returning to Harvard felt like crossing into a different reality. Washington, DC's, resonating chaos and violence, gave way to the echoing halls of academia. There, a new and unexpected chapter of my life began to unfold.

As the weeks progressed, public speaking at first was a daunting task. I stumbled over words, my voice shaky and uncertain. But with each appearance, I found my footing and started speaking with an authentic and passionate voice that resonated with those who listened. My impressions began to go viral on social media, and my words were shared across multiple platforms. My followers on Instagram surged to hundreds of thousands and growing.

In a few months, I had become more than just a student; I was a symbol, a spokesperson for a cause I deeply believed in. My ability to articulate our struggles drew admiration and attention, transforming me into a frequent guest on cable news shows with a voice that mattered.

But with this newfound fame came a haunting shadow—Gus. His work with The Vanguard embodied everything I was fighting against. Though we managed to avoid each other, I could feel his awareness of my activities. His presence was a lingering reminder of a once simpler and less painful time, a contrast to the thrilling but challenging path I was now on.

Monica became my anchor amid this whirlwind. Together, we delved deeper into the dream lab, exploring the mysteries of the spirit world. She believed my unique ability to cross into the spiritual realm could provide valuable insights, enhancing my reputation and our understanding of the ethereal universe. It was a fascinating and often terrifying journey, filled with revelations and questions.

I had a secret, something I kept hidden, even from Monica. My experiences in the spiritual world were not just visions or dreams; they were becoming tangible, affecting the physical world around me. The line between reality and the spirit world blurred, and I was caught in the middle. I began to see signs, hear whispers, and feel otherworldly beings' presence in my daily life. It was subtle at first, easily dismissed as imagination or stress. But it grew, becoming more pronounced, more insistent. I knew that something profound was happening, something that connected my newfound fame, my battles in the political arena, and my journeys into the spiritual realm.

The truth gnawed at me, a puzzle demanding to be solved. I knew I had to confront it, to face whatever awaited me in the shadows of the unknown. The time was coming when I would have to choose between the safety of ignorance and the perilous path of discovery. In the end, my decision was clear. I was not just a graduate student, a spokesperson, or a reluctant celebrity. I was a bridge between worlds, a warrior in a fight that transcended politics and reality. My path was set, and I knew I must follow it, no matter where it led.

As I stood before the mirror, preparing for another interview, I looked into my eyes and saw a resolve I had never known before. I was ready to speak, be heard, act, and make a difference. With a deep breath, I stepped into the spotlight, knowing that my journey was only beginning and that the battles ahead were not just for my country but for humanity itself. The secret I carried was a burden, a gift, a challenge, and a promise. I was ready to embrace it all.

Chapter 13
Covenant of Freedom

Fresh from the energy and adrenaline of my appearance on a local TV talk show, I returned to campus. The Student Center was bustling, but my thoughts were elsewhere, reflecting on my words and the responses they'd evoked when a young woman approached me. Her red hair was pulled back tightly, highlighting her intense, determined eyes. Her demeanor was calm, but the urgency in her voice caught my attention immediately. "Emma Zigler," she said. "You've been making quite a name for yourself."

I raised an eyebrow, curiosity piqued but cautious. "I'm sorry. Do I know you?"

She glanced around to ensure our privacy, then leaned in closer and whispered, "I'm part of the Covenant of Freedom, a movement plotting to take back what the federal government has stolen from us. The democratic system we once knew is gone. We must take our country back, no matter what."

With a squint, I stepped backward and said, "I'm sorry, but I need to be somewhere."

She reached out and grasped my hand, her eyes unwavering. "We need people like you, Emma, people who will stand up, fight, and make real change happen. Will you help us?"

The uncertainty in my heart battled with the pull of her words. I thought of the experiences of the past few months, my dream journey into the spiritual realm, the guidance of Professor Dawson, and the courage I'd discovered within myself. "I'm sorry, but I don't know you," I said, putting up my hand.

"Come on, Emma," she insisted, eyes imploring me to understand. "Just meet the leadership. Hear what they have to say, then decide."

"I don't know," I admitted, both drawn and hesitant.

Her expression softened. "I understand, Emma. But this is about more than just joining a cause. It's about standing up for what's right. Just give us a chance to explain our mission. If you're not interested, fine."

Her sincerity was compelling, and I found myself unable to refuse. "I'll meet them," I said, curious and cautious. "But that's all I'm agreeing to for now."

"That's all I ask," she replied, relief in her smile. "There's a vehicle waiting for us in the garage."

I nodded and gestured for her to lead the way. Then, realizing I had no idea who this woman was, I reached out, put a hand on her shoulder, and asked, "What's your name?"

She smiled and said, "Kaitlin Russel. Please follow me."

As we headed to the garage, my mind was filled with questions and a growing sense of purpose. I didn't have the answers, but I figured it couldn't hurt to at least hear them out.

Kaitlin and I stood in silence until the elevator reached the garage level. The doors opened, and waiting for us was an old white Ford Econoline van. The side door slid open, and Kaitlin gestured for me to get in. I took one last look around and climbed aboard.

With Kaitlin sitting by my side, the van exited the garage. We drove beyond the confines of the campus and out onto a highway.

"Where're you taking me?" I asked, my fingernails digging into the worn vinyl upholstery, anxiety churning within me.

"It's a few more minutes," Kaitlin said, patting my knee reassuringly, but her nonchalance did little to ease my growing trepidation.

After a ten-minute drive, we entered a residential community and drove for a few minutes before pulling into a garage. We only exited the van once the driver closed the automatic garage door with a clicker attached to the visor.

I followed Kaitlin into the home and was directed to sit at a round table in the kitchen, its Dutch blue décor not unlike Mother's back home.

"Would you like some coffee or tea?" Kaitlin asked, standing by the stove.

"Coffee is good. Milk and sugar if you have."

While she fussed with a French Press, a tall man with a stern face and military bearing entered and introduced himself as General Harris. Accompanying the general was a well-dressed woman who said nothing and sat across from me.

"Emma, our country is on the brink of catastrophe," the general explained, his voice laced with gravity. "We've reached a tipping point where traditional means of change are no longer effective. We believe that the government has been hijacked, and we must take it back. By force, if necessary."

I stared at him, feeling a wave of disbelief and confusion. "A coup? You can't be serious. This is the United States of America, not some dictatorship where we overthrow our leaders."

"Allow me to introduce Senator Clarke," the general said, looking at the woman.

"Senator?" I repeated with a slow nod. "I thought you looked familiar."

"Believe me, Emma," she said, leaning forward, "we've explored every legal avenue, every peaceful protest. We're at a dead end. Our democracy is being choked to death, and we must act before it's too late."

"But a coup?" I said with a grimace. "I think you have the wrong person. I'm just a student. I want to go back now."

"Hello, roomie," Monica said, entering the kitchen.

"Monica!" I cried. "What are you doing here?"

"I know this must be a shock," Monica said with a calm smile, her eyes betraying a hint of anxiety.

"You're a part of this, too?" I asked, reeling from the revelation.

Monica nodded and took a seat beside Senator Clarke. "Allow me to explain."

She paused for a moment, collecting her thoughts. "When the Covenant of Freedom approached me, I was as skeptical as you are now.

A coup in our own country? It seemed unthinkable. But as I learned more about what was happening, what's being done to our nation's principles and values, I knew I had to get involved."

"But why you, Monica?" I asked, still struggling to grasp her connection to this conspiracy.

Monica's face grew serious as she began to delve into the explanation. "Because of my expertise in dreams and sleep, the Covenant became interested in my work. They believe there may be ways to utilize the subconscious mind to their advantage. To unlock insights, predictions, and potentially communicate or influence on a level we don't fully understand."

She paused momentarily, allowing the words to sink in, then continued, "You see, Emma, this rebel force is operating in a time when traditional methods of influence and resistance may not be enough. The Covenant is against a regime that utilizes powerful propaganda, disinformation, and psychological warfare. They needed something more, something that could give them an edge."

I could see the passion in her eyes as she spoke, her words painting a vivid picture of the battle ahead. "The human mind is at its most vulnerable during sleep. Dreams can access the deepest recesses of our thoughts, fears, and desires. By understanding these subconscious layers, we could potentially reach people on an emotional level, create empathy, stir action, or even predict reactions."

Her hands moved emphatically as she continued. "The Covenant realized that they needed to fight on this battleground, in the landscapes of dreams and the subconscious mind. That's why they approached me, because of my research in this field. They saw the potential to turn something as abstract as a dream into a tangible tool in our fight."

Monica's expression softened, and she touched my arm reassuringly. "I know this may all seem overwhelming, Emma. The concept of using dreams and the subconscious in this way is uncharted territory, even for me. But the potential is there. It's a revolutionary idea that could change how we approach this struggle. It's why I was recruited and why they're interested in you. Your unique connection with the dream world and beyond could be crucial to complete this puzzle."

I leaned back in my chair, my mind whirling with the weighty possibilities of the decision before me. What Monica had just unveiled was unlike anything I could have ever conceived—a fusion of science and spirituality, psychology and politics, all interwoven into a strategy capable of reshaping our nation's future. The implications were staggering, and the burden of responsibility weighed heavily on my shoulders. Beyond that, I couldn't shake the feeling of betrayal. Why had my trusted friend, Monica, revealed my secret without seeking my consent?

Monica's voice gently pierced through the turbulence of my thoughts, her soft and resolute tone. "Reflect on it, Emma. Truly contemplate the magnitude of what we're presenting. This is an opportunity to harness your exceptional gift for something of monumental significance that could shape the very destiny of our country. I understand it's a lot to digest, but I have unwavering faith in you and our shared mission. Will you stand with us?" Her eyes locked onto mine, radiating determination and hope that was impossible to dismiss.

The room fell into a profound silence, anticipation hanging heavy in the air as my gaze shifted from Monica to Senator Clarke, General Harris, and Kaitlin. They all waited with bated breath for my response, knowing that the path I chose would not only define my future, but also the destiny of our nation.

Senator Clarke leaned in, her voice brimming with conviction. "The human mind possesses extraordinary power," she declared. "Monica's research bestows upon us unique strategies and perspectives. It grants us the ability to reach those seemingly out of our grasp, decipher the motives of our adversaries, and even anticipate their next moves. Her work in the dream lab isn't merely an exercise in scientific curiosity; it could become a revolutionary weapon in our struggle."

My anger flared, and I couldn't contain it any longer. "So you divulged my secret?" I snapped, the sense of betrayal surging within me.

"I share it out of belief in our cause," Monica replied with a steady voice. "It seemed like it could make a difference. Betraying you, Emma, was never my intention. Hopefully, you can understand that."

I stared at her, torn between anger and the realization that Monica had acted with the best intentions, however misguided. The room was silent, the tension palpable.

"Emma, we're asking a lot from you," Senator Clarke said softly. "But we're also offering you a chance to be part of something bigger than yourself. To fight for justice, freedom, and the very soul of our nation. Will you join us?"

"But to what end?" I asked, shaking my head.

They began to lay out their plan, a detailed, meticulously crafted strategy to overthrow the government. I listened, torn between fear, disbelief, and a growing sense of responsibility. They were right; something was wrong with our country. The evidence was there, the corruption, the erosion of freedom. But could I be part of something so radical, so dangerous?

Finally, it was Monica's turn to speak. Her voice was soft but firm, her words filled with wisdom and conviction. "Emma, you have a rare gift, a connection to something greater. You can certainly make a difference."

The room fell into silence, the weight of her words sinking in. I looked around, seeing the hope and expectation in their eyes. They believed in me, the possibility of change, and the power of unity.

"I need time," I said, my voice trembling. "This is too much. I need to think."

They nodded, understanding yet impatient. The clock was ticking, the window of opportunity narrowing.

It was a whirlwind of thoughts and emotions as I left the room. I was being asked to make a choice that could change the course of history, a decision that carried the weight of an entire nation. I was scared and confused, yet I felt a spark of determination. The fight was real, the stakes were high, and I had a role to play, according to the Covenant.

Chapter 14
Dream Lab

After a tense conversation in our apartment, Monica suggested we return to the dream lab. There might be helpful guidance lurking in my lucid dreams. I was initially reluctant, still grappling with Monica's betrayal, but the curiosity and hope in her eyes persuaded me to try it.

"How could you do this behind my back?" My voice was filled with frustration as we prepared the lab. "How could you just hand me over to them without first asking?"

"I'm sorry, Emma," Monica said, her voice thick with regret. "When they approached me, I was intrigued and, I'm ashamed to say, intimidated at the same time. I shouldn't have told them about your connection to the spirit world. But when I did, you can imagine their interest in you."

"But to do what?" I demanded, my anger momentarily flaring again. "Am I supposed to recruit angels to our cause? This is too far-fetched!"

"Let's see if we can find guidance," Monica suggested, her voice calm and soothing. "You've connected with the spirit world before. Maybe there's something you can learn, something that can help us understand what's happening and what our next steps should be."

We settled into the lab, and I lay down with various monitors attached, ready to delve into a lucid dream once more. Monica's fingers danced across the controls, and her soothing voice guided me into that unique space I had visited before.

Feeling the gentle hum of the monitors and hearing the last echoes of Monica's soothing words, I took a deep breath, exhaling slowly as I let go of the tension in my body. My thoughts clung to our conversation, the flare of my anger, and the weight of Monica's regret. She meant well, that much was clear, even if her choices had left me unsettled. As I closed my eyes, I made a mental note to speak my mind clearly when I woke. For now, though, I needed to let go. Let go of my frustrations and open myself to whatever guidance the spiritual realm could offer. It wasn't too hard as I felt my body growing heavier, sinking deeper into the cushioning beneath, relinquishing control and drifting into the dream world.

Images and sensations that had become familiar swirled around me. The transition was smoother now, my mind and body accustomed to this journey into my subconscious. I floated through a landscape filled with light and shadow, a place both ethereal and profound. Here, I had met the Asuras before, those mysterious entities that both intrigued and concerned me.

They appeared again, their presence like a gentle pull that I could neither resist nor fully embrace. I knew they held wisdom, secrets that could unravel my mind's mysteries, but I also needed to tread carefully. Something about them kept me cautious: a depth and complexity that I could never quite grasp. "I need guidance," I said, my dream self-poised and determined, yet not without a note of hesitancy. "I need to understand what's happening and my role."

I could feel them considering me, their ethereal forms emanating a sense of timeless wisdom and inscrutable intent. We had communicated before, but each encounter was a new dance, a careful negotiation between my desire for answers and my awareness of their enigmatic nature.

The dream held its breath as I awaited their response, the vast expanse filled with a tension of both anticipation and caution. I was on familiar ground, yet I knew that the Asuras should not be taken lightly. The answers were hidden in their silence, waiting for me to find the courage and the insight to uncover them.

The Asuras moved around me, their voices a gentle melody, filling my mind with wisdom and insight. They spoke of balance, purpose, and a path mine alone to walk. One of the Asuras approached, its form shimmering with an ethereal glow. "Emma," it said, its voice resonating like a soft wind, "your connection to our world is not an accident. It is a gift, a responsibility. You must learn to embrace, understand, and use it for the greater good."

"But what does that mean?" I asked, confusion and fear mixing within me. "What do you want from me?"

"You must be a bridge," another Asurian replied, its voice a gentle caress. "A bridge between our world and yours. Your ability to pierce the spirit world and commune with us is a key to understanding and healing the rift growing in your earthly realm."

"I'm scared," I admitted, tears forming in my dream eyes. "I don't know if I'm strong enough, wise enough."

"You have the strength," a third Asurian assured, its voice like a comforting embrace. "And we will guide you. Trust in yourself and us, and you will find the path."

"But how do I know what's right? How do I know whom to trust?" I pleaded.

The gentle melody of the Asuras' voices began to falter as doubt crept into my mind. Something felt off, a dissonance in their words and intentions. The more they attempted to persuade me, the more I grew suspicious.

Suddenly, the entire dreamscape quaked, shifting into a dazzling display of celestial grandeur. The Asuras scattered in panic as an overwhelming force manifested itself before me. In the epicenter stood an unwavering bastion of might and mercy. Towering and formidable, the figure unfurled his wings, casting forth a radiance that outshone the stars themselves. Each feather shimmered with the essence of creation. His armor gleamed as if forged from the core of a dying star, etched with runes that told of ancient victories and eternal vigilance.

The sword he wielded hummed with the harmony of justice, its blade inscribed with the wisdom of the ages. His eyes, fierce yet filled with an ocean's depth of benevolence, met mine, and I felt the unspoken promise of protection and strength that could vanquish darkness. With a voice that resonated like thunder cloaked in velvet, he spoke, and his words were a balm, as well as a herald of doom to the wicked. I found in his gaze a reminder that within us all burns a flame no shadow can extinguish.

"Amidst the swirling cosmic currents, where realms of spirit intertwine with the fragile tapestry of mortal existence, hear me, Emma." The being's voice filled the space, resonant and echoing, as his magnificent presence held me in awe. "I am the Archangel Michael, and I stand before you as a beacon of light in the vast expanse of time. Chosen by the Archangels, you are entrusted with a mission of utmost importance."

I stared, my mind reeling from the enormity of his words. "The hierarchical beings are bound by a single purpose—to nurture and safeguard humanity's journey. Yet, as shadows gather and as the fascists emerge, the very essence of humanity's evolution is imperiled. It is you, Emma, who bears the mantle of the defender, chosen to stand against this onslaught."

The space around me seemed to shift, celestial energy swirling as Michael's words vividly depicted the cosmic struggle. "In this dance between realms, Archangels take up arms, embodying fierce warriors, as the Asuras strive to unravel the delicate threads of human progress. The clash is mighty, a symphony of celestial energies and earthly struggle. Our intent is unwavering—to shield humanity from the veils of chaos that threaten to descend."

Michael's words resonated, cutting through the fog of confusion. The Asuras were not allies as they pretended but part of a greater drama, their intentions wrapped in layers of complexity and treachery. They sought to make me a pawn, but now I understood the battlefield a bit more. The answers were out there, and I was committed to uncovering them, guided by a newfound understanding of my role in this celestial dance.

"With unwavering determination, you will confront the infected forces as a vanguard against the storm," the Archangel continued. "This cosmic soliloquy echoes in the sacred spaces of your heart. You are not alone; we are your steadfast allies, our radiance illuminating your path."

Michael's voice softened, filled with profound compassion. "The symphony of battle plays on, and in your hands lies the destiny of humanity, a narrative woven with threads of courage, sacrifice, and the eternal struggle between light and darkness."

Tears welled as the weight of his words settled upon me. It was as if the tapestry of existence had been unveiled before my eyes, and I stood humbled yet resolute at the crossroads of destiny. I was stunned by the notion that my life and journey were woven into a cosmic design. It was a realization that transcended the boundaries of the ordinary, lifting me into a realm of profound significance.

As I contemplated the vastness of this cosmic tapestry, I couldn't help but feel a deep sense of purpose—each step I had taken, and each challenge I had faced, had led me to this pivotal moment. I was part of something greater, a divine narrative that had been unfolding since time immemorial. The threads of bravery and sacrifice, light and darkness, were intricately intertwined, and I was now tasked with a role in this epic drama.

My heart swelled with gratitude for the guidance and wisdom bestowed upon me by the ethereal being. It was a significant moment of understanding within the spiritual realm, a recognition of the interconnectedness of all things. With courage and determination coursing through my veins, I nodded in acknowledgment, silently accepting my role in the unfolding cosmic symphony.

In that instant, I realized my journey was not just about personal growth or individual battles. It was about contributing to the greater good, about standing as a beacon of hope and resilience in the face of adversity. As I looked to the heavens, I felt a profound sense of purpose wash over me, and I knew that I was ready to embrace the path that lay before me, whatever challenges it might bring.

Michael's gaze met mine, a deep connection transcending mere sight, delving into the very essence of my soul. "Peer inward, Emma," he urged with a voice that seemed to echo through the corridors of existence, "and behold the divine spark that resides within you, the glimmering flame of destiny that has guided your path. Born anew, you embarked upon a journey of discovery, growth, and wisdom. This path led you to the hallowed halls of Harvard University and the serendipitous meeting with Monica. Your parents, chosen by you in your beforelife, were but guideposts on this intricate roadmap of fate. As Archangels manifest their celestial power, wielding swords of light and shields of truth, you find yourself aligned with their purpose, a sentinel in the cosmic ballet, a guardian of the boundless potential that hums within the very heart of humanity."

In the wake of Michael's profound revelation, I stood at the precipice of a new understanding that transcended the confines of my previous perception of self. The imagery of Archangels wielding swords of light and shields of truth resonated within me, painting a vivid picture of my role in the grand cosmic narrative. It was a daunting responsibility that filled me with awe and trepidation. As I grappled with the magnitude of my purpose, I couldn't help but wonder how this newfound awareness would shape my path and what challenges and triumphs awaited me on this extraordinary journey.

Then, without warning, I felt myself being pulled back as if surfacing from deep water, breaking into the world of waking. The room, the lab, Monica—all materialized around me in sudden clarity. The lingering echoes of the Archangel's words reverberated within my mind, their gravity weighing heavily on my soul.

I blinked, trying to adjust to the light, as Monica's anxious face came into focus. Her eyes searched mine, filled with concern and anticipation, a million questions left unspoken. "What did you see?" she finally asked, her voice barely above a whisper, as if afraid to shatter the fragile reality of what I'd just experienced.

I tried to speak, but words failed me at first. How could I convey the majesty, the outrageous truth, the cosmic battle that had been revealed to me? How could I make her understand the significance of what had just occurred? How could I explain my role, the grand design of my life, and the purpose that awaited me?

I reached out, taking her hand, feeling its warmth and strength. The connection grounded me, helping me find my voice. "Monica," I began, trembling with emotion. "I spoke with Archangel Michael. I was shown something incredible, something far beyond what we ever imagined. He told me about my purpose," I said and paused to correct myself. "Our purpose, our destiny. It's about the cosmic struggle between light and darkness. We're part of something immense, something divine."

Her eyes widened in disbelief and wonder. "Michael? The Archangel Michael?" she stammered. "Like in the Bible?"

I nodded, tears welling up as I tried to convey the awe, responsibility, love, and trust bestowed upon me. "Yes, he told me that I was chosen, that my life was designed for this moment. Everything—my birth, my parents, meeting you, my education—led me here. It's no coincidence, Monica. We're meant to make a difference. We're meant to save humanity." The words tumbled, each heavy with meaning, my heart pounding as I poured out the truth of what I had seen and learned.

We sat there, time suspended, as I shared everything, our lives transformed instantly, the path ahead clear and shining with purpose. We were no longer just students, friends, or researchers. We were guardians, warriors, and partners in a battle transcending our earthly understanding. As the weight of that realization settled around us, we knew that nothing would ever be the same again. The journey had only begun, and we were ready to face it together.

Chapter 15
Past Lives

Monica and I shared an intimate moment in the dimly lit corner of our living room, enveloped by the hushed presence of textbooks lining our shelves. Our conversation delved deeply into spirituality and destiny while I grappled with questions about my purpose in this cosmic narrative. My voice barely above a whisper, I asked Monica the question that had been weighing on my mind: "Why me? Why you?" It was a query that hung in the air, heavy with uncertainty.

Monica's gaze never wavered; her eyes held a knowing wisdom and understanding as she said one word—"Karma."

"Karma?" I repeated.

She nodded and began unraveling the intricate concept of karma, unveiling its various forms and the profound connection it forged. "You know, Emma," she began, her voice soothing yet filled with conviction, "Steiner described various forms of karma and how it's intertwined with our journey. There's personal karma, the consequences of our actions, and collective karma, where we are tied to groups like families."

I leaned in, absorbing her words, feeling a connection that seemed to resonate on a level beyond mere friendship. "And the universal karma you mentioned earlier? How does that fit in?"

Monica's face brightened. "Exactly! Universal karma encompasses the whole human race. It's like a cosmic symphony; we are all playing our part. But, Emma, there's something more, something that transcends earthly existence. Steiner believed in the influence of the spiritual world on our lives."

I looked at her, curiosity piqued. "Influence how?"

She leaned forward, her voice dropping to a near whisper. "He believed that benevolent and adversarial spiritual beings shape our reality and can even incite conflict on a global scale."

I furrowed my brow, trying to grasp the concept. "So, you're saying the Archangels and Asuras manipulate humanity like the ancient gods of Greece?"

Monica nodded solemnly. "Yes, in a way. Steiner's view was that these spiritual beings exert their influence on human thoughts and actions, sometimes driving nations into conflict."

My eyes widened in astonishment. "Do you mean like starting wars?"

"Would you like to hear Steiner's view on World War I?"

"World War I?" I repeated, slack-jawed.

Monica nodded in response. "He saw the war as a manifestation of a great spiritual battle. Beings from the spirit world influenced human thoughts and actions, driving nations into conflict. The struggle wasn't just physical; it was a battle for the very soul of humanity."

A shiver ran down my spine as the weight of her words settled over me. "So, our connection, our shared purpose, could be part of a larger cosmic struggle?" I asked, my mind swirling with the implications.

Monica nodded solemnly. "Indeed, Emma. The choices we make and actions we take ripple through the fabric of karma, affecting our destinies and humanity's collective destiny. It's a responsibility, but it also offers the potential for immense growth and transformation."

As I pondered the concept of karma, I couldn't help but wonder about the intricate threads that bound us together throughout time. It was as if the very fabric of destiny had woven our lives into this complex tapestry of existence. Monica's words resonated deeply, igniting a sense of purpose and interconnectedness I had never felt before. I leaned forward and asked, "Could our souls have crossed paths in a distant past, and the universe conspired to reunite us now for a higher purpose?"

"It's certainly possible," Monica said.

I stared at her, the possibilities swirling in my mind. "Do you think we can find out who we were and what brought us here?"

Her eyes twinkled. "You can try by connecting with the spirit world through your dreams. Perhaps you could seek the answers there. Find out about our past lives, our purpose, and why our karma has intertwined us."

Monica reached across the table, her eyes reflecting a profound understanding. "Emma, from what the Archangel Michael has told you, we are part of something greater, intricately woven by destiny and purpose. The battle between good and evil awaits, and we have been brought together in this lifetime for a reason."

Her words resonated deep within me, and a sense of resolve welled up. I knew she was right. With Monica's encouragement and wisdom, I embarked on a journey of discovery, not just of my present purpose, but of our shared history across lifetimes.

The influence of spiritual beings, the dance of karma, and the knowledge of how the celestial realm shaped earthly events were no longer abstract concepts. They were tangible threads that wove the tapestry of my existence and our connection, a connection that spanned lifetimes, an eternal bond that now called us to stand together against the looming shadows. With determination and faith, I was ready to embrace my legacy and unravel the mysteries of my past, guided by the beings of the spirit world and the eternal dance of karma.

*

As I nestled into the familiar comfort of my bed, my spirit was anything but at rest. It yearned for the transcendental realms I'd grown accustomed to visiting in my slumber. I no longer required Monica's vigilant accompaniment; I was my own guide now. With a silent invocation, I surrendered to the nocturnal embrace, my consciousness casting its sails to the winds of the ethereal seas.

In an instant, a figure of divine majesty materialized, resplendent and awe-inspiring. It was of such grandeur that the very air around him seemed to sing with the chorus of creation. His vast and splendid wings danced with flames of a celestial palette, casting prismatic light across the boundless corners of my dreamscape. His eyes, ageless pools of benevolence, beheld me with the serenity of a thousand lifetimes.

"Welcome, Emma." His voice resonated with a symphony of warmth and authority. "I am the Archangel Seraphiel, the illuminator of paths untrodden and keeper of the soul's chronicles. The tapestry of your past awaits, woven with intricate threads of karma and destiny. Are you ready to journey through the epochs that have sculpted your being, to behold the narratives that echo within you?"

I looked at him, curiosity piqued. "Why have you come to guide me?"

Seraphiel's eyes sparkled as he smiled. "Every soul has a unique path. Yours is one of discovery, understanding, and growth. I am here to unravel the threads of karma that have shaped you."

"But why you specifically?" I pressed, eager to know more about this celestial being who had entered my life.

Seraphiel's gaze softened. "Long ago, I was chosen to guide souls seeking to understand their earthly journeys. I have walked with many through the annals of time, unveiling the lessons, the love, the triumphs, and the challenges. My purpose is to illuminate the connections, to help you see how each life has been a step toward your higher self."

I nodded as Seraphiel continued, "I help souls recall the wisdom they've gained and the karma they've woven. It's my blessing to assist you in recognizing the patterns that have led you to this moment."

His words stirred something within me, a sense of anticipation mixed with reverence. "I'm ready, Seraphiel," I said, my voice filled with determination. "Show me the way."

Seraphiel extended his hand, the air around us shimmering with a celestial aura. "Walk with me through the epochs that have sculpted you, Emma," he invited. "Every life you've lived has etched indelible marks on your soul, each filled with purpose, pain, love, and wisdom."

As I took his hand, a sacred bond enveloped my consciousness. I felt profoundly tethered to this celestial being, yet at the same time, whispers of other, subtler connections teased at the periphery of my awareness.

Our first destination transported us to 17th-century China, where I found myself in the persona of Liang, an audacious scholar known for shattering conventional barriers. In a dimly lit room fragrant with incense and filled with the rustling of parchment, I engaged in a spirited debate with Ming, a scholar of equal intellect. Surrounding us was a small gathering of fellow scholars, but Ming's words possessed an uncanny magnetic pull, resonating deep within my core. In the periphery, a servant girl observed our discourse with an aura of wisdom that belied her station. Though her role was seemingly minor, her subtle encouragement served as fuel for my audacious pursuits.

"Here, Liang, your courage became the catalyst for an intellectual revolution," Seraphiel reflected. "But remember, you did not walk this path alone. Ming, your intellectual counterpart, and the unassuming servant girl played pivotal roles in shaping your destiny."

Our journey then whisked us away to 18th-century Italy, where I assumed the identity of Isabella, a visionary artist whose creations symbolized cultural transformation. Inside a vibrant workshop pulsating with life and a kaleidoscope of colors, Lorenzo, a virtuoso violinist, enraptured my soul with his ethereal melodies. However, the enigmatic woman who frequented the art salon, always observing from a distance, held a mysterious sway over my creative spirit. Her silent presence served as the wellspring of inspiration behind some of my most profound works.

"Isabella, your artistic brilliance blossomed under her watchful gaze," Seraphiel explained, his words pregnant with significance. "While Lorenzo's music stirred your soul, the enigmatic woman's subtle influence guided your art to uncharted depths."

Our final destination transported us to early 20th-century India, where I assumed the role of Asha, a passionate educator fervently advocating for change within the Indian education system. My most engaging debates and discussions found a worthy counterpart in Anand, a fellow reformer whose gaze held a mysterious familiarity—an unspoken connection transcending mere intellectual discourse. Amongst us was also a woman who led the teachers' union. While our interactions often sparked friction, her challenges were the whetstone against which

I sharpened my thoughts and methods, solidifying my unwavering resolve.

"Asha, your zeal as an educator sparked a renaissance of thought." Seraphiel's voice resonated, imbued with timeless sagacity. "Anand's intellectual dance with your spirit, alongside the fierce leader of the teachers' union, sculpted the essence of your crusade."

Puzzled, I sought clarity. "But who were these fellow souls to me?"

"You already hold the key to this mystery," Seraphiel intoned, a knowing glimmer in his celestial gaze.

Reflection peeled back the veils of time, revealing Monica, my steadfast ally, intricately woven into each life's narrative. In the scholarly courts of Qing China, she was the maid whose silent wisdom fueled my rebellious spirit. Within the Renaissance vibrancy of Italy, she manifested as the elusive shadow, the muse whose silent whispers birthed my artistic legacy. In the fervor of Indian reform, Monica stood defiant, a leader who honed my vision with her unyielding challenge.

Gus, my heart's echo through the eons, was ever-present. As Ming, he sparked the embers of debate in ancient China. As Lorenzo, his melodies caressed the canvas of my soul in Italy, and as Anand in India, he shared a bond with me that defied mere words.

Amidst these revelations, I grasped the profound tapestry that destiny had woven—our three souls were eternally entwined, each life a chapter in an enduring odyssey. Now, as we united against the shadowy Asuras, our collective past fueled our courage to illuminate Gus's path back to grace. "These incarnations were not lone journeys," Seraphiel proclaimed, his voice a cascade through the ether. "The threads of your beings are interlaced, each life a harmonic note in the grand symphony of existence."

With Seraphiel's departure, I stood emboldened, cradled by the profound knowledge of our shared karmic journey. Armed with the wisdom of ages, I was ready to face life's trials, buoyed by the immortal ties that bound our spirits across the vast expanse of lifetimes.

Chapter 16
The Vanguard Rally

Monica and I exchanged looks, our eyes loaded with the severity of what lay ahead. Infiltrating a Vanguard rally was a tightrope act at best, steeped in peril. My presence in the media spotlight intensified the danger of being recognized, making the entire mission feel like a personal confrontation. Then there was Gus, whose uncanny familiarity with me added an extra layer of complexity I had yet to fathom fully.

Ever since my celestial journey with Seraphiel, where I'd glimpsed my past lives and sensed the presence of a mysterious soul who had touched each of them, I had difficulty believing that Gus was that soul. How could a soul intertwined with mine through various lifetimes turn into someone so morally incomprehensible?

Monica and I transformed ourselves with wigs, makeup, and garments designed to avert the most searching eyes. Pulling our hats low to obscure our faces, we melted into the crowd, marching toward the expansive hall where the rally would take place. The atmosphere brimmed with a palpable tension, electric with the enthusiasm of people seduced by The Vanguard's dogma. We moved like wraiths through this surreal world, our mission clear but fraught with unknown dangers.

My heart was a mess of contradictions, a tumult of anxiety and strange, lingering sentiments for Gus that I couldn't fully understand or wish away. I forced myself to focus. This was neither the time nor the place for existential ruminations.

Gus was the keynote speaker, now infamous for his captivating leadership within The Vanguard. As he took the stage, the crowd buzzed in anticipation, almost like an electrical current. The power in his voice and the intensity in his eyes sent a shiver down my spine. I was transported to other times, other places, where that same voice had spoken different words, filled with different intentions. It was a haunting realization I wasn't yet prepared to grapple with.

Monica nudged me cautiously. "Remember, we're here to be flies on the wall, not drawing attention. And for the love of God, make sure Gus doesn't see you."

I nodded, my eyes scanning the faces in the crowd. Each seemed to mirror an earnest yearning for something more significant. The room swelled with applause and cheers as Gus's speech continued, promising power, control, and a new expansive vision for America. I looked away, fighting back the pull of his charisma, wondering how something so dark could also feel so strangely compelling. My heart raced as I decoded the messages woven into his words. I caught Monica's eye; she was as disturbed as I was. His vision included only a select few, steeped in a disturbing ideology that threatened the very fabric of our society.

As Gus's voice crescendoed and the crowd stood, fists raised in unsettling unity, a sharp chill cut through me. This was charisma weaponized, driving a narrative of division, hate, and exclusivity. We made our way out as the crowd began to disperse, still humming with the electricity of Gus's message. Monica and I were laden with a sense of responsibility, a mandate to combat this pernicious narrative. The fight ahead was bigger than us, bigger than anything we'd faced before.

As we disappeared into the shroud of the night, I found my mind tangled with thoughts of Gus. The ethereal voyage I'd taken with Seraphiel, the inexplicable sense of déjà vu that clung to me, melded into a nebulous fog of questions and half-formed insights. How could I reconcile Gus's adversarial role in my life with the poignant connections we'd shared in previous incarnations? The discord gnawed at me.

It was like trying to piece together a jigsaw puzzle where every piece seemed to fit but didn't. A mystery inside a conundrum, as Churchill might have put it. And for some reason I couldn't yet grasp, I felt solving this paradox was the key to unlocking something monumental.

I had lived as Liang, the scholar who shook intellectual realms; Isabella, whose brushstrokes challenged the status quo; and Asha, the educator who inspired young minds. Gus had been woven into the tapestry of each life, a soul eternally interlaced with mine. Yet, here we were, opposed, standing on opposite sides of an unfathomable divide. The weight of lifetimes pressed upon me as if urging me to decipher this cosmic riddle. As we blended into the concealment of the dark, an unspoken truth whispered within me: this battle spanned not just one lifetime but many, and it was far from its final chapter.

*

I was so exhausted that when we returned to the apartment, I told Monica I needed to lie down and close my eyes. As I sunk my head onto my pillow, the uncertainty of the task ahead weighed heavily on me. The fear of failure and the enormity of what was at stake consumed my thoughts. My mind swirled with questions and doubts, and I knew I needed guidance from a source wiser than my conscious mind.

As sleep slowly enveloped me, I felt drawn into a space neither wholly dream nor reality, where the spiritual realm intermingled with my subconscious. There, surrounded by ethereal light and a profound sense of peace, stood the Archangel Michael, who possessed wisdom, love, and an enigmatic connection to me. His presence was awe-inspiring, and his eyes radiated understanding and compassion.

"Emma." Michael's voice resonated with a calm authority. "I know your fears, doubts, and questions. You stand on the brink of something extraordinary, and your path has led you here. Remember our last encounter? Your intuition has prepared you for this moment, weaving a tapestry of insight, curiosity, and courage." After a brief pause, the being continued, "You are not alone. Your dreams have been a guide, reflecting a greater cosmic understanding. Embrace this knowledge and trust in your inner wisdom. Your connection to the spiritual world, glimpsed in dreams, will be your compass."

I nodded, absorbing the Archangel's words.

"The journey ahead requires faith in yourself, empathy, and a willingness to see beyond the obvious. Remember, the seeds of change are planted in the hearts and minds of those you touch. Go forward with confidence and the knowledge that forces within and beyond yourself guide you. Embrace your destiny." Michael's ethereal voice, filled with wisdom and authority, resonated with me, but his expression grew grave as he continued, "Yet, I must warn you, Emma, a great peril awaits you. The Asuras, those chaotic beings who strive to disrupt the divine order, have their eyes set upon you. They have sensed your awakening, your growing power, and fear it. They will try to take, confuse, and bind you in their dark, sub-earthly realm."

My heart pounded, my eyes wide with determination and fear. I felt the weight of Michael's words, the reality of the unseen battle that raged around her.

"Once they take you"—Michael's voice dropped to a whisper, his eyes filled with sorrow—"there is little I, or any of the other Archangels, can do. It will be up to you to break free, to find your way back to the light. You must be strong, Emma. You must find the strength within yourself to resist their darkness, to see through their illusions."

Tears welled as my mission's magnitude and path's complexity became clear. The Archangels' guidance would be with me, but I would be the one to face the Asuras to challenge their dark influence.

"But how?" I whispered, my voice trembling. "How can I face them alone?"

"You are not alone," Michael assured me, his voice gentle but firm. "Trust in your inner wisdom and connection with the spiritual world. Remember your dreams, your visions, your past lives. They are more than mere fantasy; they echo a higher reality, a guidepost on your journey."

"Are you saying you know my destiny?" I asked, wondering if Michael could see the future.

"Of course I do," he said with a smile. "In the spirit world, time is not linear as in the physical realm. It flows and interweaves, and paths are known before they are taken. But remember, Emma, destiny is not a rigid path; it's a river that can bend and shift with your choices and free will." His words were soothing and mysterious, opening doors in my mind. I hadn't realized they were there.

"But, Michael," I pressed, anxiety bubbling, "what about the Asuras? How can I hope to face and overcome them, especially when they seek to pull me into their realm?"

Michael's eyes, filled with ancient wisdom, met mine. "The Asuras feed on fear, doubt, and confusion. They seek to disrupt, divide, and pull humanity from its spiritual core. But they have no power over love, compassion, and the innate understanding of one's true self. These are the weapons you will wield against them."

I felt a shiver, understanding yet doubting the magnitude of the task. How could something intangible, such as love or self-understanding, be a weapon against such dark forces?

"You must believe, Emma," Michael continued, his voice insistent. "Your faith in yourself, connection to your inner wisdom, and the love you carry within are more potent than any sword or shield. You have been chosen for this path because you possess the strength and the heart to stand against the Asuras."

Tears welled in my eyes, a mixture of fear and gratitude. "But what if I fail? What if they take me?"

He reached out, his ethereal hand touching my cheek. "Then you must fight, with all you are, to break free. The Asuras may be strong but cannot break your determined spirit. Remember what you stand for and why you are on this path. Hold on to your truth, and it will be your guiding star."

The words settled within me, a newfound strength blossoming. I understood now, at least partly, what I had to do and be. It wasn't about conquering or overpowering; it was about being true to myself, about embracing my destiny with courage and love.

Chapter 17
Fighting Back

I stared into Monica's eyes, my face pale, a mixture of determination and trepidation swirling within me. We were seated in the cozy confines of our living room, the gentle glow of ambient lighting surrounding us. The room felt charged with tension.

"Monica," I began, barely whispering, "I've had a vision, a warning from the Archangel Michael. The Asuras will try to take me, to pull me into their dark realm. Once I'm there, no one in the spirit world can help me. The Archangels, Michael, they'll be powerless."

Monica's eyes widened, her breath catching in her throat. She had seen me face challenges before and had been my confidante and ally throughout our journey. But this was new, terrifying.

"What do you mean 'take you'?" Monica asked, her voice trembling. "How can they do that?"

I shook my head, my eyes filled with uncertainty. "I assume upon my presence in the spirit realm. Once there, I'm not sure I can stop them. But you…" I reached out, gripping Monica's hand, my eyes pleading, "You'll have to find a way to pull me back if they succeed. You're my only hope."

Monica's heart ached at the fear in my eyes, at the enormity of the task before us. She squeezed my hand, her mind racing, trying to understand what she was hearing.

"But how, Emma? How can I pull you back? I don't know how to reach the spirit world like you."

My eyes softened, and I gave a sad smile. "I know this is asking a lot, Monica—more than I have any right to ask. But I trust you, and I believe in you. We'll have to find a way, research, and consult with those who might know. We'll need to prepare, to be ready if and when it happens."

Monica nodded a fire kindling in her eyes. This was no longer just about curiosity, exploration, or even friendship. This was about my salvation, about facing an unknown enemy in an unseen realm.

"I'll do whatever it takes, Emma," Monica said firmly, her voice filled with resolve. "We'll find a way, we'll prepare. I won't let them take you. We're in this together."

My eyes filled with gratitude, and I hugged Monica tightly, knowing that we were venturing into uncharted territory, facing a threat beyond anything we had ever imagined.

"What did Steiner have to say about the Asuras?" I asked.

"Well," Monica said, shifting her brow. "They're spiritual beings that seek to bind humanity to materialism and egoism. Their influence is subtle yet profound. They work on the human 'I' or ego consciousness, promoting a focus on the self to the exclusion of others."

My brow furrowed, my mind trying to grasp the complexity of what Monica was saying. "So, they want us to be selfish?"

"Yes, but it's more than that," Monica replied, her voice taking on an urgent tone. "The Asuras foster an excessive focus on material gain and technological obsession. They draw us away from our connection to the spiritual world, leading us into a trap of self-centeredness, disconnection, and ultimately, self-destruction."

My eyes widened, a chill running down my spine as the gravity of Monica's words sank in. "But why? What do they gain from this?"

Monica's gaze became distant, her voice dropping to a whisper. "The Asuras revel in the suffering they cause. They take pleasure in the torment of humanity, in the chaos they create. They weaken our resolve by causing us to lose our spiritual connection."

"But there must be a way to resist them, to fight back?" I asked, my voice filled with determination.

Monica smiled, her eyes filled with a glimmer of hope. "Yes, Emma, Steiner believed so. The battle is waged not only in the spiritual realm, but also in our hearts and minds. We can counter their influence by fostering empathy, compassion, and willingness to see beyond the material. Our connection to the spirit world, inner wisdom, and love for one another are the keys to resisting the Asuras."

I rubbed my chin, contemplating using compassion as a weapon of war.

"Emma, the challenge we face goes far beyond us, beyond our immediate reality," she began, choosing her words carefully. "Steiner's philosophy on the evolution of humankind is intricately tied to the very forces we're up against—the Asuras."

I felt the significance of her statement as if her words resonated within my mind and soul. It became abundantly clear that what we faced wasn't just a personal challenge, but a crucial chapter in the ongoing saga of human destiny.

"The Asuras, according to Steiner, are beings that feed on chaos and division, creating discord and pulling people away from their higher selves," Monica continued. "Their influence is like a dark shadow over humanity, hindering our collective spiritual growth."

"But how do they do that?" I asked, still trying to grasp the enormous impact of what she was saying.

Monica's face was grave as she replied, "Through manipulation, deception, and fear, the Asuras create doubt and confusion. They infiltrate our thoughts, beliefs, and institutions, subtly shifting us away from empathy, compassion, and spiritual understanding."

I felt a chill run down my spine, recognizing the truth in her words and seeing how the world around us reflected the very influence she was describing.

"Steiner believed that the future of humanity, our evolution into a higher, more enlightened state, depends on our ability to recognize and diminish the influence of the Asuras," she said, her voice filled with conviction. "It's a cosmic battle that plays out in the hearts and minds of every human being."

I sat back, absorbing her words, feeling overwhelmed and strangely empowered. Our battle, our mission, was part of a more extraordinary tapestry, a cosmic struggle for the soul of humanity.

"So, what do we do? How do we fight something so vast, so entrenched?"

She sighed, her eyes warm and reassuring. "I suppose we start with ourselves. We diminish their power by recognizing the Asuras' influence in our lives and cultivating love, compassion, and understanding. And by helping others see the same, we contribute to a collective awakening."

Her words resonated with me, touching something deep within. Our fight against the Asuras was more than saving me; it was playing a part in a greater, universal journey.

"We're part of something beautiful, Monica," I said, my voice trembling with emotion. "And we have a role to play, a purpose to fulfill."

She reached across the table, taking my hand, her eyes filled with determination and love. "Yes, Emma, we do. And together, we'll face the Asuras, guided by our inner wisdom and love for humanity. We'll stand as guardians, as warriors of light."

I smiled, appreciating Monica's support, but wondered how much she could help once the Asuras trapped me in their celestial web.

Chapter 18
Riot

The revival of the Unity for Equity movement was like a lighthouse in the fog of societal turmoil. After languishing for years, subsiding into a mere whisper of its once robust activism, it had returned with enthusiasm and unyielding intent. It felt like a sea change, a collective cry for justice and equality, a watershed moment where we could envision a better world for everyone.

However, The Vanguard saw this rejuvenation as a dangerous contagion that must be eradicated. Their violent disruption of a peaceful rally in Boston was a vicious declaration of their agenda—quelling any voice that challenged their warped ideologies.

As we watched the live streaming, The Vanguard's attack was horrifying in its calculated violence. They descended upon the peaceful march with a tactical precision that revealed premeditation. Masked individuals broke from the crowd, brandishing weapons and makeshift shields. They systematically targeted the march's leaders, disrupting the chanting and sign-waving with a chaotic mix of tear gas and rubber bullets.

The air filled with acrid smoke, and people screamed and scattered, desperately seeking cover behind cars and storefronts. Vanguard members used the momentary chaos to vandalize makeshift memorials and banners, their actions a sinister form of erasure and disrespect to the lives honored.

It was as though time itself held its breath during those excruciating moments. Each act of violence seemed to echo not just in the immediate surroundings but through the fabric of our society—each act a counterpoint to the marchers' pleas for justice, amplifying the hate they sought to eradicate.

Monica gripped the edge of the table, her knuckles white. I felt a lump in my throat, tears of frustration pricking my eyes. It was more than an attack on a march; it was an assault on hope, a direct affront to the dream of a just world for which so many had fought and died. The cruelty of The Vanguard's actions punctured our collective conscience, leaving us reeling, yet more determined than ever to act.

"We have to do something, Emma." Monica's voice was a strained whisper, her eyes reflecting the pain we both felt. "We can't let them get away with this. We can't let them be the louder voice."

"I agree," I responded almost instantly, my convictions flaring. "We need to be present, to lend our support where it counts the most."

Monica looked at me, her eyes lighting up in agreement. "Exactly; we need to stand with them. It's the least we can do. And the more visibility our actions inspire, the less room The Vanguard has to spread their twisted narrative."

So, we decided then and there to be part of the next Unity for Equity march. A movement that fought for justice, for the fundamental right to live and breathe without fear, needed allies—now more than ever.

*

Following our decision, I appeared on multiple media platforms to denounce the hatred perpetrated by The Vanguard. The words came quickly, fueled by an incandescent rage and an unshakable resolve to fight back. Staring into the camera, I addressed Gus directly.

"Gus Williams, I don't know what has twisted your soul into believing that hate is the answer." My voice trembled with emotion, teetering on the edge of anger and sorrow. "But there is still time to choose a different path, one of compassion and love instead of destruction and hatred."

As I stepped back from the camera, my thoughts drifted back to Unity for Equity. It would be a stand for justice, a stand against The Vanguard, and most puzzlingly, against Gus—a man whose connection to my past lives I still couldn't fully comprehend. It was a moment of clarity when the personal stakes met the collective, and Monica and I were prepared to put ourselves on the line. We were not just fighting for a cause; we were fighting for the soul of a nation, and in my case, wrestling with the enigma of lifetimes that connected me with the very man I was standing against.

*

The following day, I was startled by a relentless pounding on my door. Heart racing, I rushed to open it and found Gus there, hammering away with a fury. His eyes were like wild flames, and I could barely catch my breath in surprise. I had braced myself for some backlash after publicly calling him out, but I never imagined he'd storm into my personal haven to confront me.

"You have some nerve, Emma," he spat, his voice dripping with contempt.

I stood my ground, refusing to let him intimidate me. "You're the one with nerve, Gus," I shot back. "Attacking innocent people, trying to crush a movement that's standing up for what's right. You can't possibly think what you're doing is justified."

His face twisted into a sneer. "Justified? Do you think those people are innocent? They're tearing our country apart, Emma, and you're helping them."

My heart pounded in my chest. I could feel the heat of his anger, but my resolve was firm. "No, Gus, you and your cohorts are tearing our country apart. Your hatred, your violence—that's what's destroying us."

He took a step toward me, his hands clenched into fists. "Don't you dare preach to me about hatred and violence. You have no idea what you're talking about. You don't know what's really going on."

I couldn't help but feel a pang of sadness as I looked into his eyes. In a previous life, this was a man I cared for. And now, all I saw was a stranger consumed by darkness.

"I thought I knew you, Gus," I said, my voice softening. "I thought you were someone who wanted to make a difference, to build a better world. All I see now is someone lost, so filled with rage. You've lost sight of what's truly important."

His eyes widened, and for a moment, I thought I saw a flicker of something else, something vulnerable and human. But it was gone in an instant, replaced by cold determination.

"You don't get it, Emma," he growled. "This is a war; sadly, you've chosen the wrong side."

My eyes misted over as I looked at him. "Gus, you're the one who has betrayed the essence of who we could be. Your fear and anger have warped you into someone entirely unfamiliar."

"Unfamiliar?" He spread his arms wide, incredulous. "I was already the leader of The Vanguard when you met me. This is who I am."

I waved him off dismissively. "That's beside the point." Words were futile when it came to expressing the ancient connections we had. The conversation spiraled, our voices crescendoing in a tumultuous symphony of blame and hurt. The atmosphere grew electric, charged with the weight of our mutual anguish and animosity.

Finally, Gus turned to leave, his face set in a mask of cold fury. "You'll regret this, Emma," he said, his voice deadly quiet. "You'll see that I'm right, and you'll wish you never crossed me." The door slammed shut, leaving me trembling, the echoes of our argument ringing in my ears. At last, my feelings for him were extinguished, replaced by a profound sense of loss and a determination to fight even harder against the evil he represented.

I knew then that the battle with The Vanguard would get even more complicated and dangerous. But I also knew I couldn't back down and had to continue to stand up for what I believed in, no matter the cost. The future of the movement and the very soul of our nation depended on it.

I sat on the sofa, my hands wrapped around a warm cup of tea, the remnants of my confrontation with Gus still hanging heavy in the room. Monica emerged from her bedroom, her eyes filled with concern.

"I heard everything," she confessed softly, sitting beside me. "Are you okay?"

I nodded, though the truth was I felt anything but okay. "I just never thought it would come to this. I thought maybe, somehow, I could reach him. But he's so lost, Monica. So consumed by anger and hatred."

Monica reached out, her hand resting on my arm. "Maybe there's another way to reach him. One that doesn't involve confrontation."

I looked up at her, curiosity in my eyes. "What do you mean?"

She leaned back, her eyes thoughtful. "What if you approached Gus in his dreams? It could be a way to break through, to reach him in a place where he's not guarded by anger and fear. If you could pry him away from the Asuras' control and find out what's truly happening, you might be able to save him."

The idea was intriguing, though I needed to figure out how it would work. Gus wasn't like me; he wasn't lucid in his dreams.

"I don't know, Monica," I said, doubt creeping into my voice. "How would I even communicate with him? He'd just be drifting about with no focus, no awareness."

Monica's eyes sparkled with determination. "But that's where your gift comes in, Emma. You can enter his dreams, guide him, and help him see things differently."

I thought about it, the idea taking root in my mind. It was unconventional, but it felt like the right thing to do. I had to see if I could reach Gus and help him know the truth.

That night, I went to bed with a purpose, ready to take the fight to a new battlefield within the dream realm. As I delved into the ethereal landscape, I sought Gus, determined to reach him and break through the dark influence that held him captive.

At last, I found him and approached, my senses immediately assaulted by a surreal sight. It was as if the presence of evil forces had tainted the very fabric of the dream. Gus was there, his figure aimless and confused, just as I had feared, but something far more sinister accompanied him. Strange and eerie ethereal images swirled around him, like twisted phantoms taking shape in the shifting shadows.

These images were no mere figments of the dream world; they embodied the Asuras' influence, an unmistakable manifestation of their sick intent. They danced around Gus, forming intricate patterns that seemed to shield him from my reach. Dark tendrils of energy snaked through the dream, connecting Gus to these otherworldly beings and reinforcing their grip on him.

"Come on, Gus," I whispered, frustration mounting. "Focus on me. Hear me."

But he continued to drift about, lost and disconnected, his mind a jumbled mess of thoughts and emotions trapped by the Asuras' ethereal web. Their presence was undeniable, their sinister influence more evident than ever. It was as though they were taunting me, daring me to challenge their control over Gus's dream.

I realized that breaking through this protective barrier would be daunting, and confronting the Asuras directly within the dream realm would be perilous. Nevertheless, I was determined to free Gus from their insidious influence, no matter the obstacles. With every fiber of my being, I knew that this battle within the realm of dreams was crucial in our fight against the Asuras and their dark agenda.

*

The following morning, when I awoke, my heart was heavy with a profound understanding. The puzzle pieces fell into place as I reflected on the surreal encounter. It became abundantly clear to me that Gus had not willingly chosen this path of darkness. Instead, he was under the influence of the Asuras. The eerie, ethereal images surrounding him were a manifestation of the Asuras' insidious control over him.

This revelation weighed on me like a heavy burden. I had to act swiftly and decisively to rescue Gus from the clutches of these harmful beings. The fate of our eternal friendship and the essence of my mission to combat the Asuras depended on my success in the dream realm.

"There must be a way to make Gus lucid," I said, desperation creeping into my voice, "but I don't know how to do it if it's not of his free will."

Monica's eyes narrowed, her mind working. "What if we try to find Gus's soul in a previous incarnation before the Asuras' influence infected him?"

The idea sparked a glimmer of hope, and I leaned in, intrigued. "You mean go back to a point in his past lives when he was untainted by the Asuras?"

Monica nodded, her determination shining through. "Exactly."

My mind raced with the possibilities of this new approach. It was unique and had challenges, but it felt like a more direct way to reconnect with the Gus we once knew.

"If we can pinpoint that pivotal moment," I said, the excitement within me swelling like a rising tide, "when Gus's soul was pure and untainted by the Asuras, we might have the key to bringing him back to his true self."

Monica's unwavering gaze met mine, carrying a profound sense of shared purpose. "Delving into Gus's past lives will be a profound journey, Emma. And in doing so, you may hold the potential to rescue him from the suffocating darkness."

My mind was set on a singular quest—to uncover that elusive fragment of Gus's existence from his time in early 20th-century India when he was Anand, the impassioned fellow reformer whose connection with me transcended the bounds of ordinary discourse. In this incarnation, I believed I could find the essence of Gus, the unadulterated soul that the Asuras' dark influence had eclipsed.

As I embarked on this perilous journey through the annals of time, I knew I would encounter challenges and revelations. But armed with determination, love, and the unbreakable bond of friendship, I was resolute in my mission to unearth Gus's true self and lead him back to the path of light and compassion.

Chapter 19
Searching for Anand

Monica's intense gaze held mine, a silent promise of kinship in our quest. "Venturing into the depths of Gus's previous incarnations won't be without its challenges," she cautioned. "You'll need to traverse time and consciousness, Emma. I hope this is the path that will lead Gus from the shadowy grasp that holds him."

So I began an odyssey into the dream realm, a place where the temporal tapestry frayed, allowing past, present, and the possible to blend. The echoes of Gus's existence as Anand called to me, a siren song from the soul's abyss. Here, the strict lines of chronology faded, giving way to an expansive domain of existence.

I ventured night after night into a realm where the boundaries of reality faded. Each night's journey drew me deeper into enigmas I yearned to decipher.

These dreams were a kaleidoscope of experiences, a fragmented tapestry of past lives and forgotten memories. I caught fleeting glimpses of moments that seemed to belong to other versions of myself, other lifetimes where I had walked different paths. The ghostly echoes of these existences whispered to me, tantalizing and enigmatic.

Yet, amidst this swirling tapestry, my unwavering focus remained on the elusive life of Anand, the key to unlocking Gus's true self. It was as if I were navigating a labyrinth of memories, searching for the one thread leading me to the heart of Gus's soul.

In the dreamscape, I witnessed fragments of Anand's life, like scattered pieces of a puzzle waiting to be assembled. I saw him in moments of passion and purpose, his voice resonating with conviction as he stood before fellow reformers, a beacon of change in a world on the cusp of transformation. But there were also shadows, subtle hints of the encroaching darkness that threatened to consume him. In these moments of vulnerability, I sensed the Asuras' insidious presence lurking at the fringes of his essence.

Navigating the intricacies of time in the spirit world was a formidable challenge. It defied the linear progression of the waking world, a realm where cause and effect were intertwined in a complex dance. Each attempt to reach further into Anand's past required a profound attunement to the subtle currents of the soul's journey.

Many nights passed in frustration and uncertainty as I grappled with the elusive nature of time in the spirit world. But with each failure, my determination grew stronger. Monica stood by my side, a pillar of unwavering support, her belief in my mission steady.

And then, one fateful night, a profound shift occurred as I slipped into the dream state. I felt myself transcending the boundaries of the present, propelled by an inner force that guided me deeper into the past. The kaleidoscope of dreams merged into a singular vision—a moment in time when Anand's soul stood unburdened, untouched by the Asuras' influence.

I had found the thread, the connection that had eluded me. With a sense of awe and trepidation, I stepped into that moment, a witness to the purity of Gus's soul before the darkness had taken hold. I was transported to a bustling street in early 20th-century India at night. The sights, sounds, and smells were overwhelming, yet strangely familiar. I knew I had to follow the path that led me to Anand.

As I continued to explore, I could feel the vibrancy of the busy street enveloping me. The air was filled with the heady scent of spices and the sounds of merchants haggling over their wares. It was a sensory overload, both chaotic and enchanting.

My steps led me deeper into the heart of the market, each footfall echoing with intent. I followed the trail of Anand's presence, drawn to the magnetic pull of his passion and purpose. The crowd parted before me, allowing me to draw closer to the source of that unmistakable connection.

There, in a circle of fellow reformers, I found Anand. He was a beacon of light, his eyes alive with a fire. His words flowed with conviction as he spoke of change, a brighter future, and the power of collective action. Our connection was undeniable, an invisible thread of destiny that bound us together across the chasms of time. As I gazed into Anand's eyes, I felt an overwhelming surge of emotion, a recognition that stretched far beyond the boundaries of ordinary discourse.

But I also sensed the subtle undercurrents, the shadows that threatened to encroach upon his spirit. The Asuras' influence lingered at the edges of his consciousness, a looming darkness that sought to taint his noble intentions. With a determined resolve, I reached out to Anand, not with physical touch, but with the profound energy of the soul. In this ethereal realm, words were unnecessary, for our connection transcended language. I projected my thoughts, knowledge, and warnings directly into his consciousness.

I showed him glimpses of the Asuras. I revealed their insidious agenda and their relentless pursuit of power and dominance. I imparted the danger they posed to him and the very fabric of existence. Anand's eyes widened as he absorbed this otherworldly knowledge. The realization of the impending threat seeped into his being, mingling with the passion and purpose that defined him. He recognized the choice that lay before him, a choice that would shape not only his destiny but the fate of all those he sought to inspire.

In that pivotal moment, as the vibrant tapestry of the past unfolded around us, Anand's soul stood at a crossroads. The darkness that had once lurked at the periphery of his consciousness now faced a formidable adversary—awareness.

The Asuras' grip weakened as Anand's spirit ignited with newfound clarity and determination. It was a transformation born of knowledge, a realization that he held the power to resist their influence, to protect the purity of his ideals, and to safeguard the future he so passionately envisioned.

As our connection deepened, Anand's eyes met mine, filled with gratitude and resolve. The thread of destiny that bound us had not only connected our souls across time but had also woven a tapestry of hope and resilience. In that transcendent moment, I knew that the seeds of change had been planted, not only in Anand's heart but in the very fabric of existence. In his current life, Gus would carry the echoes of this awakening, the knowledge of the Asuras, and the strength to resist their insidious influence.

With a sense of fulfillment, I withdrew from the past, leaving Anand to continue his journey with newfound determination. The echoes of our connection lingered in the ethereal tapestry of time. As I returned to the realm of dreams, I realized how love, compassion, and understanding could triumph over the darkest forces.

In the waking world, I couldn't help but hope for signs of a shift in Gus, for the impact of our encounter in his past life to ripple into his present existence. The possibility that reaching back into his history might spark a change in his current life filled me with cautious optimism. It was a glimmer of hope, a beacon in the relentless darkness that had gripped him for so long.

But I knew that my mission was far from complete. The Asuras were patient and relentless adversaries and would not easily relinquish their hold on Gus. I had ventured into the past to plant the seeds of awareness, but nurturing those seeds into full bloom would require more than a single encounter. It would demand unwavering determination and a continued connection with Gus's soul, a relationship transcending time and space boundaries.

As I delved deeper into my preparations and honed my abilities, I held onto the belief that the journey ahead, though fraught with challenges, held the potential to rescue Gus from the suffocating darkness that had trapped him in the present. It was a mission fueled by love, guided by compassion, and driven by the unshakable bond of friendship, and I was committed to seeing it through to its end.

Chapter 20
Gus's Tug of Conscience

I sat in one of the opulent rooms at the White House, a heavy mahogany desk separating me from Mark Jordan, the president's Chief of Staff. The ambiance screamed prestige, authority, and an unspoken weight of consequential decisions. However, the oppressive air seemed to carry something else, a silent yet palpable tension.

Jordan, a man with unquestionable loyalty to the president, looked up from his paperwork, fixing me with a scrutinous gaze. "Gus, we've summoned you here because we believe you could be a substantial force in the upcoming Transcontinental Unity Coalition Summit. The president is adamant about taking strong action against the radical left-wing media. They've been disrupting our message, and he'll soon sign an executive order against public protesting during the event."

I felt a shiver run down my spine. The proposition seemed dangerously close to a direct assault on the First Amendment. "Mark, we're talking about a fundamental right here—the freedom of speech, the right to peaceful assembly. Doesn't this executive order go against that?"

The Chief of Staff leaned back in his leather chair, looking annoyingly comfortable with the topic. "Gus, we're aiming here for a broader picture. With control of both houses and another Supreme Court Justice soon to be confirmed, we're considering all sorts of constitutional changes."

A surge of unease washed over me, like a ripple in a still pond, quickly transforming into a wave of acute discontent. The sensation was so overpowering that for a brief second, I felt disoriented. The walls seemed to close in, the portraits of past leaders appearing to glare down at me in judgment.

For some reason, I found myself thinking about Emma, someone I hadn't thought about for months. Her voice echoed in my mind, a haunting reminder of a different kind of responsibility—a duty to a higher order and the essence of my soul. Was this discomfort, this moral ambiguity, a sign that I was straying from a path I couldn't fully comprehend?

Shaking off the disturbing thoughts, I focused on Jordan. "This isn't something to be taken lightly," I said, choosing my words carefully. "You're contemplating a profound alteration of our nation's legal and ethical framework."

Jordan smiled, the gesture void of warmth. "Well, Gus, these are unprecedented times, wouldn't you say? Times that call for strong leaders willing to make difficult decisions."

His words grated on me, amplifying the internal conflict that was turning from a flicker into a blaze. It was as if his remarks were fanning the embers of my doubts into a full-blown moral inferno. I could see Jordan's path before me, one that offered me power, perhaps even glory. Yet, I found him and it increasingly repellent.

Jordan leaned forward, interlocking his fingers as if bracing for a leap into a darker abyss. "Gus, we'd like The Vanguard to operate as a special force, reporting directly to us. We want eyes and ears on the ground, monitoring and capturing any dissident behavior that could harm the president's agenda."

The proposal hit me like a sledgehammer, making my earlier apprehensions look like child's play. He asked me to weaponize The Vanguard into a secret police force, an instrument of domestic espionage. It was an idea that evoked disturbing parallels with authoritarian regimes like Russia and China, where such practices were an open secret.

The disturbing part was that had this proposal come to me a few weeks—or even days—earlier, I wouldn't have flinched. I might have welcomed the opportunity, relishing the chance to serve my country through decisive action. So, what had changed?

"Why the hesitation, Gus?" Jordan inquired, breaking my chain of thoughts. "It's a simple yes or no. Are you with us?" Those words sounded alarmingly binary, offering no room for nuance or internal debate. Yet, I was swimming in a sea of doubts, an unsettling new consciousness gnawing at the edges of my old certainties.

"Um, yes, of course," I said, though not convincingly.

Jordan nodded, but I could see the skepticism seeping into his gaze as if he had sensed my newfound moral disquiet. I was then ushered out of the White House, and with my head spinning, I returned to my hotel. Once there, I threw myself onto the bed and lay there, trying to make sense of my unresolved discontent.

My eyes grew heavy, and as I drifted into the realm of slumber, a subtle force whisked me away from the familiarity of my hotel bed. I found myself in a place of shifting lights and elusive shadows, hovering on the border between reality and imagination. Emma stood before me in the enigmatic twilight, her gaze laden with an urgency that defied simple explanation.

"Listen closely," she implored, her hand gently clasping mine to tether me to this cryptic moment. "A sickness has infiltrated your essence. This presence casts its shadow, pushing humanity perilously close to the precipice of a dark destiny."

I furrowed my brow, a maelstrom of disbelief and intrigue churning within me. "I don't understand."

"These are ethereal parasites that thrive on humanity's baser instincts—fear, hatred, greed." Her voice was laden with gravity. "They magnify these facets, puppeteering their unwitting hosts toward nefarious ends."

A shiver coursed through me as the implications of her words sank in. "Could this be happening to me?"

Emma nodded solemnly, her eyes holding melancholic wisdom. "I've detected it within you, one that resonates discordantly with the soul I once knew. These entities have been orchestrating your thoughts, guiding your choices."

A surge of anger flared within me. "So, what do I do?" The notion that I had been ensnared, manipulated like a marionette, gnawed at my core.

Emma's countenance softened, her words measured with compassion. "The choice is yours to make. You can impede their designs and buy time for those who champion democracy to act."

My curiosity surged, drowning out the disquiet. "But how?"

"Utilize your position within The Vanguard," she advised. "Expose the government's unconstitutional maneuvers. Your influence can slow the encroaching decay, allowing the populace to mobilize and resist the encroaching tyranny."

My thoughts raced back to my encounter with Jordan—the ominous executive orders, the suffocation of free expression, and the threatening presence of the Transcontinental Unity Coalition. Could I have unwittingly contributed to the very malevolence Emma now cautioned me against?

"And if I choose otherwise?" I hesitated, knowing this query held immense weight, though I feared the answer.

"Then the descent into darkness will hasten irreversibly," she replied, her voice tinged with sorrow. "And you will be lost to it."

I jolted awake, drenched in sweat, my heart galloping as if striving to escape its cage. Though I found myself back in the reassuring embrace of my hotel room, the emotional maelstrom of the dream lingered like an intangible mist that refused to dissipate.

What truly confounded me, however, was the dream's stark lucidity. My usual dreams were elusive, their details slipping away like sand through clenched fists. Yet this dream was different, etching every word and image indelibly upon my consciousness. It bore an urgent insistence, a message that begged for immediate interpretation.

My thoughts veered immediately to Monica, Emma's confidante skilled in the enigmatic realm of dreams. I needed answers, verification, and a deeper understanding of the unsettling vision that had unfolded before me. It was a vision that had profound implications for my future and the destiny of an entire nation.

Chapter 21
Gus Visits Monica

As the glass doors to the Harvard Sleep and Dream Research Center silently slid apart, I stepped inside. A tangle of nervous energy sparked through my body as if I were hard-wired with electricity. Busily sorting through a stack of papers at her desk, Monica looked up. For a split second, she seemed to freeze, her eyes widening as they met mine.

"Gus? What on Earth brings you here?" she asked, her tone a cocktail of disbelief and curiosity.

"I had a dream," I said, deliberately measuring each word as if they were ingredients in a complex recipe. "A dream about Emma. She was warning me. It's been haunting me ever since. I've come to ask you if it's just nonsense or a trick of an overactive mind, or do dreams maybe contain fragments of truth?"

Monica's eyes studied mine briefly before gesturing to an open chair. "Have a seat," she said. "Yes, dreams can be both nonsense and wisdom. They're the subconscious mind's cryptic language, filled with symbols and metaphors. Sometimes, they merely reflect our waking lives' trivial worries and thoughts. But sometimes, they serve as windows into our deepest fears, undisclosed desires, or even hint at future events."

I sat, my curiosity piqued but tinged with skepticism. "This dream felt different. Emma spoke to me about dark forces at work as if she consciously and intentionally conveyed a message. Is that even possible?"

The air seemed to thicken as Monica pondered my words. Finally, she sighed deeply and said, "Did you know that Emma can be lucid in her dreams?"

"Lucid?" I repeated with a squint.

"It's where the dreamer becomes aware they're in a dream state. It provides an unprecedented level of access to the subconscious. Emma herself has been experimenting with it and has found it life-altering."

"Lucid dreaming?" I echoed, intrigued yet wary. "Is it a method for direct communication? Can it help me decode the unsettling messages in my dreams?"

Monica leaned back, folding her hands on the desk. "There's a lack of concrete scientific proof about dream-based communication. However, the lucid dream experience can be transformative. It allows you to delve into your subconscious while standard dreaming does not."

"Is this a skill you're saying I could acquire? Could it clarify the dreams I've been having, maybe even unravel these messages from Emma?"

Monica's eyes narrowed into slits, her face suddenly shaded with a cautious hesitation. "Lucid dreaming is powerful and possibly dangerous. It's like a magnifying glass—it can make the beautiful and the hideous more visible. Are you prepared for that duality?"

"I am, but why is it dangerous?"

Her gaze was intense, almost palpable, as it collided with mine. "Gus, you're no ordinary man. The decisions you make have repercussions that reach beyond your immediate circle. Such knowledge acquired could become a tool for wrongdoing." Her remark cut deep, tapping into the moral schism that had begun to crack open within me. It was unsettling to realize that I didn't have a confident answer.

"I've been going through some changes," I admitted, breaking eye contact for the first time. "Things I would have once scoffed at now occupy my thoughts. I need answers, Monica, whether they're comforting or not."

Monica examined my face, perhaps searching for traces of sincerity or deceit. "All right," she finally said, "but let me be clear—the world of lucid dreaming will offer no sanctuary from uncomfortable truths. It may expose aspects of yourself that you're unprepared to face. But if you're willing to confront that, I'll be your guide."

Taking a deep breath, I nodded, feeling a mixture of exhilaration and trepidation. "I have to understand what's happening to me, Monica. I have to try."

She sighed, her face softening into a blend of relief and concern. "All right, Gus. Brace yourself. You're about to set foot on a journey that will challenge everything you think you understand, everything you think you are."

Monica began by taking me through the foundational principles of lucid dreaming. "It's not just about knowing you're in a dream," she explained, "but also learning how to manipulate that dream environment. You must start with reality checks, triggers that tell you you're dreaming."

Over a series of evenings, we started with the basics—journaling my dreams to remember them better, doing reality checks throughout the day to encourage the habit in the dream world, and focusing my mind before sleep with specific intentions. Slowly but surely, I started seeing progress. My dreams became more vivid, and a few times, I even achieved a semblance of control—knowing I was in a dream without waking up.

Monica seemed pleased with my ease into the phenomenon, yet her eyes always carried an edge of caution. "You're making good progress, Gus, but we're entering treacherous waters. Remember, lucid dreaming can liberate, but it can also trap."

After several sessions, Monica proposed something that surprised me. "I think you're ready for something more radical," she said, her voice tinged with both anticipation and hesitance. "How would you feel about meeting Emma in a shared dream? She's advanced enough to make it possible. It's a controversial area of oneirology, but anecdotal evidence suggests that dreamers can sometimes share experiences."

"Oneirology?" I repeated with a grimace.

"It's the scientific study of dreams," Monica explained.

I nodded and considered meeting Emma in the dream world. The idea was electrifying but deeply unsettling. "You mean a rendezvous in a parallel universe of thought and subconscious? Is that even possible?"

"I believe it is," Monica said. "If you're convinced that Emma was trying to communicate something important, this could be your chance to confront it directly. To ask her, face-to-face, what she meant."

The weight of the choice before me settled in, akin to a slowly developing photograph that brings an obscured landscape into sharp focus. I could meet Emma, delve into the issues plaguing me, and unlock a hidden message that could be crucial for whatever looming crisis awaited.

I felt a strange confluence of fear and longing as if I were standing on the precipice of a cliff, both terrified and exhilarated. After what seemed like an eternity, I nodded.

"All right, let's do it," I said, my voice a whisper, almost drowned out by the pounding of my own heart.

Monica's eyes held a complex blend of relief, anticipation, and ever-present caution. "Very well. Prepare yourself, Gus. If you thought you were on a journey before, you haven't seen anything yet."

Chapter 22
Reunited

Hunched over the steering wheel of my car, I stared at the dimly lit entrance of the Harvard Sleep and Dream Research Center, my pulse hammering in my ears. It had been months since I last saw Emma. We'd turned a friendship pulsating with sexual tension into a battlefield of mutual loathing, yet she haunted my thoughts relentlessly. Ever since she infiltrated my dreams—a nebulous realm where reality blurs with the surreal—it was obvious that Emma had something crucial to tell me. It had been gnawing at me, pressing against the walls of my conscience like a specter demanding to be acknowledged.

Under Monica's guidance, the farfetched notion of lucid dreaming had been demystified. Over several weeks, I had not just learned but mastered the delicate art of lucidity in my dreamscapes. It felt like unlocking a secret chamber within my mind, a perplexing labyrinth fraught with the possibilities and pitfalls of my psyche. The experience was exhilarating and terrifying, pushing me to confront aspects of myself I'd rather keep buried.

My emotional journey within these dream worlds was intensifying, amplified by the looming dilemmas and moral questions that shadowed my waking life. I revisited my formative years in the Marine Corps in one hauntingly vivid dream. There I was, a fresh recruit on one of the grueling obstacle courses at Parris Island. Initially, I faltered, stumbling through the challenges. But as I gained lucidity, I excelled, impressing even the dreamscape drill instructors with my newfound agility. It left me questioning the origins of my unyielding loyalty and sense of duty— attributes now mired in ambiguity.

Then there was the profoundly unsettling confrontation with my doppelgänger, an eerie replica imbued with the darker aspects of my character. We clashed, first in a verbal sparring match and then physically, as if we were archenemies in a parallel universe. It was like grappling with my shadow, fighting against every regret, every suppressed cruel impulse. When I awoke, I felt a curious amalgam of trepidation and catharsis. I'd faced a part of myself that I'd spent a lifetime avoiding, and while the revelation was unsettling, it was also oddly liberating.

But the most psychologically wrenching experience was an exploration of alternate timelines. Amid the burgeoning political chaos in the real world, I traversed different paths my life could have taken. Would joining the rebels have made me a freedom fighter or a traitor? Would denying that dark request from the Chief of Staff have salvaged my morality or crippled my influence? Each fork in the road unveiled a cascade of consequences, leaving me grappling with the ethical complexities of my choices.

I was so lost in these ruminations that the tap on my window startled me like an electric jolt. My eyes met Emma's. Her expression was inscrutable, yet her stare—a magnetic blend of question and challenge—seemed to probe the depths of my soul. Without uttering a word, they asked: "Are you ready?"

Inhaling deeply to steady my racing heart, I lowered the window and gestured for her to enter. Whether I felt prepared or not was irrelevant; destiny was forcing my hand, guiding me down an intriguing yet precarious path. I had to confront what lay ahead, which now included navigating the intricate labyrinth of my conflicted feelings for Emma.

As she climbed into the passenger seat, I couldn't help but feel that we were both teetering on the edge of an abyss, about to dive headlong into the unfathomable depths of our shared dreamscape. And despite the labyrinthine complexities that threatened to entangle us, I was more than just willing—I yearned to confront whatever awaited.

Emma settled into the car's leather seat, her eyes briefly scanning the dashboard before resting on me. "Monica told me you've been coming," she said, her voice tinged with surprise and curiosity. "I was startled, to be honest. Never thought you'd be interested in something like this."

I shrugged, masking the storm of emotions churning within me. "Like they say, life's full of surprises. So, what about you? What brought you here?"

Emma paused, her eyes becoming distant momentarily, as if collecting her thoughts or maybe fortifying herself for a confession. "I was having nightmares," she finally said. "Intense, debilitating nightmares that made every night a horror show."

"Oh my," I muttered.

Emma nodded and said, "Monica taught me how to control them through lucid dreaming and how to take the reins instead of being a helpless passenger in my subconscious. I learned to navigate my dreams to change their course. I never thought that path would lead me back to you, especially after the way things ended between us."

"The universe does work in mysterious ways." I mused at the cliché, now touched with a newfound reverence, marveling at the twisted but purposeful lines that had drawn us back into each other's orbit.

"Or it has a wicked sense of humor," she countered. "So, what are you hoping to find, venturing into the dream world with me? Monica says she's never tried to sync up two dreamers before. We're like her little science experiment."

"I'm at a critical juncture," I mumbled, fixing my gaze on the dashboard like a compass pointing to hidden truths. "These dreams, they're forcing me to confront aspects of myself. And I can't shake the feeling that you're somehow connected to what comes next."

Emma's eyes met mine, their glow intensified by the dim light within the car. "I also sense that something pivotal is happening. But this journey we're considering—it's not for the faint of heart. Are you sure you're up for this?"

"You mean in there?" I asked, nodding toward the Dream Center's looming entrance.

"In the realm of dreams," she clarified. "It's a place where we might find some answers, or at the very least, the right questions to ask. But it will be an intense experience. So, if you have any reservations, now's the time to voice them."

The significance of the choice filled the air, amplifying the unspoken tension that had long existed between us. I reached out, cautiously taking hold of her hand. The sensation was electric, as if a dormant circuit had suddenly been completed. "I'm ready," I confirmed, a sense of excitement mirrored in the subtle tightening of her grip.

A genuine smile broke through her usual reserve, transforming her entirely. "Then let's venture into the uncharted, Gus. Prepare yourself; reality is about to get a whole new rulebook."

There, enveloped by the night and the soft glow of the car's interior, we committed to a path neither could predict. A journey through the tangled mazes of dreams awaited us, a quest for clarity about who we were and what we might be to each other. Hand in hand, we took that figurative leap into the unknown, both anxious and exhilarated by the revelations that lay ahead in the shadowy realms of the subconscious.

Chapter 23
A Shared Awakening

The recliners felt like extensions of the dark, wood-paneled room, upholstered with a soft fabric that promised comfortable passage into the dream world. Monica had set them close together, a bank of monitors and electrodes arrayed around us like high-tech sentinels.

She looked at us solemnly. "I'll be monitoring your brain activity throughout. If either of you goes too deep or anything seems off, I'll wake you up."

"Ready?" Emma asked, her eyes meeting mine.

"As I'll ever be." I sighed.

Monica suggested we hold hands, claiming it might help enhance the connection between our dream states. As our fingers interlaced, a familiar thrill shot up my arm, a sense of intertwined destinies settling in my soul.

"Sleep well," Monica whispered, hitting a switch.

A peaceful ambiance filled the room as soft sounds from the audio system merged with the quiet hum of machinery. I felt the recliner adjust ever so slightly to cradle my body better. My eyes grew heavy, but sleep was elusive. The thrill of holding Emma's hand played over and over in my mind, like a catchy tune you can't shake. The anticipation was electric, each second ticking away on an invisible clock.

I took slow, deep breaths, recalling Monica's guidance on entering a state of relaxed awareness. Each exhale seemed to carry away a small portion of my nervous energy. Slowly, the excitement transformed into a kind of focused calm. My mind's eye saw colors morphing, blending, a prelude to the dreamscape I was about to enter. The world went hazy, then dark, then exploded into a vivid clarity that could only belong to the dream world.

I stood in a lush garden, the colors more vivid than any waking reality. A small brook meandered through the scene, its surface dancing with light. And there Emma was, under the spreading boughs of an ancient willow tree.

"Welcome," she said, her voice threaded with a melody harmonizing with the rustling leaves and bubbling water. We lowered ourselves onto the verdant grass, and for a few timeless moments, we existed, holding hands, feeling a kind of unity that had eluded us in the waking world.

"It's strange, isn't it?" I finally broke the silence. "Being awake in a dream. It's like I'm fully here but also aware that there's another reality waiting for me."

Emma nodded, her eyes reflecting the intricate dance of light and shadow in the dream world. "I know what you mean. Here, every sense is amplified, every emotion poignant. It's freeing and yet disorienting. You're aware you're dreaming, but the line between dream and reality blurs. I often prefer my dream world life to my waking life."

"Exactly," I agreed. "I always felt bound in the waking world—by expectations, responsibilities, and the sheer physicality of everything. But here, those boundaries seem to dissolve. It's exhilarating and a bit terrifying."

She squeezed my hand reassuringly. "The fear is natural. After all, this is uncharted territory. But the exhilaration—that's the taste of true freedom, of a mind unfettered. Don't you think that's worth the risk?"

"Absolutely," I said, a newfound conviction cementing in my soul. "This is like exploring a new frontier, except the frontier is inside me. I never thought I'd become an explorer of internal landscapes, yet here we are."

"Ah, internal landscapes," Emma mused. "Such fertile ground for exploration and change. And it's better navigated together, don't you think?"

"I couldn't agree more," I said, the synergy of our connected hands amplifying the emotions surging within me. "If this is what it's like to be awake in a dream, I can't wait to see what other surprises await us deeper in."

Emma looked at me, her eyes twinkling like distant stars in the night sky. "Then let's not wait any longer."

"Wait any longer for what?"

"We can go further, Gus. This is just the edge of the dream world. We can go where the living dare not tread until their earthly lives are over and they transition to the spirit realm." My eyes widened, but any words of skepticism died in my throat. I looked into her eyes, those endless, mysterious eyes, and knew she spoke the truth.

"In that realm, we can explore the reasons for our connection," she continued. "Why destiny, or fate, or whatever you want to call it, keeps pulling us together. We can learn about our past lives, the intricacies of our souls, and perhaps even catch a glimpse of what the future holds." She paused, searching my eyes for any sign of hesitation. "If you're not ready, tell me now."

I felt the weight of her words, heavy with promise and peril. But as I looked around at this world we had entered, at the woman beside me who seemed as much a part of it as the brook and the willow, I knew there was only one answer. "I want to go further," I said. "Lead the way."

Her face lit up, radiant and filled with cosmic relief. She reached over, and as we touched, the garden around us began to shimmer, dissolve, and then re-form into something infinitely more mysterious.

I tightened my grip on Emma's hand, and together, we took the first steps into a world beyond the veil, following a path that promised answers to questions we had not even thought to ask. Despite the uncertainty, for the first time in a long while, I felt truly alive, bursting with anticipation that made even the dream world seem pale in comparison.

Chapter 24
The Akashic Records

The dream world melted away as if washed by a tidal wave of ethereal light. The garden, the willow, the brook—they all dissolved into a mist that shrouded us briefly before vanishing. Emma and I stood in a place unlike anything I'd ever seen—even in my most outlandish dreams.

"Welcome to the soul world," Emma whispered, awe filling her voice.

The transparent crystal ground shimmered like a sea under the full moon. Overhead, the sky—if you could call it that—swirled in colors that had no worthy name, a celestial dance of iridescent hues. The air was electric, filled with a harmonious hum that resonated with my essence.

"Are you sure about this?" I looked at Emma, trying to find my bearings.

"We've already crossed the threshold, Gus. There's no turning back now. But don't worry, we're safe as long as we stay connected."

We moved through the radiant landscape, drawn by an unspoken agreement toward a gathering of figures in the distance. As we approached, I noticed that these were not humans, but rather beings made of pure light. They emanated wisdom and an overpowering sense of peace.

One of them approached. Its form was fluid, like living, luminescent water, but its eyes—oh, its eyes—were deep pools of ancient knowledge. "Ah, young dream travelers," the being projected, its thoughts seamlessly entwining with ours. Their communication transcended mere language, flowing effortlessly into the depths of our minds. "You seek answers."

"We seek understanding," Emma responded, her voiceless reply resonating with the profound energy of this realm.

"You wish to examine the tapestry of your past lives, the threads that have bound you together time and again," the being intuited, its thoughts embracing us in a warm, empathetic embrace, more felt than heard.

"Yes," we both affirmed, our collective consciousness reaching out to embrace the shared history we longed to uncover.

A second radiant figure materialized beside the first, their ethereal forms intertwining like tendrils of light. Together, they seemed to conjure a mystical dance in the very air around us, weaving intricate patterns of luminescence that wove together our pasts.

Images emerged, evoking emotions and memories transcending time and space's boundaries. Scenes played out before us like shimmering apparitions—the two of us existing in different epochs and forms, yet undeniably recognizable. There were moments of unbridled joy and profound sorrow, times when we had selflessly saved each other, and times when we had, regrettably, failed one another.

"These are your shared pasts," the being conveyed, its thoughts imbued with a reverence for the intricate tapestry of our intertwined existence. "In each life, you two have been destined to cross paths, to teach each other lessons that one lifetime could not encompass."

With a deep sense of curiosity and a tinge of trepidation, I dared to seek further insight. "And what is our lesson in this life?"

"That is for you to still discover," the being responded, its thoughts gently cascading over us like a soothing cosmic breeze. "The weave is not yet complete. You are both thread and weaver, co-creators of the narrative that unfolds in the grand tapestry of existence."

As Emma and I absorbed these revelations, our connection to the beings of light deepened, and a sense of awe permeated us. The cosmic dance of understanding and self-discovery unfolded in this surreal realm, where past, present, and future intertwined in a mesmerizing display of spiritual illumination.

Emma squeezed my hand tightly, pulling me back into focus. "We should go," she said. "We've seen enough for now."

"Remember," the being projected as we turned away, "the soul world is but a reflection of your inner world. Understand one, and you understand the other."

We walked hand in hand, my mind buzzing with revelations, my soul feeling both heavier and lighter. As we moved away, the crystalline ground beneath us blurred, giving way to the dream world from which we had initially departed.

"We'll talk about this, won't we?" Emma looked at me, her eyes more alive than ever.

"Yes," I replied, "but words will never do justice to what we've just experienced."

And with that understanding, we stepped back into the realm of dreams, forever changed yet still ourselves, bearing the shared secret of a realm far beyond waking comprehension. When we woke in the recliners, our hands were still interlocked, our souls forever entwined in a mystery transcending time and space.

Monica looked at us as we regained consciousness, her eyes on the monitors displaying our brain activity. "You're both awake. How do you feel?"

"Like I just came back from another universe," Emma responded, her eyes meeting mine.

"And you, Gus?" Monica turned her gaze toward me.

"Incredible. Overwhelming. It's hard to put into words," I said, recalling the ethereal landscapes and beings of light we'd encountered.

Monica's eyes widened. "Please, tell me everything. Leave no detail out."

Emma and I recounted our journey through the dream world, describing the lush garden, the brook, the willow tree, and our foray into an even deeper realm. We talked about the beings we encountered, the sensations of existing in multiple timelines, and the strong sense that we were connected through past lives.

"Intriguing," Monica finally commented, pulling up her chair to face us. "You ventured beyond where I thought you would go. Your brain activities were synchronized in an unprecedented way. You journeyed into what Steiner called the *Akashic Records*."

"The Akashic Records?" Emma echoed, her curiosity evident.

"Yes," Monica elaborated. "Steiner described it as a sort of 'cosmic library,' a repository that records every soul's thoughts, actions, and emotions. He believed that through disciplined spiritual development, one could access this dimension."

"It felt like we were there," I said, still in awe of the experience. "Could the beings we met be guardians of some kind?"

"It's a possibility," Monica conceded. "Steiner would likely say that they could be advanced spiritual entities that oversee the soul's evolution. The mind is still a mystery we've barely scratched the surface of. Through lucid dreaming, what you've done today is truly groundbreaking."

Emma looked over at me and smiled.

Monica adjusted her glasses and leaned back, a mix of professional curiosity and personal awe dancing in her eyes. "What's fascinating about the Akashic Records is that they're not just a static library but a dynamic, constantly evolving reservoir of cosmic wisdom. Accessing the Akashic Records provides insights into past lives, future possibilities, and the interconnectedness of all existence."

She paused, letting the words sink in before continuing. "If you encountered beings during your journey, they will likely serve a purpose within this cosmic repository. Guardians, guides, advanced spiritual entities—call them what you will. Their role might be to aid souls in interpreting and understanding the vast swathes of information stored there. In other words, they could be akin to cosmic librarians, helping you navigate through endless halls of spiritual knowledge."

I looked at Emma, who seemed to be processing the information; her eyes widened slightly in awe and curiosity. "So, you're saying the Akashic Records could guide our actions, decisions, and spiritual growth?"

Monica nodded, her face earnest. "Exactly. The insights gained can be transformative, enlightening, but they also come with a great responsibility—to oneself and the collective soul of humanity."

She leaned forward, a hint of caution in her voice. "What you've managed to do through a scientific approach to lucid dreaming could be the tip of the iceberg. You've ventured into territories often only explored through many, many years of spiritual practice."

Emma and I exchanged glances, realizing the magnitude of what had unfolded. This was no longer just about dream exploration; we had stepped into a realm that promised answers to the mind's mysteries and a deeper understanding of our soul's journey, past, present, and possibly future.

As I squeezed Emma's hand, it was clear this was just the beginning of a much larger journey. Our adventure into the dream world had opened doors neither of us expected, doors we were eager to explore further. Monica's revelation about the Akashic Records added another layer of profound mystery and curiosity.

"You have had a rare experience," Monica emphasized, looking at us intently. "But remember, each journey is unique. And while you're exploring this other realm, you're still tied to this one. Proceed with caution, respect, and intent."

"We will," Emma assured her, her eyes locking with mine. "Trust me," she whispered, "this is just the beginning."

I smiled, my heart filled with a sense of adventure and wonder. "And we have so much more to explore," I said.

Chapter 25
A Change in Gus

I strode into The Vanguard's headquarters, the ethereal remnants of the dream realm still clinging to me like a second skin. The atmosphere inside was as tense as ever, but today it felt like a discordant note in a symphony.

Derek, my loyal second-in-command, was quick to greet me. "Gus, listen up. We've got a situation. Unity for Equity is pushing its agenda to advance civil liberties, selling it as a matter of national security. They're gaining traction and fast."

I eased into my chair, feeling its formality more acutely than before. "What are our options?"

"We could go on the offensive, leak some damning facts about the leaders and disrupt their momentum," Derek said, his eyes narrowing with a sort of tactical glee.

Normally, I would have jumped at the chance to disassemble an adversary. But today, I hesitated. "How about a different approach? What if we engage them in open dialogue?"

Derek's eyes bugged out. "Dialogue? Are you serious?"

Before I could respond, my phone buzzed with an email. It was a request for an interview from *Radical Views*, a far-left-leaning cable network. My initial instinct was to decline; I'd been on that show before, and the combative nature of the interviews left me drained.

But now, I saw an opportunity. I handed the phone to Derek and said, "Book the interview. It's time to shift the narrative."

Walking through The Vanguard's headquarters, I became keenly aware of the stifling, rigid, tense atmosphere. I noticed the anxious glances of my team members as I passed their workstations, the slight stiffening of their backs, and the subdued conversations that fell silent in my presence. They feared me, and why wouldn't they? I had cultivated a culture of intimidation, valuing results over rapport.

As I passed by Sarah, one of our social media experts, she almost recoiled, visibly preparing herself for a terse interaction. And then, for the first time in what felt like ages, I smiled at her—genuinely, warmly. She did her best to return the expression, which appeared pained and confused.

I continued my stroll through the labyrinthine office, making a point to connect with as many team members as possible—a smile, a nod, a word of appreciation to each. When I reached my office, a subtle but palpable change permeated the air. Faces were less tense; conversations were less hushed.

Settling into my chair, I pondered this miniature transformation, my heart lightening. It was so simple yet so impactful. The journey with Emma into the spirit world had stripped away the hardened layers around my soul, allowing a softer, more humane aspect to surface. A ripple effect was already unfolding, its promise yet unknown but deeply hopeful.

As I booted up my computer, I caught my reflection on the screen, a man simultaneously familiar and foreign to me. I liked what I saw for the first time in a long time.

This was just the beginning, indeed.

*

"Welcome back, everyone. Today, we have Gus Williams, the controversial leader of The Vanguard of Purity, a political consultancy firm known for its hard right-wing tactics. Gus, thank you for joining us," said Clara, the show's host, her voice tinged with skepticism.

"Thank you for having me, Clara," I responded, amazed by the even tone of my voice. *Was this really me speaking?*

"So, let's get straight to it," Clara said, leaning forward. "First of all, I'm surprised you accepted this invitation to speak with me on air."

My mouth opened, and out came words I never thought I'd say: "But why? I have nothing to hide." My honesty surprised me; a ripple from the spirit world with Emma seemed to have subtly altered my disposition.

Clara gestured expansively. "Your organization has been accused of supporting policies that erode civil liberties and pushing the far right's agenda. How do you respond?"

Again, the words flowed from me like a calm river. "I appreciate the opportunity to address that issue head-on," I said, maintaining eye contact. "We live in complex times where security and freedom often seem at odds. What I've come to realize, however, is that it's not a zero-sum game." I couldn't believe I was saying this. The old me would have been on the attack by now.

Taken aback, Clara blinked. "That's a departure from your typical hardline stance."

"Sometimes we have to be willing to evolve," I found myself saying, with words that even I struggled to recognize as my own. "In this instance, it seems we could make more progress by finding common ground, by addressing the fears and anxieties that underlie these political movements rather than attacking them outright."

The studio fell silent. Clara looked as though she was recalibrating her entire script in her mind. "So, you're saying you're open to dialogue with those advocating for reducing civil liberties?"

"Exactly," I affirmed, somewhat astonished by my resolve. "And not just a dialogue among politicians and pundits, but an inclusive conversation that involves the citizens who will be directly affected by these policies."

Clara's skepticism melted into genuine curiosity. "Wow, I must say, this is not what I expected from you, Gus Williams."

"I believe in the potential for change, in the possibility that we can do better. And that starts with conversations like this one," I said with an engaging smile.

As the interview concluded, Clara looked genuinely surprised. "Well, this has been enlightening. Thank you for coming on the show. We'll all be eager to see where this new path takes you."

After I removed my microphone and walked out of the studio, a strange blend of vulnerability and empowerment washed over me. For the first time, I had chosen dialogue over confrontation and empathy over authority.

As I walked into the world beyond the studio, my steps were fueled by a newfound perspective. Yes, it was daunting but also exhilarating. Emma's whisper from that ethereal realm echoed in my mind: "This is just the beginning."

And I knew, deep down—it truly was.

Chapter 26
Emma in Trouble

The shrill ring of my phone shattered the quiet in my office. Monica's name flashed on the screen.

"Hello, Monica," I answered, already sensing the urgency in the silence that followed her name.

"Gus, do you have a minute to talk?" she asked, her voice laced with tension.

"Sure, one second," I replied, waving at Derek to leave my office. After the door clicked shut, I continued, "What's going on?"

"It's Emma," Monica began hesitantly. "She ventured into a lucid dream, aiming to explore the spirit world further. She's been there for over twelve hours, and I can't wake her."

My pulse quickened. "Have you tried everything to bring her back?"

"Of course!" Monica snapped, her voice breaking. "I tried everything. It's like she's… too far removed from this realm."

"So, what do we do?"

"You need to go find her," Monica urged.

"Find her?" I said, standing up and grabbing my jacket. "All right, I'll come over."

"It's deeper than the dream world you'll have to navigate," Monica added, her tone even graver.

"Yeah, I get it, the soul world," I said, a note of resolve settling in.

"I haven't told you what you need to know before you go."

"What is it?" I questioned, eager for information.

"I can't explain it over the phone," Monica advised cautiously. "You need to hear it in person."

"All right. I'll head over to the center."

"No, don't go there. Come to my apartment," Monica insisted.

"The apartment?" Confusion swept over me. "Why's Emma at the apartment?"

"Just come," she urged, ending the call abruptly.

*

The tension was palpable when I entered Monica's apartment. Though her face was etched with worry, a glint of hope remained in her eyes. "Come in," she murmured, leading me to a dimly lit bedroom.

Emma lay on the bed, her face serene as though locked in a peaceful dream. "Emma," I whispered, giving her a gentle shake. She didn't stir.

"Why isn't she at the Dream Center?" I asked Monica, turning to face her.

"Emma's lucid abilities have matured; she doesn't need all that equipment," Monica explained, gesturing vaguely as if dismissing the plethora of machines and devices in her lab.

"I've never done this without all the… gear," I confessed. "Can we be certain I'll even reach her?"

Monica sighed, her eyes searching mine. "The truth is, I don't know. But your connection with Emma transcends machinery. You'll have to trust that."

I nodded, uneasy yet determined.

"But there's something else you should know," Monica began, her voice dropping to a near whisper. "The region of the spirit world Emma wanted to explore—it's a dangerous place."

"Dangerous, how?"

Monica took a deep breath, as if weighing how much to reveal. "Have you ever heard of Asuras?"

The word was foreign, filling the room with an even deeper sense of foreboding. "No, I haven't."

"In spiritual cosmology, Asuras are entities you don't want to mess with. They feed on spiritual energy and capture souls that venture too far or get too close. I think Emma might have… attracted their attention."

I felt a chill go down my spine. The stakes were suddenly higher, making my initial concern about reaching Emma without equipment almost trivial.

"So, what do I do if I run into these Asuras?" I said, as if I had eaten something sour.

Monica's eyes locked onto mine as if she were peeling back layers to reveal a truth I had long forgotten. "The Asuras recognize the lust for power in individuals, and you were an easy target for them early on. That's their modus operandi. They find those who crave power, infect them, and use them to spread their disease."

The air seemed to thicken, and I felt the weight of her words deep in my chest. My previous notions of where my powers had originated were crumbling, replaced by this darker, more malicious source.

"So, you're saying my abilities are not… my own?" I stammered, my voice tinged with both disbelief and a creeping dread.

"Your abilities are your own," Monica said. "But your intentions were hijacked."

"So they know me, these Asuras."

Monica nodded. "But that's not necessarily a bad thing. Use their recognition of you. Let them believe you're still susceptible to their influence. That might give you the edge we need to save Emma."

I looked away, my thoughts spiraling into the darker corners of my mind. So, all this time, it wasn't just ambition or drive. Some baneful force had its hooks in me. This realization added a grotesque layer to the tapestry of my life, as though an invisible hand had been guiding me, exploiting my vulnerabilities, orchestrating my rise and potential fall. Was my entire life just a product of this dark influence? Am I even capable of making choices that are truly my own?

The questions loomed large in my mind, casting a shadow over every achievement and every battle won. All my life was an illusion, or worse, bait in a trap I'd been too blind to see. The room seemed smaller than before, as if the walls were inching inward.

"All right," I said, settling onto the bed beside Emma's unmoving form. "If my connection to the Asuras can be advantageous, then I'll use it."

As I lay down, preparing to descend into that perilous realm, one thought eclipsed all others—find Emma. I would venture into the spirit world with the guidance of angels and a risky gambit involving the entities I needed to evade. I was resolute, whether driven by love, guilt, or the uncomfortable truth of my nature.

The room blurred, and I plunged into the convoluted layers of the spirit world, each layer a new terrain of risks and possibilities. But no matter what lay ahead, I carried the dual lights of hope and strategy.

Chapter 27
The Gates

As I ventured further into the enigmatic corridors of the dream world, a profound transformation began to unfold. The once-ethereal fabric of this realm coalesced into a monumental gate that towered like a celestial monument before me. It possessed a haunting majesty, veiled in an iridescent mist, set against a kaleidoscopic sky adorned with swirling nebulas and cosmic wonders. And within this surreal scene, a magnificent entity materialized—awe-inspiring and radiant, its aura pulsating with timeless wisdom and unfathomable depth.

"Augustus." The voice reverberated, invoking my given name. "You now stand at the threshold of the spirit realm. Tracing this ethereal domain while firmly rooted in the earthly realm is a rare privilege, but it is not without its perils. You must demonstrate your worthiness."

The reality around me shifted and transformed before my eyes. Suddenly, I found myself enclosed in a chamber—a sanctum of mirrors, each reflecting a facet of my life, a tapestry of triumphs and tribulations.

"Choose a mirror," the voice continued, its resonance filling the chamber with an aura of solemnity that could be felt in the air.

A sense of trepidation permeated the chamber, thickening the atmosphere with anticipation. After what felt like an eternity, my gaze settled upon one reflection that tugged at my conscience, filling me with a profound sense of regret and sorrow. It depicted a pivotal moment from my past, when, as the leader of The Vanguard of Purity, I had carried out orders that had resulted in widespread suffering. The arrogance and self-assuredness that had driven me then now created blades of remorse piercing my soul.

Summoning courage, I stepped toward that mirror and, with resolve, entered it. The past enveloped me like a fog, revealing the immediate consequences of my actions and the far-reaching ripples of suffering—

anguished faces, shattered lives, and broken communities—all echoing from my decisions. The sorrow overwhelmed me like a tidal wave crashing against the shores of my consciousness.

"Now, you have an extraordinary opportunity," the voice intoned, its echo intensifying the chamber's emotional weight. "The chance to renounce your past is seldom granted before the cycle of life and karma runs its course in another existence. Here and now, in this very life, you can begin purifying your soul."

Tears welled up, unbidden yet welcomed, as they streamed down my cheeks. "I denounce my past actions," I declared, my voice imbued with newfound humility and a profound acknowledgment of my fallibility. "I recognize the pain I have inflicted and reject those deeds and the part of me that was capable of such actions."

The chamber seemed to respond as if it were sentient. Its walls rippled, and the air vibrated with energy. The mirrors momentarily fogged over, then cleared, revealing a different version of me—one with open eyes, humility, and readiness for redemption.

"You have chosen wisely," the entity declared as my surroundings shimmered, and I found myself once more before the celestial gate. "Your soul embarks on its purification today, but understand that this is only the opening chapter. The spirit world is a labyrinthine tapestry, with both darkness and light."

I stood there, frozen, unable to move or speak.

"It is imperative," the entity continued, its voice growing more solemn as the gates groaned open, flooding the space with an otherworldly glow, "that you first seek the counsel of the hierarchical beings. They alone possess the strength to shield you from the Asuras, who are no strangers to your earthly existence."

Taking a shuddering breath, I crossed the threshold, the gateway closing behind me. My resolve solidified, fortified by my life-altering decision and the immense responsibility ahead: to rescue Emma and confront the devilish entities for whom I had once been a pawn.

As the realms melded around me, drawing me deeper into an unfamiliar world, every atom of my being aligned with a singular purpose. In that transformative moment, I found the possibility of redemption for the part of my soul that had strayed so perilously far from its source of light.

After crossing the threshold, a new reality unfolded—radiant and pulsating with an energy that resonated through my very essence. I stood in a meadow adorned with vibrant, otherworldly flora, surrounded by an intoxicating fragrance, unlike anything I'd ever known. Within this surreal landscape, an angelic figure descended from a sky illuminated by streams of iridescent light.

"Augustus, I've been sent to guide you," the angel said, its voice a harmonious chord that reverberated throughout the world around us.

"Guide me?" I questioned, a note of urgency in my voice. "Can you guide me to Emma?"

"All in due time," the angel reassured, its eyes brimming with a wisdom that transcended time and space. "First, you must understand why you are uniquely positioned to confront the Asuras."

I placed a hand on my chest and asked, "Why would they be concerned about me?"

"You possess a latent power," the angel began. "A power that makes you a threat they sought to neutralize by leading your soul astray, pushing you toward harm instead of healing. Now that you have renounced your past and embarked on the path of purification, you have again become a true adversary to them."

The weight of the angel's words settled upon me like a mantle of responsibility. "But what power do I hold over them?"

The angel's countenance grew even more severe. "Your power emanates from the very essence of your soul, your unwavering commitment to truth and justice. The Asuras thrive on deceit and chaos. When fully realized, your untapped potential can unravel the dark tapestry they have woven, disrupting their control over the human realm.

The higher beings—the Archangels and deities—rely on you to tip the balance in favor of light."

"However," the angel continued, "your strength will remain incomplete without Emma. She holds the key to unlocking your full potential. Your destinies are intertwined in ways you have yet to fathom. You must find her to thwart the Asuras and offer a cure for the virus they have inflicted upon humanity."

The enormity of the task set before me began to sink in. Not only to rescue Emma, but to confront these malevolent entities and shift the cosmic balance toward good? It felt overwhelming, yet a spark of recognition ignited deep within me.

"Then take me to Emma," I resolved, "so that together, we may do what must be done."

The angel extended its hand toward me, and as our fingers touched, the meadow around us dissolved into a cascade of light and shadow. We were on the move, journeying deeper into the realms of spirit and destiny, where I would find Emma and, with hope, the strength to fulfill the mission entrusted to me by the higher beings.

As the celestial gates closed behind us, I turned to the radiant being. "May I know the name of the angel guiding me through this perilous journey?"

"I am Uriel," the angel replied, emanating a comforting glow illuminating the nebulous path before us. "I serve as a guiding force for souls embroiled in matters of cosmic significance."

"Uriel, what is the nature of this realm I'm to enter?" I questioned, grappling to grasp the enormity of my quest.

"You will be led to the darker, more materialistic sub-earthly realms inhabited by entities like the Asuras—hindrances to human spiritual progress. This is where you will find Emma, though I can guide you only to its threshold."

"Can you not accompany me all the way?" I asked, with the weight of my solitude in this challenge suddenly dawning upon me.

"Hierarchical beings are not permitted to pass through these lower realms," Uriel explained, a tinge of sorrow clouding its luminous eyes. "The laws that govern our existence prohibit such acts, as they would disrupt the delicate balance of free will and destiny."

The realm Uriel spoke of was unlike any I had envisioned. I pictured a world shrouded in shadows, where the air was thick with maleficent intentions.

As we ventured closer to the boundary of this treacherous realm, Uriel offered a final piece of counsel: "Remember, the Asuras feed on spiritual discord. Your newfound purity will be your armor and your weapon. Yet, for your mission to succeed, you must find Emma. She is your lodestar; you cannot utilize your full power against these nefarious beings without her."

Uriel encased me in a protective auric shield with a sweep of its magnificent wings. "May this light guide you when all others fade," the angel whispered, as if bidding a final farewell.

I looked into Uriel's eyes, drawing strength from its celestial gaze. Then, with a heavy heart but an indomitable spirit, I crossed the threshold into the sub-earthly realm, armed with the newfound knowledge and the responsibility it carried.

The gloom gathered around, yet the ember Uriel sparked within me refused to be stifled. I stood resolute, ready to find Emma and confront the Asuras. I bore a nascent radiance, a threat to the shadows yearning to snuff it out. The realm transformed, its air denser, its darkness deeper, laced with an eerie allure. Colors here bled with an intensity that was mesmerizing yet unnervingly askew, as if refracted through a dream turned sinister. Above, bizarre constellations flickered, their formations as captivating as they were disconcerting.

This was no place of enlightened spirits; it was a quagmire of stagnancy, veiled in the remnants of thwarted dreams and malevolent wills. Here, illumination was a stranger, devoured whole by an abyss ravenous for all that shimmered with virtue.

"Be wary of the enchantment that surrounds you," Uriel cautioned. "The Asuras' domain may mimic paradise, but it is a malevolent mirage—its splendor but a snare to entangle the unwary."

"So, what should I expect?" I asked, trying to prepare myself for the unknown terrain that lay ahead.

"Expect nothing. Assume nothing," Uriel replied plainly. "For assumptions are the first seeds of deception. See with your heart, not with your eyes. Your newfound purity will be your compass. Rely on it to guide you through the subterfuge." We hovered for a moment at the gateway that separated the realms. It was a swirling vortex, less a door than a rip in the very fabric of existence. I felt a sense of foreboding crawl up my spine.

"I can accompany you no further," Uriel said solemnly. "From here, you go alone. But remember, you have been granted a unique power— the ability to harm the Asuras and disrupt their influence. They will do everything they can to disarm and corrupt you again. But they are also frightened of you."

I swallowed hard. "And Emma?"

"She is essential. Without her, the scales could tip in the Asuras' favor. You must find her, not just for your sake, but for the balance of spiritual energies that affect all of humankind. She is in the darker, more materialistic realms, those sub-earthly pits where the Asuras exert their influence. They have taken her there, thinking they can break her, but they underestimate the strength that comes from love. Go now; time bends strangely in their realm. The longer she stays, the greater their influence over her."

Taking a deep breath, I nodded.

"As above, so below," Uriel intoned as it retreated, its form dissolving into a cascade of light particles that sped skyward, rejoining the tapestry of the heavens.

I focused my intent, reinforcing my mental shield and plunging into the vortex. As I passed through, I felt like I was being squeezed and stretched simultaneously—an unsettling, disorienting sensation. But as quickly as it came, it was gone.

I found myself in a landscape that defied logic, a place where the laws of physics held no sway. It was both beautiful and grotesque, like a paradise that had been tainted. Twisted trees with iridescent leaves loomed above, while the ground below shimmered with an ethereal light that seemed to come from nowhere.

I had entered the realm of the Asuras, a place of spiritual quicksand that pulled relentlessly at the edges of my consciousness. But fortified by Uriel's wisdom and driven by my indomitable purpose—to find Emma and to cleanse my soul—I took my first steps into the abyss.

Chapter 28
Emma is Trapped

I found myself in a place that defied easy description. The walls appeared made of liquid metal, always moving yet never altering the room's dimensions. The colors were disturbing, a blend of deep purples and blacks punctuated by acidic greens and yellows, as if the hues were alive and malicious.

The air was heavy, filled with a musty scent that seemed to be trying to choke my essence. Sounds were warped; haunting whispers were everywhere but unintelligible, heightening my sense of isolation. This prison seemed designed to contain, disorient, and break my resolve.

I sat with my back against a wall that pulsed as if it was alive while I tried to think of how I'd ended up here and if Gus or Monica knew my whereabouts. I'd been freely navigating the spirit realms, my lucid abilities giving me a range of movement most could only fantasize about. This time, however, I had ventured too deep, lured by a mysterious resonance that I couldn't resist.

That was when they ambushed me. The Asuras hadn't shown themselves in a form I could understand; they felt more like a cumbersome weight, an overpowering force that pulled me into this disorienting prison. They used my sense of resonance to lure me in.

My thoughts were interrupted by a sudden ripple in the wall beside me. Faces—twisted, filled with malice—materialized briefly before melting back into the wall. They were observing me, attempting to break into my consciousness.

In a flash of inspiration, perhaps desperation, I decided to use my lucid abilities to free myself from the Asuras' grip. I focused my energies, mustering all the willpower I could, recalling the times I'd exercised control in the spiritual realms. It felt like it was working; a tingling sensation radiated from my core, hinting at the potential of breaking free.

But the Asuras seemed to sense my attempt. The walls pulsated more violently, and the colors turned even more menacing as if to mock my feeble efforts. My concentration broke, and my energies scattered, leaving me trapped and emotionally drained. It was a stark, humbling reminder of my captors' overwhelming power and the unique challenge they posed.

Even in the face of this failure, I clung to my resolve like a drowning sailor to a piece of driftwood. These Asuras temporarily thwarted my efforts, deflected my energies, and left me emotionally drained, but they failed to comprehend the tenacity of the human spirit when fueled by hope.

It was that tiny flicker, that barely there luminescence in the depths of my soul, which they vastly underestimated. In their ancient wisdom and overwhelming power, they missed the simple strength of a single earthly soul connected to others by invisible threads of love and friendship. They could see my isolation but not the links that connected me to the earthly world I had left behind—a world that held living souls like Gus, who could search for me.

However, a new uncertainty gnawed within: would Gus even know how to find me? We had journeyed through spiritual realms together, but this was different. This was an abyss, a space disjointed from the natural flow of spiritual landscapes we had come to know. It was as if I'd been removed from the tapestry of existence and placed in a drawer of forgotten mismatched socks. My predicament seemed not just a geographical challenge but a metaphysical one. Could love and connection penetrate a space designed to eradicate those things?

But then, I realized this worry was another of the Asuras' tricks—another attempt to chip away at my resolve. To assume that Gus couldn't find me was to underestimate him, just as the Asuras had underestimated me. I knew the extent of his abilities, the reach of his intuition, and the depth of his love. Moreover, it wasn't just Gus. It was also my mother and friends whose love had infused me with purpose; it was every soul I had ever touched or been touched by. They were my beacon, their collective hope and love shining through the layers of realms, piercing even the impenetrable darkness around me.

So, even if I was isolated physically, I was far from alone in a realm beyond realms. This was the Asuras' strategy flaw—the glitch in their otherwise perfect prison. And it was this gap, this tiny oversight, that I intended to exploit. If hope and love could survive in a place like this, so could I.

I took another slow, purposeful breath, readying myself for whatever would come next. The atmosphere remained oppressive, but I refused to be crushed by it. Help was coming; I could feel it.

Just as I fortified my mental barriers, a vibration rippled through the room—different from the ones the Asuras had used to torment me. This time, it was an audible hum, a garbled yet strangely melodic language that seemed to come from the very walls themselves.

"So, you have decided to defy the boundaries of your realm." The hum coalesced into a voice chillingly articulate. "You wander where mortals should not. For what purpose?"

My mind raced. How could I explain myself in a way these beings would understand—or care to understand? But before my thoughts could form into words, the voice continued.

"Do you know what eternity feels like, Emma? We could show you—eternity spent in a horror-driven existence, an endless maze of your worst fears, a prison crafted from the darkest recesses of your soul."

The walls writhed in tandem with the voice, morphing into grotesque faces with eyes like burning coals. A wave of dread washed over me. Was this a preview of the eternity they promised?

However, instead of succumbing to the terror they sought to instill, I found the grotesque display almost grounding. It fortified my resolve, reminding me that I had faced darkness before and come out stronger and wiser. The Asuras didn't know about my past battles, my debilitating nightmares, the ones that had prepared me for moments like this.

"Do you think I ventured here out of naivety?" I finally found my voice, projecting an air of confidence I didn't fully feel. "I came seeking understanding, not just for me but for lost souls who deserve another chance at redemption. Isn't that a goal worth trespassing boundaries for?"

Silence fell over the enclosure, the walls freezing mid-writhe as if contemplating my words. Then, the voice spoke again, softer this time, tinged with curiosity.

"And you believe your puny human soul has the resilience to withstand the repercussions of such a quest?"

"I don't just believe it," I said, my voice steady as my eyes scanned the room, seeking any sign of weakness in my captors. "I know it. I have something you don't—a connection to a power you can't fathom, relationships that strengthen me, love that sustains me. Your horrors might be eternal, but so is my hope."

As I spoke, a new vibration filled the room. It was different—warm, inviting as if someone had struck a celestial chord. I couldn't be sure, but it felt like help was imminent and already here. Could it be Gus? Or had my defiance caught the attention of something else—something even these dreaded Asurians feared?

"Interesting," the voice mused, its tone unreadable. "It appears you're not alone."

The walls suddenly retracted, pulling away from me as though burned by my conviction. For the first time, I felt the Asuras' grip on me weaken, just a fraction, but enough to breathe easier. Enough to keep fighting. And in that moment, I knew—whatever game the Asuras thought I was playing, they hadn't seen anything yet.

Chapter 29
An Audacious Plan

Gus looked at me, his eyes shimmering with an ethereal glow that was familiar and profoundly otherworldly. For a fleeting moment, we were cocooned in a sphere of tranquility, starkly contrasting the toxic abyss we had just escaped. It was as if we were both standing at the threshold of a new realm, brought together by love and guided by divine intervention.

"Monica was frantic," he said, his voice tinged with a sense of urgency that belied the celestial calm surrounding us. "You had fallen asleep, and she couldn't wake you. She sensed that your soul was in peril and called me to help."

Gus's eyes sparkled with a celestial luminescence as he recounted his journey. "I, too, tried, but you stayed asleep. Then Monica suggested that I venture into the dream world. Of course, I did and became lucid almost immediately, driven by my desperate need to find you. I made my way with the help of the angel Uriel. But when I entered the sub-earthly realm, I could not find you. Just when I thought all was lost, a rift—a tear in the dream materialized before me."

He paused, his gaze locked onto mine, filled with awe and revelation. "I was drawn into that rift, and there, standing amid an ethereal radiance, was the Archangel Michael. He explained that even he, a being of immense celestial hierarchy, couldn't venture into the sub-earthly realm of the Asuras. However, he could empower me to do it. He told me your life was a crucial point of light in a grand cosmic struggle between the celestial and the demonic. For that reason, he made me his surrogate—imbuing me with a fragment of his divine essence to locate you and bring you back."

Gus's grip tightened, and a surge of warmth radiated from his touch, enveloping me in a unique blend of human love and divine grace. It was as if this connection transcended the physical realm, and we were weaving together a new tapestry of existence. In that moment, I sensed a connection between us that extended beyond our shared emotions and into the celestial forces that had led us to this pivotal point.

He began to speak of his journey through the spirit realm, and his words carried an aura of awe and reverence. "With the Archangel's guidance and the celestial power he bestowed upon me," Gus explained, "I embarked on an extraordinary odyssey. It was a journey through a labyrinthine maze of ethereal landscapes, each more enigmatic than the last. In this realm," he continued, "time and space seemed to fold in on themselves, creating a surreal landscape that defied earthly logic. I traversed landscapes of surreal beauty, where the boundaries between dream and reality blurred. I moved through cascading rivers of light, passed through forests of iridescent trees, and ascended crystalline mountains that seemed to touch the very heavens."

Gus's voice filled with wonder as he told of his encounters. "Along the way, I encountered beings of pure light. They radiated wisdom and an overwhelming sense of peace. They were my guides and protectors, reassuring me that I was on the right path. My mission wasn't just a personal rescue; it was a vital part of a grand cosmic strategy. The deeper I ventured into the spirit realm," Gus explained, "the more I sensed the threads of destiny weaving around me. It was as though the cosmos itself had conspired to bring us together, aligning our fates in the ongoing battle between good and evil. Each step I took was more than a physical movement; it was an intense spiritual revelation, drawing me closer to realizing our shared purpose."

"In the heart of that labyrinthine maze," he recounted, "guided by the divine essence bestowed upon me by the Archangel Michael, I found a shimmering gateway. It was a portal to a place where the boundaries of reality and dreams merged—a place where you were held captive by the Asuras. I stepped through that gateway with determination and unwavering faith, prepared to face the darkest depths of the sub-earthly realm to rescue you."

With determination burning in his eyes, Gus continued, the weight of our shared experiences pressing upon his words. "As I entered, the presence of the Asuras surrounded me. It was a realm shrouded in darkness and despair, starkly contrasting the celestial beauty I had traversed." His voice quivered with intensity as he described the harrowing encounter. "The Asuras tried to deter me, to break my resolve, but I clung to the divine essence bestowed upon me. It was a beacon of light in that abyss."

Gus's gaze never wavered as he shared his pursuit of the elusive thread that connected him to me. "I followed the faint trace of your presence through the oppressive darkness, determined to find you. Sensing my purpose, the Asuras unleashed their defenses, creating illusions and nightmarish visions to obstruct my path." He paused, the memory vivid in his mind. "But I pressed on, guided by the unwavering love and the divine mission that had brought me here. Then, I heard your voice, Emma."

His grip on my hand tightened as if to reassure himself that we were together now. "I followed your voice through the labyrinthine maze of the Asuras' domain. It led me to a chamber where they held you captive, trapped by their dark magic." Gus's voice showed a steely resolve as he described the final confrontation. "The Asuras surrounded me, their power formidable, but I drew upon the divine essence, the celestial power that surged within me. It was a battle of wills, of light against darkness."

"With every ounce of strength and love I possessed," he continued, "I reached out to you, Emma, and together, we shattered the chains that bound you. The Asuras recoiled from the radiance of our connection, and in that moment, we overcame them." Gus's narrative continued as he delved deeper into the pivotal moment of our escape from the Asuras' grip. "In that dire chamber where they held you captive, the malevolent energy of the Asuras was palpable. It weighed upon me like an oppressive darkness, threatening to engulf us both."

He paused momentarily, his eyes fixed on mine as if reliving the experience. "I knew that breaking their hold on you would require something more than physical strength—it demanded the essence of our love and the celestial power entrusted to me. It was a battle on multiple fronts—the earthly and the metaphysical." Gus's words were charged with emotion. "With every ounce of strength, I summoned the love that bound us together. It was a force more potent than any dark magic the Asuras could conjure. In that moment, I reached out to you, not just with my physical touch but with the entirety of my being, our souls entwined in a profound connection."

He painted a vivid picture of the moment. "As I touched you, our combined energy radiated like a brilliant beacon, a fusion of our love and the celestial power within me. The Asuras, beings of darkness and malice, recoiled from this radiant connection. Our love and light were anathema to them, a force they could not comprehend or withstand." A sense of triumph and relief colored his voice. "In that climactic instant, the chains that bound you, the dark magic that imprisoned your soul, shattered into a thousand shards. The Asuras, overwhelmed by the brilliance of our unity, were pushed back, their power waning in the face of our shared strength."

Gus's gaze never left mine as he concluded. "And so we overcame them, Emma. We emerged from that sub-earthly realm, our love and determination prevailing over the forces that had sought to keep us apart. The power of our connection, the fusion of love and celestial essence, shattered the chains and banished the darkness." Gus's voice softened. "And here we are, reunited, our souls forever entwined, having defied the darkness and found our way back to each other. Our story," Gus whispered, "is far from over. By facing this ordeal, we've stepped into new roles and greater responsibilities in a cosmic drama. It's clear now that we're not passengers on this journey but active, vital participants in a much larger, divine plan."

"But you can't deny what you've been a part of, Gus," I said, unable to ignore the remaining tension between us. "The regime you supported has wreaked havoc on countless lives, even if you now recognize that we're part of a greater plan. Cosmic destiny doesn't absolve you of your earthly actions."

Gus sighed, his eyes clouding over with a mix of regret and a painful form of enlightenment. "I know," he admitted, "and I've been doing a lot of reflection. What's happened in the past can't be undone, but we can affect the present and the future. This divine plan… it's not an excuse for what I've done or supported. Instead, it's an opportunity for my redemption."

I considered his words carefully, my heart a maelstrom of conflicting emotions. It was hard to reconcile this spiritual, insightful man with the person who had so vehemently stood on the opposite side of a moral divide. Yet, here he was, beside me, not a warrior of earthly ideologies but a fellow soldier in a much grander scheme.

"You understand that I can't just let go, right?" I looked into his eyes, searching for sincerity. "I will fight that regime with everything I have. Your epiphany doesn't change that for me."

"I wouldn't want you to change, Emma," Gus said, his eyes meeting mine with a newfound clarity. "Your relentless commitment to justice—it's one of the reasons I… it's one of the things that helped me wake up. I've witnessed your light, even from the depths I was in, and it guided me out."

I nodded, the weight of our shared experience and the challenges that lay ahead settling around us like a mantle. Looking back at the celestial horizon, it seemed to shimmer as though validating our intentions.

"So, what now?" I asked, curious if Gus had a plan.

"We fight," he said, gripping my hand tighter. "We fight on every front, in every realm, because that's what we're destined to do. And I'll fight beside you this time, not against you."

"Those are lovely sentiments, Gus," I replied, relieved and elated that he was finally on my side. "But 'fight on every front' is a bit vague. Do you have any specifics? Strategy is just as important as will."

He sighed, the weight of our dilemma momentarily clouding his eyes. "You're right, of course. Strategy is crucial. I've been considering maintaining my position in The Vanguard, fighting from the inside. But I can only maintain the charade for so long before they catch on."

I nodded, understanding the limitations of his role. "Being a double agent has its risks, but having someone on the inside is tempting. Still, what if we can set up something that leads The Vanguard to its downfall? Something so damaging it'll be impossible for them to recover."

His eyes sparked with interest. "I like where you're headed with this. You're thinking of making them unravel from within?"

"Exactly," I said, my mind racing through the possibilities. "We leak false information, set traps, and create internal conflicts so severe they'll begin to question their leadership and mission."

"We'd have to be incredibly careful," Gus cautioned. "They're clever and will look for betrayal, especially as tensions rise."

"True," I admitted. "We'll have to be even smarter. Our plan should be so intricate and layered that even if they catch onto one part of it, the other mechanisms will continue to operate undetected."

He smiled, reinvigorated by the idea of an audacious plan. "Then let's do it, let's dismantle The Vanguard of Purity from within. And once that's done. …"

"Then we move on to the next obstacle, whatever that may be," I said, finishing his sentence and gripping his hand as if sealing a pact. "We keep going until we've torn down every institution that stands in the way of universal freedom and equal justice."

We stood at the precipice of a new chapter, filled with the sort of challenges we could never have anticipated but were now eager to face. We were ready to take on the world, not just because destiny demanded it, but because our love was the one true constant, encouraging us to fight the battles ahead.

Chapter 30
Return to The Covenant

As we sat in the dim light of our apartment, waiting to leave for the meeting, Monica took the opportunity to brief us on Senator Clarke and General Harris. "Listen, Emma, I know you met them before, but let me share some background. Senator Diana Clarke is a Democrat from New Jersey, around forty years old, and an ex-Marine. Her military background influences her political strategies, so she's not someone to mess around with. She's serving her second term and is constantly ruffling feathers in the administration. Trust me, they're watching her like a hawk," Monica said, pausing to sip her coffee. "Any slip-up, and they'll crucify her."

I nodded, absorbing the background.

She continued, "And let's not forget about General Mark Harris. He was at the helm of NATO forces when Russia escalated to nuclear in the Ukraine war. After notching up an already violent conflict and finally reaching a peace agreement, it all fell apart when the president was elected to a second term, essentially giving Russia free rein over Ukraine. To say General Harris is furious would be an understatement. He's committed to bringing down the president by any means necessary."

Monica leaned back, looking intently at us. "Together, Clarke and Harris created the Covenant of Freedom. They've managed to recruit some big names from the government and military. We're not talking about some fringe group; these people are serious about staging a coup." She paused, allowing the gravity of her words to sink in. "But they're also up against a fortified administration. The president has pretty much insulated himself, making it almost impossible for a coup attempt to succeed. That's why I think they'll be very interested in what you guys bring to the table—something more than just brute force."

"Are you suggesting we offer them the power over our dreams?" I asked, my eyes meeting hers as I realized the weight of what she was proposing.

Monica nodded, her gaze unwavering. "Exactly. What you've seen and done in the spirit realms can't be ignored. Your ability to navigate otherworldly terrains, your interactions with celestial beings like Uriel and Michael, and the insights gained could be game-changers. Imagine using the dream world as a strategic dimension—somewhere we could gather information or directly influence events in our physical world." The idea hung in the air between us, both audacious and fascinating.

Gus shifted uncomfortably. "But what about the ethical implications? We've always agreed that the dream realm is sacred, that we'd never misuse our powers."

Monica sighed. "You're right, and I'm not suggesting we throw ethics to the wind, but the Covenant is facing a deeply entrenched, authoritarian regime. They need more than just political strategy or military might; they need a new kind of arsenal that can tip the balance in favor of liberty."

I pondered this, recalling my experiences in the lower realms, where corrupt inclinations and unfulfilled desires weighed like anchors. What if we could influence the moral compass of those in power, tilting them away from their darker impulses?

Gus looked skeptical but intrigued. "If we were to share this power, it'd have to be with the utmost caution and rigorous oversight. The risk of misuse is too great."

Monica smiled, seeming to anticipate his reservations. "Of course. And that's part of what would make this partnership so potent. We would insist on ethical guidelines, a form of checks and balances to prevent corruption or abuse of this new dimension of power."

"As intriguing as this is," I finally said, breaking the thoughtful silence, "there's another layer we're not considering. The celestial beings we've encountered, like Uriel and Michael, made it clear that cosmic laws govern these realms. We'd need to tread carefully not to disrupt the balance between free will and destiny."

Monica nodded, her eyes acknowledging the depth of our concerns. "Agreed. But the world outside is in chaos, and perhaps it's time to consider whether your unique abilities might be the missing piece the Covenant needs to restore balance here."

And so, as we sat, bathed in the dim light, we weighed the gravitas of Monica's proposition. It was not just a tactical move, but an ethical dilemma that could redefine the essence of earthly and celestial balance. Then again, desperate times called for desperate measures, and we were nothing if not desperate for change.

*

As we pushed open the door and walked into the cozy space, memories of my first meeting with the Covenant leadership flashed before me. Around this simple, weathered kitchen table, I had heard the revolutionary plans discussed for the first time. The mismatched chairs and the lingering smell of food gave the space an air of warmth and humanity, but the atmosphere felt different this time—a tension threatened to eclipse the room's homey comfort.

Senator Clarke and General Harris sat at the table, papers scattered about, and their faces immediately shifted from expectation to astonishment when they saw Gus.

"Surprised?" Monica quipped, slicing through the tension as she moved to take a seat.

"Are you kidding me?" The general's chair groaned as he leaned back, skepticism filling his eyes. "You bring the founder of The Vanguard here, Monica? Explain."

"It's no joke," I interjected, drawing Gus closer to the table. "He's here because he's committed to our cause. Moreover, he can help us shift the narrative right from the heart of The Vanguard."

The senator rose from her chair, eyes narrowing. "An epiphany, Gus? Or a trick to gain intel?"

Gus met her gaze without flinching. "I'm not asking for your trust, just for the opportunity to prove my commitment. I can help create a revolution that goes beyond physical combat—a shift in the collective consciousness that's both subtle and powerful."

Monica began to pace slowly, locking eyes with each person around the table. "Isn't that what we've talked about? Changing minds and hearts? Now we have the means to penetrate those we considered impenetrable."

The senator arched an eyebrow skeptically and said, "So, the founder of The Vanguard is now our ally? Just like that?"

Monica stood beside me, nodding. "It's complicated; I realize that. But his recent experiences have fundamentally changed him. He's completely committed to our cause and will be able to provide immeasurable value."

Gus met their challenging stares. "I've been on a journey that's shown me a different way, a path that goes beyond violence and coercion," he said. "I want to be part of a meaningful change."

The room held its collective breath until the senator finally nodded. "Fine. Let's say, for argument's sake, we believe you. What's your plan?"

"Instead of meeting force with force, we change people's hearts and minds."

The general nearly laughed himself off his chair. "Hearts and minds won't help us when the secret police are beating down our doors. We don't have time for this consciousness-raising mumbo jumbo."

I glanced at Gus and Monica and decided it was time to play our hand.

"Maybe there's something else we should tell you," I started cautiously. "We've had experiences in the soul world. Gus and I received guidance and insights from higher beings—Archangels if you will—that inform this approach."

The general shared a look with the senator and said with a healthy dose of doubt, "Angels? You're seriously talking about angels?"

The senator leaned forward, suddenly very interested. "Wait, are you telling me you can access other realms?"

Gus and I momentarily held each other's gaze, acknowledging the gravity of what we were about to reveal. We nodded in tandem as I took a deep breath. "You must understand the depth of what we've been through," I started, my voice imbued with an earnestness that seemed to hang in the air. "This isn't just lucid dreaming; it's astral projection—voyages to parallel realms that co-exist with our own. In these realms, we've encountered beings of all sorts, both benign and destructive."

Gus took over, his voice steady. "Among the evil beings are the Asuras, ancient entities that feed off negative energies. They're a driving force behind the divisiveness and chaos we witness today. They're the real enemies of humanity, operating behind the scenes, sowing discord."

I allowed the words to penetrate before I resumed. "It might sound outlandish, but Gus was under their influence while with The Vanguard. These Asuras can manipulate thoughts, making us believe we're acting on our convictions when fulfilling their agenda of division and hate."

Gus nodded in acknowledgment. "That's right. I broke free from their hold only after I realized the depth of the darkness I was entangled with. And trust me, if I could break free, it's possible to liberate others as well. It's part of a broader spiritual strategy that has the power to end fascism not just in the United States but worldwide."

"This is where our plan comes in," I added. "I propose, instead of meeting force with force, which is precisely what the Asuras want us to do, we aim to instigate a change from within. We intend to use the same methodologies The Vanguard employs, but this time to spread unity, compassion, and enlightenment—values that are anathema to the Asuras."

Gus concluded, "By doing this, we won't just be fighting against an external enemy. We'll be purging the true enemy that lurks in the shadows, influencing us from realms we're just beginning to understand. And as we change, these realms will also change, setting off a chain reaction that will ultimately benefit humanity."

Our words hung in the air, both a revelation and a challenge. Now, it was up to our riveted audience to decide whether they were ready to embrace this unorthodox approach that operated not just on a political or physical battlefield but also on a spiritual one.

"I'm confused," the senator said, shaking her head. "Who are these Asuras, and how did you meet them?"

Gus and I exchanged glances before nodding in unison. I then elaborated on our spiritual experiences, sensing that a brief overview wouldn't convince these hardened non-believers. "Through a process of first learning how to lucid dream, courtesy of Monica," I began, pointing to her, "I'm able to traverse the dream world in an awakened state."

"Are you serious?" the senator asked, wide-eyed.

I nodded and continued, "It's wonderful; anyone can learn."

The senator gestured for me to proceed.

"Well, once I was comfortable in the dream world, I delved further and discovered a way into the soul world. That's where I had encounters with beings like the Archangel Michael and the malevolent Asuras. Later, Gus acquired this ability and could explore the realms as I did. But when I got trapped by the Asuras, Gus intervened and set me free."

"I think my mind's going to explode," the general said, clutching his head.

"This is not some figment of our imagination," I insisted. "These realms hold energies and beings that guide the collective human experience. We've received messages and insights that have made it abundantly clear: The change we seek in our world starts from within, from our consciousness. It's an internal shift that reflects outwards."

The general crossed his arms, visibly skeptical. "You expect us to believe that celestial beings are offering geopolitical advice? Why would entities from another dimension care about our earthly matters?"

Gus chimed in, "The notion might seem far-fetched if you're looking at it purely from an earthly standpoint. But think about it—our world is interconnected in ways we can't fully comprehend. If we're part of a larger cosmic plan, every move we make resonates in those higher dimensions."

I added, "It's not about them offering us a military strategy. It's about realizing that the energy we put into the world—love or hate, peace or violence—has ripple effects that transcend our earthly realm."

The general scoffed. "Sounds like a bad sci-fi movie."

However, the senator leaned forward, captivated. "This is unlike anything I've ever heard. If your words hold even a kernel of truth, it's a potential game-changer. It would be foolish not to explore this avenue."

Turning to the general, the senator continued, "Can we afford to dismiss this out of hand? Their inside information from The Vanguard is invaluable on its own. Now, add this extra layer. This could be our secret weapon."

Still eyeing us cautiously, the general finally nodded. "Fine, explore it. But don't expect me to buy into this mystical stuff until I see proof."

The senator smiled. "That's fair."

"Agreed," Gus and I said in unison, a sense of hope invigorating the air. We had crossed a threshold, not just in convincing the Covenant leadership but also in understanding the gravitas of what lay ahead. We were about to mesh the material and the spiritual in a fight for the very soul of humanity.

Chapter 31
Who is Gus Williams?

Monica pulled on her jacket, slinging her bag over her shoulder. "All right, I'm heading to Newport to visit my dad for a few days. You two behave," she said, a teasing smile dancing on her lips.

"Safe travels," Gus called out as Monica exited the apartment, the door closing behind her. Her departure left a void, a silence that seemed to beckon us to explore the untold aspects of our lives. I turned my gaze to Gus, realizing how little I knew about the man who had walked beside me through previous lifetimes.

"So," I began, sitting across from him, "I feel like I know your soul and the tapestry of our past lives, but I'm curious about the Gus Williams of this lifetime. Tell me?"

Gus leaned back, a nostalgic smile playing on his lips. "It wasn't always politics and The Vanguard," he began, his voice wistful. "In a time before all that, I was just a kid from Chicago."

As he spoke, he painted a picture of a simpler life, a childhood filled with the love of family and the dreams of a boy who the world's complexities hadn't yet touched. "My dad was a mechanic, my mom a schoolteacher. We weren't wealthy, but love was our currency. We shared dinner every night, and weekends often led us to Lake Michigan for picnics. They instilled in me the values of hard work, integrity, and the importance of family."

He chuckled, the memories of his youth filling the room. "I was a diligent student, always eager to learn. But my true passion ignited on the debate team. That's where I felt alive and found my purpose—arguing points, swaying opinions, fighting for what I believed was right. We even won several state championships in high school. I truly believed I could change the world."

I nodded, absorbing the foundation of his life story. "And college?" I inquired.

Gus tapped a finger on the arm of the sofa. "I came here to Harvard."

I couldn't help but express my surprise. "Harvard?"

He nodded, his eyes reflecting the intoxicating allure of those academic years. "Yes, it was at Harvard that I felt I stood at the center of everything. I excelled in history and political science, and my professors saw in me the potential to shape the world. There, I met a mentor who believed in my vision and introduced me to influential figures—early backers of The Vanguard."

As he continued, I could sense the transformation, the subtle shift in ideals that ultimately led him down a different path. His words painted a picture of a man who had once been driven by noble intentions, now clouded by unforeseen influences. "But," Gus confessed, "as The Vanguard grew, I started to change. My once-clear ideals became muddled. I was… influenced. It was subtle, not a specific moment I could point to and say, 'That's when I went astray.' But with the growth of The Vanguard, my moral compass spiraled out of control. That's when the Asuras must have begun to tighten their grip on me. I became a vessel, amplifying their message without fully understanding it."

His eyes met mine, vulnerable and human, despite our shared experiences in the realms beyond. "I wanted power, but not for its own sake. I believed I could change the system from within and make it work for the people. But it changed me, Emma, and not for the better. All the while, I was building an organization designed to sow chaos and division." Gus released a heavy sigh as if he had unburdened himself.

Listening to his account, I felt like I was finally seeing the whole man before me, a complex soul shaped by the choices of a lifetime. It wasn't a story of inherent evil but a warning about how even the noblest intentions could become twisted. My curiosity surged as the weight of his narrative settled in the room. "That's a good start," I said, leaning forward. "But let's dive into the details. What about your love life? Were you ever married, divorced, or in a serious relationship? Any children or former lovers I should know about?"

Gus raised an eyebrow, his discomfort masked by a hint of amusement. "No children," he began. "I never made it down the aisle, though I came close once. She was a passionate environmental lobbyist. But as I delved deeper into The Vanguard, our paths diverged. My ambition and darker influences drove a wedge between us." He paused, considering whether to divulge more. "There were other relationships, but nothing serious enough to mention. Most of the time, I was married to my work, to the mission—or at least what I thought it was."

I nodded, absorbing the earthly details that colored the canvases of our lives. "It's interesting how we've shared our souls across time and space, yet we're still unraveling the layers of who we are in this lifetime."

Gus met my gaze, a thoughtful expression crossing his face. "It's as if we have an eternal connection, yet we're still strangers in this life. We need to bridge that gap, especially if we're going to be partners in every sense."

His words hung in the air, marking a pivotal moment in our journey. It felt like we were standing at the threshold of something meaningful, a challenge that would test us as individuals and as a team. One thing was clear: I wanted to walk this path with Gus, no matter where it led.

Gus locked eyes with me and changed the focus of our conversation. "Okay, now it's your turn. We've traversed universes and faced unimaginable cosmic forces, but what about you? Any past romances I should know about?"

A blush crept onto my cheeks as the focus shifted to me. "Well," I began, slightly flustered, "I've had a few relationships, if you can call them that. There was Kyle, a boy back home. But we agreed to see other people. Most of the time, they were distractions, fleeting moments that felt significant at the time but turned out to be empty."

"And?" Gus prodded.

I met his gaze, choosing honesty. "I've lived life, Gus. I assumed you did, too. We weren't exactly waiting for each other in that sense."

He chuckled, acknowledging the complexity of our shared pasts. "Fair point. Neither of us was a saint. But here we are, bound by something far more profound."

I shifted the focus again, breaking the enchanting spell that had enveloped us. "What do you think about the Asuras?" I blurted out the question, wanting to understand the depths of his transformation. "Could you possibly pinpoint when their influence began?"

He twisted his mouth, lost in thought, and then said, "I think it was when I became obsessed with power, influence, and the belief that the end justified the means. I thought I was doing the right thing, protecting the nation. But in reality, I was feeding into a darker agenda, influencing people to spread hate and fear. Looking back now, it's like I had blinders on."

I leaned in, captivated. "And what woke you up?"

He met my gaze, a profound sense of realization in his eyes. "It's obvious, isn't it?"

"Tell me," I teased.

"You did, Emma. Our encounters in the spirit world, our shared past lives, the messages we received, and our confrontation with the Asuras—all culminated in a profound awakening. It was as if a veil had been lifted, and I saw the destruction I was causing, the lives I was affecting. It terrified me, but it also became a catalyst for change."

We sat silently, the weight of his transformation and our shared experiences sinking in. I felt a bond strengthened by the knowledge of who he had become and who he once had been. "Thank you for sharing that," I finally said, a sense of hope filling the room. "We have a significant task—changing minds, shifting collective consciousness, and confronting the true enemy. But knowing who you are now and who you once were makes me believe we can succeed."

Gus nodded, a mixture of regret and determination in his eyes. "I'm with you, Emma, till the very end."

I couldn't help but smile. "I thought eternity had no end?"

As we locked eyes in that dimly lit apartment, it felt like two souls, having traversed time and space, had finally found their common ground. We were prepared for whatever challenges lay ahead, or so we believed.

Chapter 32
A Pact

That night, we crossed a threshold that felt both new and ancient. As Gus and I made love, the walls of the physical world seemed to dissolve, leaving behind a space where only our souls existed. Every touch and kiss felt like echoes of lifetimes past, as if our spirits were rejoicing in a union they had been aching for.

I had been intimate before, a few times, but it had never felt like this—never so profoundly spiritual and grounding at the same time. It was as if our physical forms were merely vessels, conduits for something far deeper, a cosmic alignment of souls that transcended the flesh and bone that encased them.

As I looked into Gus's eyes, I felt the magnetic pull I'd experienced in countless other lifetimes, a love that had always found its way back to us. I felt grateful and, strangely, complete. I realized then that the love I felt was the culmination of millennia, an undying flame that had weathered the storms of lifetimes.

And as we basked in the afterglow, a serene silence filling the room, I knew we had rekindled something sacred. Our love had withstood the test of time and defied the bounds of the physical world. It was the stuff of soulmates, a love that could empower us to face the insurmountable challenges ahead.

In that still, intimate space, tranquility settled over me like a gentle veil. Regardless of the uncertainties and dangers that awaited us, I had an unwavering conviction that Gus and I would navigate our way through—just as we had done in past lives.

As this comforting thought lingered in my mind, my gaze rested on Gus, who had already drifted off to sleep. A smile graced my lips as I welcomed the presence of this extraordinary man into the tapestry of my life, and I closed my eyes, crossing the threshold into the realm of dreams.

*

As I fell asleep, the tranquility that had cradled me shattered abruptly. Like being jerked from one reality into another, I found myself beyond my dreams and in the spirit realm. It wasn't a space of celestial wonder or mystic landscapes; instead, it was a plane of palpable, oppressive darkness, oozing noxious energy that seemed to stick to my soul like molten tar.

Before me towered a figure that was the embodiment of darkness, so profound it felt like an affront to the very notion of light. His form consumed every luminescent speck around him, drawing it into an abyss of unending night.

"Welcome, Emma," it said, its voice a resonant growl that seemed to reverberate through the very fabric of this twisted realm. "I am Azogrim, of the Asuras. You stand in my dominion."

Its introduction confirmed my worst fears; I was in the presence of a being of unimaginable darkness and malice. Azogrim stood like a monumental sculpture, its essence so overpowering that it threatened to drown out all hope and light in an eternal night sea. Yet, even in that moment of overwhelming darkness, I felt a flicker of resolve ignite within me, refusing to be extinguished.

"You are the audacious human who believes she can oppose us," Azogrim snarled, his voice a harsh symphony of gravel and rusted metal. "Let me grace you with a preview of what awaits your pitiful species." With a sweeping gesture, he altered the scenery. The world around us transformed, offering me a horrifying glimpse of Earth under Asurian control. The sky was a convoluted swirl of pitch-black clouds, ignited intermittently by bolts of crimson lightning, giving the appearance of a celestial sea of fire. Once lush and full of life, trees were now skeletal, their branches twisted in contorted shapes like anguished limbs of damned souls, as though each was emitting a silent scream of everlasting torment. Oceans formerly brimming with colorful life were now bloody cesspools, their surfaces covered in a sheen of sickly, opalescent oil that reflected the abominable skies.

Cities had become charred ruins, skeletons of their former selves, inhabited by what remained of humanity—shell-shocked, hollow-eyed wanderers, their spirits crushed and drained, rambling aimlessly amid the wreckage. Every single living thing, every piece of verdant land, every droplet of clear water had been corrupted, transmuted into its most vile form.

The vision unfolded like an orchestrated masterpiece of suffering, a symphony in which every discordant note resonated with an aspect of unimaginable anguish, culminating in a cataclysmic finale of complete and utter despair. I felt Earth's agony penetrate every fiber of my being, so intense, so overwhelming that my very cells seemed on the brink of disintegration.

"Do you understand the magnitude of what you're seeing?" Azogrim's voice dripped with vicious delight. "This is your world devoid of its childish yearnings for love, for compassion—a ceaseless maelstrom of suffering, each soul a note in our eternal requiem of despair."

As his words reverberated, I felt myself nearing an edge, a precipice beyond which there would be only unending sorrow. Yet even then, I clung to something indefinable but unbreakable within me. "This isn't the only possible future," I protested, my voice laced with desperation and determination. "Love, hope—these aren't just words; they're the anchors of our existence. You cannot extinguish that light."

Azogrim erupted into derisive, jarring laughter. "Your feeble hopes are like candles in a tempest. Do you honestly believe you could hold back the flood of eternal night we have unleashed?"

As if on cue, I was jolted awake, pulled violently back into the waking world by Gus, who had sensed my turmoil and had shaken me from my voyage. As I lay there beside him, the familiar contours of my bedroom, the softness of my sheets, felt like an asylum, a sanctuary from the visceral horror that Azogrim had revealed. Yet the impression it left was indelible, carved deep into the core of my soul, fanning the flames of my resolve.

Gus cupped my face, his eyes searching mine as if trying to banish the remnants of that realm. "You're trembling," he noted softly.

I hesitated, fearing that voicing my dream would give it more power. But I knew I had to share it. "I met this Asurian. He called himself Azogrim and showed me Earth as it would be under their complete control—a world in agony, a symphony of suffering. Everything was twisted, warped into a form of eternal torment. The sky, the trees… humanity itself. He mocked me, made me feel powerless."

"It's okay," he said, stroking my face.

"I'm afraid to go back to sleep," I confessed, my voice barely a whisper. "If the Asuras can infiltrate my dreams, make me witness such horror, how can I ever find rest? They've invaded a sanctuary I thought I had protected by learning how to go lucid. Now, this haunts me."

Gus sighed, his eyes filled with a mixture of resolve and a pain I knew mirrored my own. "Then we must turn our vulnerability into strength. If they can reach us in our dreams, we must also be prepared to face them there. To protect each other, even in their realm."

"What do you mean?"

"We dream together; stay connected in the spiritual realm as we are in this one," he explained. "Sleep can no longer just be a pause, a momentary escape from the waking world. It must now be another battlefield, another realm in which we continue our fight. We must be warriors, both awake and asleep in the physical and spiritual worlds."

His words resonated deeply, fanning the embers of my resolve into a roaring flame. I nodded, tightening my grip on his hand. "Then let's promise to be each other's guardians in all worlds and through all challenges. Because I can't imagine facing any of this without you."

"And I, you," he responded, sealing our pact with a kiss that seemed to transcend realms, a manifestation of love that could defy even the darkest of nightmares.

Chapter 33
Gus at The Vanguard

When I walked back into Vanguard headquarters, the tension in the air was almost tangible. My right-hand man, Derek, looked up from his desk as I entered. He set aside the papers he'd been scanning and fixed me with a gaze that always felt like it could pierce through steel.

"You've been gone," he remarked, leaning back in his chair. His voice had that disquieting mix of curiosity and veiled accusation.

"I was attending to pressing matters," I replied, maintaining a calm exterior. "My duties aren't always in the spotlight."

His eyes narrowed slightly, not entirely convinced. "We've always been transparent with each other, Gus, since the beginning. There's talk; some say you've lost your fire after that interview with *Radical Views*. The edge in your orders has softened. What's going on?"

I forced a chuckle, trying to diffuse the growing suspicion. "If I've lost my edge, the world must be soft." I laughed. "Don't worry, Derek, I've something planned to quell such rumors."

Derek sat up straighter, interested but cautious. "Something big?"

"Big enough to make the city take notice. We're going to ramp up our operations and show our strength. Let people know The Vanguard isn't playing games," I assured him, a strategic lie designed to keep him in line for a while longer.

His eyebrows lifted, skepticism fading into a look of genuine intrigue. "That sounds more like the Gus I know. So, tell me about it."

"Ah." I waved a finger. "Not just yet. I still have to iron out some specifics. But be ready; it will require a full team mobilization."

He nodded, seemingly satisfied, but how he held his eyes on me a second too long stirred a sense of foreboding deep within me. Derek was shrewd, ferociously loyal, but most importantly, ruthless. That combination could either save us or doom us, and right now, I was afraid it would be the latter.

*

Later that night, I shared my unease with Emma. "Derek's getting suspicious. He seems close to uncovering my real motives. If he discovers my plan to dismantle, there'll be hell to pay."

Emma considered this before speaking. "What if you could reach out to him in the dream realm, soul-to-soul? I reached you, and your soul heard me. Maybe Derek could hear you, too."

I nodded, considering the idea.

"But we should do this together," Emma suggested. "It's what we promised each other that we would do."

"All right," I said with a deep breath. "Tonight, we'll search together for Derek's soul."

*

That night, Emma and I prepared ourselves for a different kind of battle that would take place in the ethereal realms of sleep. Lying beside her, I felt her hand gently squeeze mine, grounding me with her comforting touch.

"Ready?" she whispered.

I nodded, and we took a deep breath, willing ourselves into the dream realm. Emma led the way at first, guiding us through the astral landscape—a landscape I'd come to know but still found mystifying each time. But this journey was unlike any other. Instead of the tranquil valleys or ethereal forests I was accustomed to, Emma directed us downward, far beneath the shimmering surface, into a darker, more oppressive space.

"We're entering the domain where the Asuras dwell, and I assume that's where you'll find Derek." Emma's voice echoed softly in my mind. "Be on your guard. I'll wait here for you. If you need me, call out; I'll hear you."

She paused, holding onto what seemed like an invisible boundary, her gaze filled with concern and resolve. With a nod, I ventured alone

162

into this abyss, this subterranean realm of darkness and despair. It felt like stepping into the Asuras' den, their very birthplace—an environment steeped in darkness so intense that it nearly swallowed me whole.

Navigating through a labyrinthine underworld, I finally located what I was searching for—Derek's spiritual presence. It was as twisted as the surroundings, a fortress of hostility that seemed to reject any intruders outright. As I approached, attempting to penetrate his soul's barriers, I felt an invisible force push me back. The Asuras were protecting him.

A wave of disquiet enveloped me as I navigated back through the otherworldly labyrinth. The Asuras had just upped the ante in our cosmic chess match; Derek's soul was beyond my reach, wrapped in a protective shield of energy. My heart sank as the gravity of the situation settled in.

Without recourse, I rejoined Emma, where she waited at the invisible boundary. Her eyes met mine, filling with concern as she discerned the weight of my thoughts. "You look troubled," she noted as we both willed ourselves to return to the waking world.

Emerging back into consciousness, I found Emma's eyes already searching mine. "What happened?" she asked, her voice tinged with worry.

I exhaled deeply, my words heavy with newfound apprehension. "Derek's soul is shielded, fortified by the Asuras. Attempting to touch his essence felt like throwing stones at an impregnable castle. We've hit a wall; they're manipulating people and securing their loyalty in the spirit realm. This adds an insurmountable layer of complexity to our quest."

Emma's eyes narrowed in thought. "Then we need to rethink our strategy. If they've figured out how to strengthen souls in their favor, we must learn how to break or bypass that defense. We're dealing with cosmic stakes here; it's not just about altering the course of humanity anymore, but about freeing souls enslaved across dimensions."

As I absorbed her words, the magnitude of what lay ahead seemed almost unbearable. We were waging war not just on the physical realm but on a cosmic level that extended to spiritual dimensions, facing an enemy sophisticated enough to fortify its assets.

Yet, amid these growing complexities, a sliver of hope ignited within me. Love had been my salvation, pulling me back from the depths of the Asuras' malevolent grasp. If there was any force potent enough to pierce these seemingly insurmountable barriers, I couldn't help but believe it was the transformative power of love. And if love had saved me, then perhaps—just perhaps—it could save others, too.

Chapter 34
Gus Is Taken

I was halfway between my car and The Vanguard office when two broad-shouldered men abruptly emerged from the shadows. Before I could react, they seized me, one gripping my arms while the other pinched my wrists with a zip tie and slipped a canvas bag over my head—blinding me. No words were exchanged, only a guttural command to remain silent.

The next thing I knew, I was bundled into a vehicle, my mind racing through countless scenarios. The tension escalated when I was transferred from the car to an awaiting helicopter. The rhythmic thumping of rotor blades reverberated through the airframe, creating a disorienting and tense atmosphere. With each passing minute, the uncertainty of my situation weighed heavily, and the isolation intensified. The muffled sounds of the helicopter's mechanical workings and the occasional distant voices added to the surreal experience. It felt like an endless, anxious journey through an abyss, with only the sensations of motion and sound to tether me to reality.

As the helicopter landed and the engines gradually wound down, the tension in the air remained palpable. Moments later, hands firmly gripped my arms, guiding me out of the aircraft. Still blindfolded, I stumbled along the uneven surface of a parking lot, the distant hum of the helicopter fading behind me. The transition from the aircraft to solid ground was disorienting, my imagination racing with images of what could lie ahead.

With each step, the pressure in my chest mounted. My captors remained silent, their grip unwavering as they led me through an uncharted path. The anticipation of the unknown added to the weight of my predicament. Finally, I felt a change in the environment—a shift in the air pressure, perhaps—indicating we were approaching an entrance.

The moment we crossed the threshold of the doorway, the bag over my head was abruptly removed, and my eyes blinked against the sudden influx of light. I found myself in an unfamiliar room and began scanning the surroundings, trying to make sense of the situation. It was then that I saw Emma sitting on a chair, her expression a blend of relief and worry.

I mouthed the words, "Are you okay?"

She nodded ever so slightly, her lips forming the words, "And you?"

I gave a slight nod, my mind far from reassured. If I, as the leader of The Vanguard, were a target, that was one thing; I'd been in dicey situations before. But involving Emma? That was another level of complexity that fueled my already simmering anger and inflated concern.

Our silent exchange was interrupted by the opening of the interrogation room door as General Harris and Senator Clarke entered.

"Gus and Emma." General Harris spoke first, his voice laced with stern formality. "We've brought you here to get to the bottom of your so-called abilities. And we have the means to provide irrefutable evidence."

The senator stepped forward, her eyes piercing as she looked us over. "Your claims have caused quite a stir in circles you can't even imagine. If what you say is true, it changes everything. And we need to know if it is or not."

I looked at Emma, who just shrugged.

"We have technology here that's not even available at Harvard," the general continued. "We can monitor your REM cycles, map your neural activity, and actually see what you see in your dreams. Are you willing to cooperate?"

Emma glanced at me, her gaze both searching and assertive. The unspoken consensus passed between us; despite the clear risks, we had gone too far to back down now.

"Fine," I said, my voice tinged with resignation and a hint of defiance. "Though I wish you had been a bit less *Black Ops*. Being accosted was certainly unnecessary."

The general sighed and, with a flick of his hand, signaled for us to follow him into an adjoining room where a high-tech laboratory awaited, bathed in the sterile glow of overhead lights. The room was a futuristic marvel, surpassing anything I encountered at Harvard's Sleep and Dream Center.

In the center of the room, two sleek loungers beckoned us. Surrounding these chairs was an impressive array of monitors, their screens displaying intricate graphs and charts that hinted at the complexity of the equipment's capabilities. Cables snaked across the floor like complex webs, connecting the monitors to the chairs and other devices.

Against one wall stood a towering console, its control panel adorned with many buttons, switches, and touchscreens. It was a testament to the technological prowess of this covert operation, leaving no doubt that we were about to embark on an entirely new level of dream analysis and exploration.

Yet, as I walked toward the lab setup, I felt a strange surge of optimism. This uninvited detour could provide us with the ammunition we so desperately needed, not just for our earthly battle but also for the cosmic struggle we were locked in. A struggle that now had high-ranking military and political figures vested in its outcome.

The lab was bathed in sterile light, a clinical ambiance that starkly contrasted with the mystical realms I'd recently navigated. A technician appeared from behind the banks of equipment, dressed in a white coat and wearing black-rimmed eyeglasses. He gestured with his skinny arm for Emma and me to climb into the chairs.

"My name is Jesse," he said, while attaching the sensors to our foreheads and temples, securing them gently. "Take your time," he encouraged, his voice a soothing counterpoint to the room's medical austerity. "Get comfortable, and then allow yourself to drift into deep sleep."

I exchanged a last determined glance with Emma, ready to embark on this unprecedented journey into the depths of our subconscious minds. My eyelids grew heavy, and I allowed them to close, but sleep didn't immediately seize me. Instead, I was in a twilight state—conscious but teetering on the edge of the dream world.

I focused on my breathing, each inhalation pulling me farther away from the sensory inputs of the lab, and each exhalation distancing me from my waking concerns. My mind started to churn out shapes and patterns, abstract swirls of color that danced behind my eyelids. They needed to be more cohesive, like a painter splattering hues on a canvas without form or plan.

I took another deep breath, centering myself, imagining my body sinking into the chair, becoming one with it, tethering my physical form to the room so my mind could roam freely. The swirls began to make sense, to merge and fuse into recognizable shapes and figures. And then, the transformation occurred. A subtle click, like unlocking a hidden door, signaled my transition into a lucid dream. In that moment, the boundaries of reality melted away, replaced by an exhilarating sense of freedom. It was as if I had stepped into a boundless realm where the only constraints were my imagination.

Eager to demonstrate the wonders I'd mastered, I willed myself aloft, embracing the sky's embrace with effortless grace. Beneath me, a tapestry of earthly splendor—towering peaks, vast blue oceans—rushed by, a mere backdrop to my ascent. The wind's caress against my skin was a vivid reminder of this realm's visceral reality. I alighted upon an ethereal isle adrift among the clouds, my every movement a dance of deliberate elegance.

With focused intent, my human frame metamorphosed, taking on the mythic form of a dragon, scales as armor and limbs stretching to majestic lengths. A roar escaped me, fierce and exultant, as flames erupted skyward, a fiery spectacle born from my draconic maw. Yet, this display was but a prelude; once more human, I delved into the esoteric, articulating tongues foreign to my conscious self—each word a testament to the limitless potential within this lucid dreamscape. This realm was my domain, my cognizance honed to a razor's edge, ready to slice through the veils of reality itself.

As my time in the dream realm ended, I slowly opened my eyes, and the laboratory surroundings gradually became focused. Emma, who had already awakened, caught my gaze. "How did it go?" I asked, genuinely curious, as she stretched and returned to the realm of wakefulness.

She flashed a grin. "I visited my childhood home, sat on the front porch, and enjoyed iced tea with my mother. It was a pleasant dream."

"That sounds lovely," I replied, propping myself on my elbows. My attention then shifted to the technician, who remained fixated on the bank of monitors. "What did you see?" I inquired.

Suddenly, emerging from the shadows, General Harris and Senator Clarke approached us. Their expressions held a mix of astonishment and calculation. The general spoke first, his eyes darting between the screens displaying our REM activity and our expectant faces. "Your neural mappings were nothing short of revolutionary," he began. "Gus, you were flying, changing shapes, speaking in languages we couldn't identify. And, Emma, it was as if we took a trip to your childhood home. Remarkable."

I exchanged a glance with Emma, a mix of validation and unease washing over us. "So, our experiences matched your observations?" I asked, seeking confirmation.

"Seems so," Senator Clarke affirmed.

"With that done, we have a proposition," the general said, his tone becoming grave. "We're curious if this ability could be useful. Specifically, can you infiltrate the president's dreams? Perhaps execute actions that would have real-world implications. Even taking a life in the dream world or, if necessary, in the spirit realm?"

The air in the room seemed to turn icy. Emma and I locked eyes, sharing a moment of shock and horror.

"No, of course not!" Emma blurted out. "We've been exploring these realms for the betterment of humanity, not to weaponize our abilities."

"You're asking us to go against the very principles that guide us," I added, my voice tinged with disbelief.

"And what principles would those be?" the senator asked, with a dose of sarcasm.

"Love," Emma stated firmly. "Our motive has always been love. We believe it's the key to overcoming the dark forces trying to control humanity. Our journeys into the spirit realm have been about fostering connection, understanding, and empathy. Not violence."

The general and senator exchanged glances, clearly unprepared for such a response.

"Ethically, we can't comply with your request," I said.

Emma reached over and squeezed my hand. We both knew our real mission had just taken an abrupt turn. The stakes had suddenly turned higher.

"Then you leave us no choice but to proceed with our tests regardless," the general said, his voice leaving no room for debate.

"What does that mean?" I asked, sharing a look of concern with Emma.

The general flipped his hand, signaling for the same two men who forced me into the car to approach. "You'll be staying with us while you figure things out."

"What do you mean figure things out? It's figured. It would be best if you let us go," I demanded as the men grabbed Emma and me and forced us through doors and into what appeared to be a fully furnished apartment.

Emma glanced at me, her eyes narrowing as the door shut behind us. "So, this is our gilded cage, huh?"

"It seems so," I replied, looking around the apartment designed to look inviting but intended to be more like a prison cell.

Emma's voice trembled as she leaned close to me, whispering, "We've got to get out of here, Gus. They've completely twisted the purpose of our journey. The thought of them using our gift for something so vile is unbearable."

A cold shiver ran down my spine. "I know, Emma. I know. So, what do we do? How do we get out of this godforsaken place?"

Her hands clenched, and she jiggled the locked door handle forcefully. "We need to escape, or at the very least, make sure we don't give them what they want."

My chest tightened, a sense of foreboding overtaking me. "They can invade our dreams, Emma. They can coerce us."

She looked into my eyes, brimming with a blend of resolve and vulnerability. "But remember, lucidity is a choice. We decide to become aware in our dreams. If we don't will it, they can't force us."

I grimaced, jaw clenched. "Don't underestimate them, Emma. Don't underestimate the lengths people will go to when driven by power, fear, and greed."

Chapter 35
Dreams for Humanity

Our rooms were comfortable enough, even though they were a mock-up of domesticity with a noticeable sterile aftertaste. It was as if someone had decided to create the illusion of home, only to remind us how far we were from it. Emma and I settled onto the only bed in the room, its sheets smooth and cool. It was time to sleep, or at least attempt it. In the morning, our efforts were to figure a way out of there.

"We should practice," Emma said, shifting her brows.

"Practice what?" I asked, with several unlikely scenarios playing out in my head.

"Trying not to lucid dream."

"Why do we need to practice?"

Emma shrugged. "It might not be as easy as you think. We should try it tonight, so we'll be ready tomorrow."

I paused, feeling the weight of her question. "Should we be doing this?"

Emma looked thoughtful. "Do we have a choice, Gus? They're monitoring us. Anything we dream—anything we do in the spirit realm—they'll know."

I sighed, running a hand through my hair. "I know, but the idea of suppressing something so natural feels wrong, almost like we're betraying ourselves."

She nodded, her eyes softening. "I feel that too. Our dreams have been our refuge, playground, and even our teacher. But we need to practice, so tomorrow when they hook us up, we won't give them any satisfaction."

"We spent months learning how to control our dreams," I said, the irony not lost on me. "And now we have to unlearn it, just like that?"

Emma touched my hand gently. "Not unlearn… hold back. For now. Until we figure out how to get out of this mess."

"What if we inadvertently go lucid? Then what?"

"We handle it like we handle everything else," Emma replied, her voice tinged with apprehension and determination. "Together."

I looked into her eyes and saw my fears and hopes reflected back. "All right, let's try not to lucid dream," I said, lying on the bed.

We turned off the lights, plunging the room into darkness. Lying beside Emma, I felt her fingers entwine with mine, offering a semblance of comfort in this bizarre reality.

Closing my eyes, I tried to empty my mind, not to summon that particular sense of awareness that kicks in when I go lucid. I let the silence envelop me, and for a moment, I felt like I was floating in an endless void.

And then, without warning, I found myself standing in a dense forest, the light of the moon filtering through the canopy of leaves above. I instantly knew I was dreaming, and therein lay the problem. The moment I became aware, the forest became more vivid, the rustling of the leaves louder, the scent of earth more pungent. I was lucid, and there was no turning back. I tried not to control or let the dream unfold, but it was too late. A shimmering lake appeared before me, its waters a surreal hue of blue reflecting the silver moon. Catering to my wishes, the world bent and shifted. Animals—creatures born of fantasy and fear—soared overhead, their wings adorned with feathers that sparkled like diamonds. It was both exhilarating and heartbreaking. I wanted to relish the limitless possibilities before me, but I knew that each action and thought carried potential consequences far beyond this realm.

Finally, I awoke. Emma was already sitting up, her face etched with worry and wonder.

"You too, huh?" she asked, as if reading my thoughts.

"Yeah," I said, "the moment I became aware, it was like flipping a switch I couldn't turn off. I tried not to be lucid, Emma. I really did."

She shook her head and offered a sad smile. "You know, I found myself in my childhood home. Standing in the middle of the kitchen, it felt so real. I could smell Mom's apple pie and hear the laughter of family in the next room. I wanted to be in the moment so badly, not to know it was a dream. But the second I realized this, everything changed. The pie started levitating, and the laughter turned into whispers speaking in languages I'd never heard. I was lucid, and that was that."

We looked at each other, the gravity of our situation settling in. In a world where our abilities could be weaponized, our intentions perverted, lucidity was both a gift and a curse.

Emma rolled on her side, bringing her mouth close to my ear, and softly whispered, "If we can't stop ourselves from being lucid, why don't we just embrace it? Dream bigger, bolder, and more defiantly than before. We can control the narrative provided to the Covenant by creating what we want for humanity in our dreams."

"Yeah," I said, popping up onto an elbow. "That's brilliant."

"But what do we want?" Emma said, lowering her tone to emphasize the question.

I took a breath and released a sigh. "That's a good question."

"We need a vision, a plan of where we want to end up, and the process of how to get there."

I leaned back into my pillow, contemplating the gravity of Emma's words. "So, we're talking about dreaming up a sort of utopia, then?"

"More like dreaming up a world on the road to utopia," she corrected. "A better direction for humanity, a course correct."

I looked at her, her eyes shining even in the dim light of the room, and felt a newfound sense of purpose. "A shift from greed to generosity, hate to love, ignorance to wisdom."

"Yes," she nodded. "From disconnection to unity, not just among people but between humanity and nature. A world where intellect is not just an individual endeavor but a collective pursuit."

"That's wonderful," I said, a slight smile forming. "So, how do we put this into dreams? How do we dream this into reality?"

"We dream in layers," Emma said, her voice tinged with excitement. "We start by visualizing the values we want to see—love, empathy, wisdom—and then we dream of scenarios where these values defeat the darker forces. Slowly, we build on that."

"And how do we make sure this doesn't backfire? What if the general and senator catch wind that we're deliberately manipulating our dreams?"

"If our dreams are strong enough and resonate, they might sway even the skeptics. If we control the narrative, we can also control how much they see and interpret."

I nodded, feeling a wave of relief wash over me. We had a plan and a vision, and, most importantly, we had each other.

"Let's do it," I said. "Let's dream a better world into existence."

Emma smiled, her face glowing in the ambient light. "It's a big dream, but that's the point. It's a dream big enough to fit the hopes of all humanity."

Closing my eyes, I felt the comforting weight of Emma's hand in mine as we drifted to sleep. With a unified purpose now etched in our minds, it was time to dream and to dream big. Our souls were ready to dive into the uncharted waters, challenging not just our captors but the current state of humanity. We were no longer dreamers but visionaries, and our new mission had just begun. And the two of us together, even if the world tried to bend us to its will, we would shape our destiny, one dream at a time.

Chapter 36
Day One

It was morning, and Emma and I sat on the bed, staring at the door that locked us away from the outside world. The irony wasn't lost on either of us. We were physically confined, yet mentally, we were about to embark on the most ambitious adventure of our lives.

"So, how do we pull this off?" I asked, turning to her.

Emma thought a moment. "We need a strategy. A well-thought-out plan to make our dream as powerful as it can be," she said, her eyes intense but brimming with enthusiasm.

"Okay, so what's step one?"

"First, we sync our emotional states," Emma began. "We must be harmonious to connect in the dream world properly."

"Emotional sync, got it," I nodded. "And then?"

"Visualization. We focus on our key values—love, empathy, and wisdom," she continued. "We practice projecting these ideals mentally so that they take form in the dream."

"All right, sounds good," I said, feeling the adrenaline course through me.

"And before we close our eyes, we verbally confirm our objective. Anchoring us and keeping us focused."

"Making sure the Covenant can't corrupt our dreams," I affirmed.

"Exactly. So, once we're in, we have to find each other," Emma continued. "Think of it as establishing our 'Dream Wi-Fi,' connecting our consciousnesses."

"And we manifest a safe space. A sanctuary of sorts," I added.

"Yes. A place filled with symbols of love, empathy, and wisdom. It could be a garden or a tranquil beach—anywhere peaceful."

"Sounds idyllic," I said.

"But that's when we switch gears and create a dystopian setting." Emma's eyes grew intense as she explained.

"Why dark?"

"To challenge ourselves, seeking scenarios where love triumphs over hate, empathy defeats apathy, and wisdom topples ignorance."

"So we role play. I can represent wisdom, and you can embody empathy," I suggested.

"Exactly. We enact scenes that demonstrate these values beating back darker forces."

"But how do we elevate it from there?" I inquired.

"We exaggerate their darker plans to a point where they look absurd, self-destructive even."

"Making it obvious that their way is unsustainable. I like that."

"And we counteract with elements powered by love, empathy, and wisdom," Emma concluded.

"We end by showing a glimpse of what the world could look like with these values. A utopian outcome," I surmised.

"And we seal it. We create a ritual or a symbol in the dream that solidifies these values into our reality."

"Leaving a mark even in this illusion." I smiled.

"And then we need a wake-up plan. A safe signal to pull us out simultaneously," Emma stressed.

"A bird song?" I suggested.

"Perfect. We'll know it's time to wake up when we hear the nightingale," she said.

"And once we're up, we document everything. Compare notes. Validate each experience."

"Exactly," Emma concluded. "In this way, we defy the Covenant's objectives and build a blueprint for enacting these values in the real world."

"And we do it together," I added, grabbing and squeezing her hand.

"Always." She smiled back, her eyes locking onto mine.

At that moment, as we finalized our dream strategy, it felt like the beginning of an incredible journey through layers of consciousness that would defy our captors and define a better future.

Just as we were about to delve into the intricacies of our dream strategy, there was a sharp knock on the door. It jolted us out of our reverie.

"Come in," I called out, releasing Emma's hand and shifting to a sitting position.

The door opened, and Jesse entered. His sallow skin seemed to almost glow under the lights. He had the air of someone who knew more than he was letting on. "It's time for your dream session," he announced.

"But we just woke up," I protested. "How are we supposed to sleep again?"

"The sedative we'll administer will take care of that," he responded, a clipboard clutched in his bony hands.

Emma frowned. "Won't a sedative interfere with our ability to lucid dream? It might distort the dream layers, even mess with our objectives."

Jesse looked momentarily uncomfortable, shifting his weight from one foot to another. "I have my orders," he said finally, his voice tinged with an almost apologetic tone.

Emma and I exchanged a concerned glance. The sedative was an unpredictable variable that could nullify our entire strategy or, even worse, render us vulnerable in a realm where we had hoped to wield control.

"Let's just go with it," Emma whispered, almost as if reading my thoughts. "We'll adapt."

"Yeah." I nodded, taking a deep breath to steady myself. "We can't control the variables, but we can control our response."

We followed the technician from our quarters to the lounge chairs, surrounded by the array of equipment meant to measure and observe our dream state.

As we lay down, Emma and I shared another meaningful look as Jesse prepared the sedative. This was just another obstacle on this bizarre journey. And if there was one thing we'd learned, it was that together, we could navigate anything—even the unknown landscapes of induced dreams.

Jesse approached with a syringe, I felt the needle prick my skin, and Emma's eyes were the last thing I saw before everything faded to black. Even in that void, I sensed her presence, like a beacon guiding me into the dream layers we had meticulously planned. Despite the sedative and the uncertainty it brought, we journeyed into our collective dream space, armed with a strategy and bound by a connection that not even the Covenant could sever, or so we hoped.

Chapter 37
A Fractured Sleep

The sensation of sleep's pull felt bizarre this time, almost as if I were being sucked into a vortex. When the dreamscape materialized, it was fragmented—vivid hues that should've composed the garden were splattered like errant brushstrokes on a canvas. I found myself standing next to what seemed like a fountain, but the word inscribed on its base was garbled and shifting.

"Is this our sanctuary?" Emma's voice echoed from everywhere and nowhere. Her figure appeared, flickering like a glitchy hologram.

"Connected? Are we?" I stammered, my words not quite forming as they should.

"Values… base? Love. Empathy. See?" She tried to point to inscriptions, but they kept distorting into illegible symbols.

The fractured world around us started changing again. The sky didn't just turn cloudy; it splintered into shards. We were in something resembling a city, but the buildings seemed to melt and twist as though made of wax. Faceless figures roamed, not despondent but erratic, their movements jerky and unpredictable.

"Lead… take the… I'll." Emma's voice disintegrated into static as she raised her hands. The streams of light were erratic flashes, like a broken strobe, touching these bizarre representations of people who didn't so much transform as they glitched into different forms.

"Empathy… that's," she managed, but her wink flickered in and out. The building I reached out to exploded into a cloud of numbers and symbols. When it cleared, a school was there but not solid.

"Your turn" were the words I think I said, but they felt hollow and meaningless.

Our world was again distorted, and we were now in a war room that was both present and absent simultaneously. Soldiers—or at least I think they were soldiers—muttered incomprehensibly, their plans not exaggerated but randomized, shifting from warfare strategies to nonsensical recipes for baking.

"Watch," Emma said, but her gesture only scattered the fragmented reality further. "We… not… done," she tried to say. But before she could finish, we jerked back to what should have been our sanctuary. It wasn't brighter or effervescent; it was unstable, vibrating at a fascinating and nauseating frequency. "World… aim… could this." Emma's words were getting lost, her eyes not shimmering but glitching.

The fountain that should have been marked "Humanity" was there, but it was a kaleidoscope of fluctuating forms. I reached out to touch it, and the sensation that shot through me was uncontrolled static, like touching a live wire. A cacophony of sounds erupted, none resembling the melodious tune of our agreed wake-up signal.

"Wake up," I heard Emma say, but her voice was layered with other sounds, garbled and distant.

My eyes fluttered open. Emma was beside me, her eyes also opening. The sensations of that disjointed dream still clouded my senses. "We… did?" I tried to say.

"Yes, we… sort of," she replied, equally puzzled.

The sedative injected into our bloodstreams had turned our dream layers into a chaotic jumble. We had ventured into a realm we couldn't control, our vision hijacked and twisted. Yet, even in that disarray, I sensed the seeds of rebellion we had tried to plant. Emma and I were still blinking away the remnants of the fragmented dreamscape when I noticed them—the general and senator standing at the far end of the room, eyes fixed on the monitors that had just displayed our chaotic dream world.

Emma sat up abruptly, a fire in her eyes. "You can't force us to sleep. The sedatives interfere with our consciousness; you saw the results."

They exchanged glances, then turned back toward us. "That was… unexpected," the general forced himself to admit, his face betraying his internal struggle to understand what he had just witnessed.

"Incomprehensible," the senator added, her eyes widening.

Emma seized the moment. "Exactly. Then, let us sleep naturally and build our dream world as we know how. Your interference distorts."

The general seemed to contemplate her words carefully. "Very well," he said, "we'll abandon the sedatives for now. But I hope you understand what's at stake here. You two are unique, and we want to understand how to harness this… phenomenon."

"Then let us show you," Emma retorted, her voice firm but her eyes pleading. "Let us show you a dream world shaped by values, not your interference or drugs."

The senator nodded. "Fair enough. We'll allow you a natural sleep cycle next time."

As we returned to our rooms, Emma and I exchanged glances, and I said, "As much as I'm relieved about the sedatives, we're still not in a natural setting. I can't help but wonder if that's messing with our dreams, too."

Emma nodded, her eyes narrowing as she considered the thought. "That's a valid point. This lab, the tech, the constant surveillance—it's not conducive to the kind of lucid dreaming we're trying to achieve."

"And yet, it's the world we're stuck in for now." I sighed. "I suppose we'll have to adjust our expectations and build stronger mental barriers."

Emma puckered and nodded, giving it thought. "Or maybe it's not about barriers, but rather adaptability. If we create these layered dreams, filled with the values we want to bring into the world, maybe we need to learn how to bring them into less-than-ideal conditions. It's good practice for manifesting them in the real world, right?"

I considered her words, feeling the weight of their significance. "That's an intriguing perspective. A dream, after all, isn't just an escape; it's a rehearsal for life."

Emma narrowed her eyes. "What do you mean?"

I leaned back, contemplating the question for a moment. "Well, think about it this way. In dreams, we can explore scenarios, emotions, and challenges in a safe environment. It's like a playground for our minds, free from the constraints of reality. When we face difficulties or decisions in our waking life, our dreams often allow us to work through them. It's as if our subconscious mind is saying, 'Hey, let's practice this situation and see how it feels.' Dreams allow us to test the waters without real-world consequences, whether a confrontation, a problem-solving scenario, or even the pursuit of a goal. When awake, we can learn from our dream experiences and apply that knowledge to similar situations. So, when we dream together and consciously navigate those dreamscapes, we're essentially practicing for the challenges and adventures life throws at us. It's a way to become more skilled, resilient, and adaptable in our waking lives."

"I love that!" Emma said, her eyes gleaming with renewed excitement. "So, let's take what we've learned today and use it to go deeper and bolder in our next attempt. If we can dream it here, under these conditions, we're one step closer to making it a reality out there."

Her words filled me with a newfound sense of purpose. Our dream strategy was more than just a resistance against the Covenant's aims; it was a blueprint for a better world, and every hurdle we faced was a challenge, helping to refine that blueprint further.

The game was far from over, but as we contemplated our next moves, I couldn't help but feel a surge of optimism. With Emma by my side and our shared dream taking shape—even if only in the depths of our minds—I knew we were laying the groundwork for something extraordinary.

Chapter 38
Searching for the President

The haunting strains of an elusive melody lingered at the edges of my consciousness as I fought the encroaching waves of sleep. Gus and I had spent what felt like an eternity confined to our chambers, waiting for the elusive permission to rest. These sterile, windowless rooms had become our prison, and the only respite lay in brief visits to a makeshift gym, where we mechanically rowed and pedaled, going nowhere in the process. Despite our physical exertions, the relentless grip of sleep deprivation clouded our minds and dulled our senses. Midnight loomed on the horizon, and I yearned for the solace of slumber. Just when it seemed within reach, a sharp knock shattered the stillness, punctuating our exhaustion with an unwelcome interruption. Jesse entered and held the door open with one hand while beckoning us to follow with his other.

He ushered us, half-conscious, into the dream lab, where I locked eyes with Monica as we exchanged baffled glances and unspoken questions. Why was she part of this midnight ritual?

"Monica? Didn't expect to see you," Gus said, his eyes narrowing with a blend of surprise and suspicion.

"I've been conscripted to supervise your next foray into the oneiric depths. Given your last—shall we say—reckless expedition, they thought my expertise would be useful," Monica replied. Her tone was a dry martini of irony, but her eyes were pools of genuine concern.

Just as we absorbed Monica's presence, the door to the outside was flung open, admitting Senator Clarke. She radiated an almost palpable force field of urgency, filling the chamber with unspoken impatience. "I trust Monica has clarified her presence here?" she snapped, bypassing any semblance of cordiality.

"In broad strokes," I answered cautiously.

"Fine. Here it is: you're to locate the president's soul in the astral realm and obliterate it. Although I realize this is purely speculative, that action should result in his mortal termination." She laid out our grim assignment.

The moral weight of her words hung in the air like a dark cloud, casting shadows on our ethical compasses. Obliterate a soul? This was a sacrilegious venture into uncharted territories, a Pandora's Box I had no desire to unseal. But in that suffocating moment, I realized we were beyond the government's jurisdiction once we stepped into the dream realm. We had free will there.

I took a deep breath. "We need a moment," I finally said.

Alone together, Gus and I grappled with the weight of our decision. Our primary objective was locating the president's soul within the dream realm. But the order to kill it was a chilling prospect.

I turned and whispered to Gus, "What if we find his soul, and instead of destroying it, we try to heal it? Infuse it with love and understanding, not violence. It's the only morally defensible path I can see."

He met my eyes, a mixture of resolve and concern in his. "I agree, Emma. Let's do this, but with our hearts in the right place. We'll search for his soul; if we find it, we'll try to bring back his humanity."

Monica took on the solemnity of an ancient priestess as she prepared us for our journey into the realm beyond. Each electrode she affixed to our scalps was like a ceremonial seal, locking us into a covenant with the unseen. "Ready?" she asked, her voice tinged with an apprehension that mirrored ours.

"As we'll ever be," I replied, stealing a last glance at Gus, whose eyes reflected a sea of complex emotions—fear, uncertainty, and a glimmer of daring.

Monica initiated the sequence, and the world around us began to dissolve. But it wasn't a rapid disintegration; it was more like a graceful retreat of the senses. First, the ambient hum of the room's electronics receded, like the tide pulling back from the shore. The sterile scent of the lab seemed to evaporate, replaced by an earthy aroma that hinted at ancient forests. Then the lab walls started to blur, their edges softening as they faded into a blank canvas of infinite possibilities.

Our consciousness became unhinged from physicality, floating upward into a transition space—a liminal realm that was neither here nor there. We were on the precipice of dreams, that mysterious borderland where the earthly and the ethereal bleed into one another. Below us were the familiar territories of sleep and their benign landscapes of forgotten memories and unspoken desires. But ahead loomed a kaleidoscope, swirling with colors and forms, its depths shimmering with the light of countless souls.

Gus and I, our astral forms tethered by an invisible link of shared purpose, ventured forth. The dreamscape welcomed us like a moral crucible, a test of our deepest convictions materialized in surreal geography. The mystical woodlands we traversed were trees with silver bark and leaves like shards of sky. We floated over rivers where the waters were not liquid but molten gold, flowing with a celestial rhythm, and the air—oh, the air—was a living tapestry, weaving threads of forgotten myths and legends around us.

The beauty of this astral realm was a stark contrast to what awaited us. As we delved deeper, the luminous environment shifted, deteriorating into a grotesque tableau. We crossed the threshold into the sub-earthly soul realm—a subterranean cavern of nightmarish visions that seemed conjured from humanity's collective dread. Here, the rivers were not of gold but of ink-black sorrow, and the trees bore fruits of despair. The air was thick with an unsettling energy, its weight pressing upon us like a palpable fog. We understood that we had arrived at our daunting destination, and whatever choices we made here would echo in both realms.

The soul in question was hovering amidst a ballet of ghostly illuminations—a mutable, dark orb. It writhed and pulsated, shape-shifting into forms that defied earthly description: a serpentine abomination, a twisted visage of torment, a gnarled monolith. It was flanked by the Asuras, shadowy sentinels that manifested as insidious wraiths, their forms convulsing with sickened energy.

"What do we do now?" Gus's voice quivered.

"Let's enlighten, not annihilate," I proposed, drawing from a reservoir of resolve.

Our ethereal forms radiated brighter, challenging the Asuras' dark barricade. I summoned tendrils of purifying light to penetrate their defenses, but the beams were swallowed whole, vanishing into a soul-sucking abyss. Gus conjured a tunnel of luminescence, only to watch it collapse under the Asuras' oppressive force. The atmosphere pulsated with their energy, imbued with a palpable dread. With a mutual, desperate glance, we conceded our dwindling options.

Gus's voice rose to a thunderous roar, filled with a desperate energy that reverberated through the dreamscape. "Let us pass!" His command clashed against the impenetrable wall of Asurian energy, a spiritual battleground where sound and intention met dark resistance. His words didn't merely vanish; they were devoured, absorbed into a maw of swirling shadows that lashed back at us. In an instant, the Asuras unleashed their wrath, pulling us into a chasm that could only be described as a subterranean abyss—a realm of nightmares too awful to put into words yet too vivid to dismiss as imagination. It was a void saturated with the cries of forgotten souls and a darkness that felt almost sentient, clawing at our beings.

In that moment of infinite despair, a spark—a flicker of understanding—kindled between Gus and me. Through a mingling of instinct and inspiration, we devised a maneuver, a trick woven from the fragile threads of dream logic. It wasn't a trick of complexity but rather one of profound simplicity. We visualized the maze not as a series of walls and corridors but as a living organism, its pathways like arteries, each leading to the heart.

As we navigated through the labyrinthine pit, our approach allowed us to skirt past lurking monstrosities that had previously seemed unbeatable. They seemed almost to step aside, recognizing the newly found harmony in our movements. The traps that had threatened to ensnare us appeared to disarm themselves, their mechanisms freezing as if confused by our new strategy.

Then, just as abruptly, we were pulled upward, soaring through layers of consciousness as if ejected from the bowels of the nightmare. Reality's threshold appeared before us like a celestial gate, starkly contrasting the abyss that had just removed us. As our eyes flickered open, we were met with a tableau of human emotion—Monica's eyes vast with mingled relief and concern, and the senator's once-impassive face, now a crumbling edifice of hope, turned to disappointment.

"We couldn't," Gus declared, his voice tinged with fatigue from battling literal and ethical demons. It was a simple statement, but in that moment, it bore the weight of worlds untraveled, of choices made and moral lines uncrossed.

"Perhaps a change in tactics is needed," the senator said, her face a swirling storm of frustration and deep thought.

Before she could elaborate, Monica chimed in. "Might I suggest a paradigm shift? Rather than going for an aggressive confrontation, we could aim for a redemptive connection with the soul?"

Gus and I exchanged a knowing glance. "That was our intention," I confirmed. "We also believe that redemption is a more powerful strategy than destruction."

As we disconnected from the mass of wires and electrodes, a flood of mixed emotions engulfed me—relief laced with bone-deep fatigue. We had ventured perilously close to a moral event horizon, teetering on the brink of ethical damnation. Although we hadn't accomplished the task laid out for us, we had returned with our moral compasses intact. At that moment, the victory seemed less about fulfilling an objective and more about preserving the integrity of our souls—an accomplishment far weightier than any mission success.

Chapter 39
A Spiritual Strategy

The laboratory had been repurposed into a tactical command center for humanistic endeavors, where strategies for fostering empathy and understanding were meticulously crafted. The once bare white walls were adorned with elaborate blueprints of interpersonal networks, each representing the intricacies of societal interrelations. These visual representations served as a stark reminder of the invisible lattice of relationships that form the backbone of our social structures.

Beside them, meticulously crafted charts detailed potential empathy hotspots, each line and curve representing the unique patterns of human behavior and emotional response. These charts served as our guide, directing us to the locations in the real world where empathy had waned and suffering had taken hold. We studied these behavioral patterns with curiosity and determination, knowing they held the key to rekindling compassion within humanity.

In the corner of the room, a timeline stretched across the wall, a complex tapestry of events that attempted to map our previous efforts in the field—a realm where the boundaries of reality were clear and our actions had a tangible impact. Though organized in appearance, the timeline resembled a complex narrative, each entry marking a significant chapter in our mission's unfolding story.

As we delved into exhaustive planning, our minds navigated the intricate pathways of possibility. We were intellectually drained from the weight of our task, but beneath the fatigue lay a cautious optimism. We believed in the potential for change, in the power of love and compassion to transform even the most entrenched beliefs. In this clinical setting, we forged our battle plan, ready to embark on a journey that would test our intellect and the essence of our souls.

"From what you've observed, the Asuras offer a formidable defense," Monica began, her eyes glancing from her clipboard to the intricate charts on the wall. "We don't know if they guard the president's soul or if they're just the resident energy of that realm."

Gus shook his head, admitting, "They overwhelmed us. Their intensity is massive."

"That's why a more compassionate approach might be worth considering," Monica said, walking toward a blank whiteboard section. "As we said, if brute force doesn't work, we should attempt to resonate on a frequency that aligns with healing or restoration."

The words hit home. Gus and I exchanged a knowing glance.

"Let's think this through," Monica continued, uncapping her marker. "How did you maneuver through the Asurian realm?"

Gus looked at me, then back at Monica. "Honestly, it was more like stumbling in the dark, testing the waters."

Monica paused, her marker hovering above the whiteboard. "Before we dive into potential strategies, let me explain why I'm considering something like a mantra," she began, locking eyes with both of us. "Mantras have historical and spiritual significance. They're not just collections of words; they're frequencies and vibrations. They've been used for millennia to bring about specific changes in reality. In this case, the aim would be to tune into a frequency that might disrupt or neutralize the defensive energies in the Asura realm. Think of it as a spiritual disarmament tactic. Does that make sense?"

Gus and I nodded in agreement. "It does," I said. "Especially since we're entering a realm where the usual rules don't apply. The idea of using something as ancient and universal as a mantra adds a layer of, well, plausibility to what we're trying to achieve."

"Exactly," Monica replied, capping her marker. "So, with that reasoning in mind, what kinds of phrases or languages resonate with both of you for this mantra? It should carry a deep, personal meaning so that its energy can be most effective."

Monica's rationale lent credibility, making a mantra an integral part of our spiritual strategy. I felt better equipped to venture into the uncertain territory that awaited us.

Gus thought momentarily. "What about something like peace and unity? We want to convey that we're not a threat."

"That's good," I added. "Perhaps something that combines the essence of love with the intent of peaceful coexistence."

Monica put her marker down and looked thoughtful. "How about *Om Shanti Prema*? It's Sanskrit for universal peace and love. The vibration of those words could resonate in that realm. What do you think?"

Gus scratched his head. "It's simplistic to think that chanting a mantra would disarm entities as defensive as the Asuras. They aren't exactly a welcoming committee."

"That's true," I said. "While the mantra sounds powerful, we should prepare for the possibility that it won't disarm the Asuras as we hope."

Monica took a deep breath, considering our concerns. "It may not work, but sometimes the simplest of intentions—peace, love—can transcend complexities. It's not just the words but the energy behind them. Remember, you're both powerful mediums in your own right."

I nodded. "I'm sure those words are not common in the Asuras' world; maybe that's an advantage."

"We're also bringing psychology into a spiritual war zone," Gus interjected, looking around at the charts and diagrams surrounding us. "That's quite a risk. The Asuras might not respond as humans would."

Monica picked up her marker on the tray below the whiteboard, taking a step back to gauge our reactions. "Before I go further, have you heard of the term *Sphere of Empathy*?"

Gus and I exchanged glances, shaking our heads.

"All right," Monica continued. "It's a concept used in certain psychological therapies, primarily for individuals grappling with trauma or deep-seated emotional issues. The aim is to create a safe space in which the individual feels secure enough to lower their defenses and confront their vulnerabilities."

Moving closer to ensure she had our full attention, she said, "So, what if we apply that principle to the spiritual realm? Envision a metaphysical sphere around the president's soul, filled with unconditional love and understanding. The goal would be to disarm any defensive energies and make it more conducive for introspection or dialogue."

Looking around at the charts and diagrams surrounding us, Gus said, "Again, the Asuras might not respond as humans would."

"We're talking about creating a bubble of unconditional love and understanding around his soul," I said.

Gus held up a finger. "But what if it's perceived as an intrusion?"

Monica nodded, her face a mix of concern and determination. "It's true the very tool designed to facilitate healing could be misinterpreted as a threat. But as we've discussed, this mission is fraught with risks and unknowns. It's the best-calculated risk we can take under these uncertain circumstances."

After a pause, Gus nodded. "Let's try it."

Monica dimmed the whiteboard. "We move forward, armed with our mantra and *Sphere of Empathy*, aware of the risks, but open to adaptability."

Gus gave my hand a reassuring squeeze. With a plan fraught with uncertainties but backed by the best of our collective knowledge and intuition, we felt as prepared as possible for our perilous expedition back into the Asurian realm, a journey to touch a soul in desperate need of redemption.

Chapter 40
Prophecy Revealed

Gus and I resumed our seats, the electrodes attached. Our roadmap, newly drawn and full of many possibilities, was fresh in our minds. We closed our eyes, took deep breaths, and prepared to enter the dream world. This time, we were not mere explorers but travelers with a purpose. As our consciousness slipped away, a newfound confidence surged within me: we were ready, and this time, we had a plan.

The lab walls dissolved, giving way to a kaleidoscope of colors and shapes, swirling like mist. Then, with a final surge, we were thrust into another world entirely. The spiritual realm we found ourselves in was an unsettling mix of beauty and horror. Massive pillars of light touched a sky filled with ever-changing constellations, while an undercurrent of darkness seemed to pull at us, urging us deeper into the subterranean layers of the spirit world. Gus and I floated, disoriented, trying to find our bearings. Our tether to the physical world was already starting to feel tenuous.

"We need to move," Gus said, his voice tinged with urgency. "The Asuras won't just wait for us." So, we pushed on, navigating through a labyrinth of translucent caverns and neon-lit jungles. Phantasmal beasts and figures that resembled but were grotesquely different from humans observed us curiously from the shadows. As we started to feel hopelessly lost, the ground quivered beneath us. A monolith erupted from the earth, covered in ancient symbols that seemed to writhe and shift. It beckoned us closer, humming with a resonant energy reverberating through our souls.

"Do you think this is it?" I asked, my eyes fixed on the cryptic symbols.

"Only one way to find out," Gus said, reaching out to touch the monolith. The moment he made contact, the world around us dissolved.

We found ourselves in an amphitheater made of what appeared to be crystalline quartz, refracting rainbows in every direction. At its center stood a female figure, ageless and ethereal.

"Welcome," she said, her voice echoing through the chamber. "I've been expecting you."

The words struck me with a sense of destiny, as if every step we took had led us to this moment. We were here to venture into the unknown and confront a prophecy that tied our fates to something more significant. The figure unfurled an astral scroll that appeared to hover in the space between us. Her words were a floating message revealing that the Asuras were not mere guardians but manifestations of collective energies—energies that had found their way into our world, fueling fascist, authoritarian regimes, hatred, and intolerance. "As it is in the higher realms, so it is in the lower," the deity proclaimed. "To mend one, you must mend the other."

"We seek to achieve disarmament through empathy," Gus explained, his eyes narrowing as if caught in a delicate dance of doubt and realization.

The oracle fixed us with an unsettlingly penetrative gaze as if scanning the codices of our souls. "Yes, but let me be clear: empathy is the seed, not the tree. Your quest spans two realms, intricately linked between the physical world and our ethereal energies. The *Sphere of Empathy* you aim to forge must meld your inherent strengths with those you'll unearth in the world around you. It should pulsate with universal compassion that your earthly realm so sorely lacks, compassion so scarce that it has forged the very barriers that keep you divided."

Drawing nearer, the oracle continued, "In your earthly domain, you must pinpoint three loci of dissonance—specific places or situations where the absence of empathy has resulted in suffering. These could be homes shattered by misunderstanding, communities torn apart by prejudice, or nations fractured by political discord."

Gus nodded, his mind racing to comprehend her cryptic message. "Loci of dissonance," he repeated, committing the phrase to memory.

I felt the weight of the oracle's words press upon me. Her guidance was clear—we had a mission and a sacred duty to fulfill.

"In these loci," the oracle's voice lowered to a whisper that was almost inaudible, "you must plant Seeds of Compassion that inspire empathy and unity." The words hung in the air, heavy with significance.

The oracle's message was mysterious and profound, leaving me with an unshakable sense of purpose. I felt a calling to heal the fractures in our world with the soothing balm of understanding. But doubts crept into my mind, and I couldn't help but voice them. "How could such simple acts make a difference?" My voice trembled with uncertainty. "The world is crumbling in so many places. Can three acts of kindness truly be enough?"

The oracle regarded me with otherworldly wisdom as if she had expected these questions.

"Simple acts," she replied, barely audible, "can set profound changes in motion. Even a single thread can alter the pattern in the vast tapestry of existence. Seeds of compassion are not just acts of kindness; they are catalysts for change, sparks of empathy that can ignite a transformation."

Her words resonated within me, offering a glimmer of hope.

"The world may be fractured," the oracle continued, "but the process of mending begins with individual hearts, like drops in an ocean that create waves. By planting these seeds, you become stewards of empathy, sowing the potential for healing."

I absorbed her wisdom, my doubts giving way to a newfound determination. I realized that I had a role to play in sowing Seeds of Compassion and nurturing empathy in a world that desperately needed it.

Gus looked intrigued but puzzled. "Once we satisfy this request, what then?"

"Once you've completed your tasks on Earth, you will return to the ethereal realm," the oracle continued, "where you must journey through the three Rivers of Essence: the River of Sorrow, the River of Joy, and the River of Tranquility. These rivers hold the collective emotions of all sentient beings. By navigating them, you will learn to embrace emotional complexity in its purest form. Your vessel for this perilous journey will be none other than the *Sphere of Empathy* itself. Only when you have absorbed the lessons of these rivers can your sphere be powerful enough to disarm the Asuras and penetrate the labyrinthine defenses around the soul you seek to redeem."

The weight of these words seemed almost too much to bear. We weren't just talking about an expedition to another realm; this was an expedition into the depths of emotional and spiritual existence, which demanded a transformation at every step.

"You see," the oracle intoned, "only a *Sphere of Empathy* born of such a comprehensive journey—one that addresses the earthly and the ethereal, the individual and the universal—can shatter the barriers your target has erected around himself. More importantly, it can serve as a beacon that calls forth the foundational empathy lacking in your world. Break one wall, and you may find that others begin to crumble in a cascade of awakened compassion."

My hands trembled as the oracle's essence permeated my being, the resonance of her words striking a chord within me that I hadn't known existed. This was not merely a quest but a spiritual symphony that had to be composed with precision, courage, and boundless love.

With an ethereal wave, the oracle vanished. The grand amphitheater disintegrated into a mist, leaving us in space simultaneously nowhere and everywhere. Yet her words remained indelible, not only in our minds but deep within the foundational structure of our souls.

Gus and I exchanged a solemn glance. Much was to be done in both the seen and the unseen realms. One thing was sure: the roadmap had been laid out, and the compass was set. It was time to embark on the most significant expedition of our lives, armed not just with a mantra and a theoretical *Sphere of Empathy* but with a newfound understanding of the profound interconnectedness of all realms and beings. We hoped not just to bring down a single wall but to initiate the crumbling of divisive barriers worldwide.

Chapter 41
Strategy Revealed

Gus and I awoke to the soft, ethereal glow of the monitors permeating our secret hideaway. The oracle's words still echoed in our minds. In that moment, we were not just ordinary individuals; we were chosen vessels for a mission of cosmic significance that held the power to heal the very essence of existence itself. It was a responsibility that bore down on us, urging us to devise a strategy that could match the gravity of our task.

The room, bathed in the soft luminescence of technology, seemed like a bridge between the mundane and the mystical. Our trusted ally Monica sat poised at the control panel, her fingers moving with a grace born of mastery. Her presence radiated a calm authority that concealed her inner excitement for all we had accomplished so far.

"Monica," I began, my voice heavy with the weight of the oracle's message, "it appears we've been chosen for a mission that transcends ordinary understanding—a mission guided by a being we can only describe as an oracle."

"Oracle?" Monica repeated, her eyes widening with curiosity and reverence.

Gus nodded, his gaze unwavering. "Our mission is to seek out three places where the very essence of empathy has withered, leaving behind only the haunting echoes of suffering. In these places, we bear the sacred duty of planting what the oracle called the Seeds of Compassion."

Monica leaned forward, her curiosity tangible, and her fingers momentarily paused on the control panel as she absorbed the profound nature of our task. "I don't understand."

"The oracle calls these three places the loci of dissonance," I explained.

"What does this mean?" Monica inquired, her voice filled with genuine curiosity and a touch of bewilderment.

"Loci of dissonance," I began, "are places or situations where the absence of empathy has sown seeds of suffering. They are points of discord and pain in the fabric of existence, like a melody that has lost its harmony. These could be homes torn apart by misunderstanding, communities fractured by prejudice, or nations divided by political hatred."

Monica nodded slowly, her brow furrowed as she absorbed the explanation. The weight of our mission was becoming increasingly apparent to all of us, and her unwavering support was crucial as we delved deeper into the complexities of our task. "And this oracle wants you to do what at these places?" Monica inquired, her curiosity piqued as she sought to grasp the full extent of our mission.

I took a deep breath, trying to convey the depth of the oracle's message. "We are entrusted with a sacred duty—to plant the Seeds of Compassion. Our mission is to mend the fractures in our world with the soothing balm of compassion and understanding."

Monica nodded in contemplation, her eyes reflecting the gravity of our task. The profound nature of our mission was becoming increasingly clear, and we all felt the weight of the responsibility placed upon us by the oracle's enigmatic guidance.

"But to what end?" she inquired.

"The oracle believes that our actions will set in motion a chain of events that will ripple through humanity," I explained with a sense of determination that transcended skepticism.

Gus added, "By transforming these three focal points of despair into beacons of empathy, it's possible we can ignite a transformative wave of change."

Monica's skepticism lingered, and she asked, "By just changing three places of discontent?"

I sighed, acknowledging the audacity of our mission. "Perhaps our celebrity and influence could amplify the message in ways we can't predict."

Monica leaned back, her gaze fixed on the distant horizon. After contemplating, she posed another crucial question, her voice tinged with uncertainty. "How would you know you've succeeded?"

I considered her question carefully, realizing that the measure of success in our mission was as enigmatic as the oracle's guidance. "We don't know," I admitted honestly. "We'll just have to wait and see. Success might reveal itself through the ripples of empathy we create, the stories we change, and the lives we touch. It's a journey into the unknown, but we're willing to take that leap of faith."

Gus nodded in agreement, emphasizing the importance of our roles. "It's certainly worth a try," he affirmed.

Monica then focused on the next crucial step, her gaze probing. "And after you accomplish this?" she inquired.

"Then," I replied solemnly, "we must embark on a quest back into the spirit world—to traverse the three Rivers of Essence: the River of Sorrow, the River of Joy, and the River of Tranquility. These rivers, guided by the oracle's enigmatic wisdom, are the keys to cracking the Asuras' formidable defenses."

Monica rubbed the back of her neck as she absorbed my words.

I regarded my friend with wonder and determination, ready to share what we knew. "At these rivers," I began, "our mission will take on a new dimension. I don't precisely know what we're supposed to do there. I suppose we would uncover the specifics as we progress in our quest."

Monica nodded thoughtfully, her curiosity leading her to speculate, "I assume these rivers aren't real."

I met her gaze with a knowing smile. "We believe, as they exist within the spirit world, that they carry the essence of emotions rather than water."

Monica's concern shifted to a practical matter. "But what about the Covenant?" she questioned, her eyes flicking toward the door as if expecting them to intrude at any moment.

The mention of the Covenant raised a significant dilemma for our mission. We knew that the general, a stern and unwavering figure, might not look kindly upon our globe-trotting quest to spread compassion and empathy. His perspective had always been firmly rooted in a more traditional and forceful approach to change. The idea of two of his prized operatives setting off on a journey to perform acts of goodwill might not align with his worldview.

Though I shared Monica's reservations, I also held onto a glimmer of hope. I recalled the senator's surprising openness to shifting their initial strategy, a willingness to explore a more compassionate path toward change. It had been a pivotal moment in our discussions, a sign that even within this formidable organization existed room for a change of heart and approach.

As we contemplated the general's and senator's potential reactions, it became clear that navigating this delicate situation would require tact and strategic communication. We knew that seeking their permission would be crucial, but we also understood the need to present our mission in a light that would resonate with their values and objectives. The challenges were apparent, but our commitment to our mission was unshaken, and we were determined to find a way to align our quest for compassion with the ideals of the Covenant, however challenging that might be.

Monica's commitment to our cause shone through as she nodded unwavering agreement. "I stand with both of you," she declared firmly. "We must craft a path to accomplish this mission and usher in the profound change the oracle envisions."

With our resolve solidified, we focused on the following critical challenge—identifying and successfully transforming the three loci of dissonance. It was a task that demanded meticulous planning and unwavering determination. "I've got an idea," I said, my mind racing with options. "We should use our visibility. I could take on the role of a spokesperson, using the news channels to push for empathy, unity, and the importance of sowing the Seeds of Compassion. Perhaps I could look for a cause that helps the plight of abused women."

Gus nodded, looking deep in thought. "I'll keep leading The Vanguard, using my influence to promote understanding and empathy within our ranks. Together, we can create a wave of change that goes beyond borders."

Monica, always practical, joined in with determination. "You can count on me. I'll support both of you, using my expertise in navigating your dreams to amplify your efforts and ensure your message reaches far and wide."

Amidst our brainstorming, we also unearthed a path to identify the loci of dissonance. We planned to conduct extensive research, reaching out to global communities, humanitarian organizations, and grassroots activists. As influential figures, we would use our unique positions to gather information and stories from those who had experienced suffering and lacked empathy in their lives.

With our plan meticulously laid out and the revelation of our breakthrough against the Asuras, we embraced a renewed sense of purpose and readiness to embark on our mission. Though yet to be discovered, these represented challenges and opportunities to make a profound difference. Our journey had truly begun, and we remained steadfast in our commitment to fulfilling the sacred duty entrusted to us, undeterred by the formidable challenges ahead.

Chapter 42
The Three Loci

In our hidden sanctuary, we gathered once more, determined to choose the three loci of dissonance that would serve as the fulcrum for the earthly portion of our mission. The oracle had set us on this path, and we were poised to make choices that could reshape lives and perceptions.

Monica had several monitors open, each displaying maps, images, and data related to potential areas for our mission. The screens flickered with the suffering of humanity in various parts of the world while the promise of transformation hung in the air like an ethereal melody waiting to be composed.

We knew our choices had to be calculated, strategic, and resonant with the profound message of compassion we aimed to convey. The weight of this decision was palpable, each option representing a unique opportunity to sow the Seeds of Compassion and usher in change.

Gus, embodying his role as a leader, sat with a sense of gravity. His task was to select a locus directly under the influence of the current administration in Washington. It was a daunting endeavor, one that would require unwavering commitment and resilience.

I, too, felt the magnitude of my responsibility as I considered my locus—a place in the world where I could help women who had suffered unimaginable hardships.

Monica leaned over the table, her eyes scanning the monitors with a deep sense of purpose. "All right," she began, her voice resonating with the solemnity of our mission. "Your choices must have far-reaching consequences. Each locus represents a unique opportunity to sow the Seeds of Compassion but comes with complexities."

Gus nodded, understanding that our mission transcended mere acts of kindness. "We need to be strategic and practical," he emphasized. "Our mission is about illuminating the path toward empathy and understanding, resulting in real change for the people we touch."

Monica's fingers hovered over the map of Kabul, Afghanistan. "There's no place on the planet where women have suffered more. Since the United States' abrupt withdrawal, the Taliban's cruel control over Afghanistan's women has grown. They have enforced a regime of oppression and cruelty, denying women even the most basic rights. The abuse and the constant threat that hovers over the women of Afghanistan is a grim reminder of dreams shattered and voices silenced."

Monica's voice trembled as she continued, "Under Taliban control, women are subjected to unimaginable suffering. They are denied access to education, healthcare, and employment opportunities. The freedom to move about and even speak freely in public has been brutally curtailed. Women who were once doctors, teachers, and leaders in their communities have been forced into the shadows, their talents and potential wasted."

She paused, her gaze fixed on the map of Kabul. "The abuses are heart-wrenching. Forced marriages, child brides, and domestic violence have become tragically common. Girls are robbed of their childhoods, and their dreams are crushed under the weight of oppression. The world needs to know their stories to understand the resilience and strength of Afghan women who continue to fight for their rights against all odds."

Monica's description painted a stark picture of women's dire situation in Afghanistan, emphasizing the urgency of their mission to bring about change and offer hope in the face of despair. I couldn't help but ponder the possible influence of the Asuras upon the Taliban's reign of terror. The description of such pervasive suffering and cruelty seemed like a symphony orchestrated by forces beyond the mortal realm. A chilling thought added another layer of complexity to our mission.

As the weight of this monumental task settled upon my shoulders, I couldn't help but feel a sense of responsibility. Kabul, a city scarred by tyranny, stood as a stark reminder of the urgent need for change. The thought of venturing into such a challenging environment, where women had endured such horrors under the Taliban's rule, initially sent shivers down my spine. Thoughts raced as I considered the challenges ahead, looming like a specter and demanding my attention. I contemplated the risks, the sacrifices, and the long road. Could I truly make a difference in the lives of these women? Could I help them regain their freedom and dignity?

Images of Kabul, a city I had only seen on news broadcasts and in documentaries, flashed before my eyes. The war-torn streets, the stories of oppression, and the resilience of the women who had endured it all weighed heavily on my conscience. The dangers of entering this volatile and unpredictable country were undeniable, and the hurdles seemed insurmountable.

Taking a deep breath, I straightened, determined to face this daunting task head-on. "Kabul is a crucible of resilience," I said, my voice filled with trepidation and conviction. "I'm ready to accept the challenge. I'll do everything in my power to bring hope and safety to the women who have suffered for far too long under the shadow of the Taliban and to help them reclaim their rightful place in society."

My commitment resonated in my words; there was no turning back once I'd voiced my decision. Gus placed a comforting hand on my shoulder and shook his head with concern. "No, Emma, that's too dangerous. You'll be risking too much."

I met his gaze. "I don't believe it's too much, Gus. We must shake up the status quo and make a real difference."

The room was thick with unsaid words, heavy with the gravity of what lay ahead. "Emma," Gus said, his voice steady but laced with fear, "the perils are greater than you imagine. Not just the physical dangers, but the cultural and political complexities that can turn even the simplest act into a life-threatening situation."

I nodded, aware yet unwilling to let fear dictate my actions. "I know the risks. But think of the impact, Gus. If we can empower just one woman, it could be the spark that ignites change. I can't stand by when I have the means to help."

Gus sighed, the weight of the world in his eyes. "It's not just about being a woman in Afghanistan. It's about being a foreign woman, alone, in a land where even local women face unimaginable restrictions. You'll be scrutinized, possibly targeted."

"I will be cautious," I assured him, "and I won't be alone. I'll have support, contacts… I won't be reckless."

Gus's hand tightened on my shoulder, his resolve faltering. "Promise me you'll reconsider, Emma. For all our sakes."

Staring into the depths of his concern, I felt the enormity of my decision. Yet, the call to action was too powerful to ignore. "I promise to plan every step with the utmost care. I can't promise to step away from this path. It's too important, Gus."

He nodded. "Very well," he conceded with a thoughtful nod. "I've also made a decision," he began, his voice carrying a sense of purpose that filled the room. "But I understand that transforming The Vanguard won't be straightforward, especially with Derek and many of my staff committed to our current ideology. We need a strategic plan to make this change happen seamlessly."

Monica's eyes lit up with approval, her enthusiasm matching the gravity of the challenge ahead. "That's a wise approach," she declared, her voice filled with optimism. "To shift The Vanguard's direction, you'll need to build bridges and gain the support of key members. It won't be easy, but it's essential for creating lasting change."

Gus nodded in agreement, his expression thoughtful. "Let me start by initiating a series of open dialogues within the organization. I can create a platform where different viewpoints are heard and respected. This will allow me to identify individuals open to change and willing to embrace a more compassionate approach. But," he paused, "we need to be cautious."

I leaned forward, my gaze locked on Gus. "What are the risks?"

Gus took a deep breath before continuing. "The truth is, powerful forces within The Vanguard won't tolerate dissent, especially from its leader. I'm ashamed to say it, but we have an unpleasant way of dealing with dissidents."

Monica's eyes widened, and a heavy silence hung in the room. Gus's words conveyed a chilling reality that we couldn't ignore.

"We make people disappear," he added, his voice lowered as if afraid of being overheard. "I need to be prepared for that possibility."

The weight of the revelation settled on us like a leaden shroud. The path ahead, already daunting, now seemed fraught with danger. But it only fueled our determination to make a real difference within The Vanguard and the broader world, even if it meant confronting the darkest aspects of the organization. I leaned in, eager to hear about our final locus. "What about the third locus, where Gus and I combine forces?"

Monica's eyes danced back and forth between us, her expression thoughtful. A subtle smile played on her lips, hinting at the potential for transformation in this endeavor. With a few deft keystrokes, she summoned the digital presence of RightView News, a far right-wing news station known for its polarizing rhetoric and divisive content. The screen displayed a constant barrage of headlines that often fueled prejudice and hatred.

Monica leaned in, her voice carrying a mix of determination and hope. "This station," she began, "represents a community deeply motivated by prejudice and hatred. It's a tough nut to crack like they all are. But together, you two will try to change the conversation. Your mission? Swap out their fake news with the real deal and try to get folks to see the truth."

Gus and I exchanged glances, silently acknowledging the mountain we were about to climb. Turning a media platform with its heels dug in would be challenging. Still, we were driven by our commitment to the cause of compassion. The thought of having a real impact in a space known for divisive talk gave us some steel.

Gus leaned forward, his eyes locked on Monica's. "We get how important this is," he said with conviction. "We'll dive into conversations with their audience, lay down the facts, and make space for folks to talk without throwing punches. The idea is to mend bridges between different views and spread some empathy where it's been missing."

I said, "By pushing open, respectful discussion, we aim to break the walls of bias and hate that have separated people for too long. It's not a quick fix, but even taking baby steps toward understanding can set off bigger changes down the road."

Monica's smile widened, radiating confidence in our abilities. "You guys together have the potential to turn not only the story on this platform but also the minds and hearts of those who tune in," she reassured us. "Remember, compassion's the power to break even the toughest shells."

With our game plan set for the final locus, we were ready to tackle the challenges that spanned physical action, social change, and media influence. As we geared up for our missions, the endless possibilities of what we could achieve together filled the room, stoking our spirits with hope and resolve.

We locked eyes, fully aware of the magnitude of what we proposed. "Let's aim to rewrite the script," Gus said, and I nodded in agreement. As we cemented our decisions, we knew the road ahead was paved with obstacles and uncertainties. Success wasn't guaranteed, but we firmly believed that love, compassion, and unyielding determination could spark transformation, even in the darkest circumstances. Our journey had begun, and the horizon stretched before us, waiting to be embraced. "I guess that's it," I said. "Now, all we have to do is find a way out of here."

The door swung open just as the words left my lips, and Senator Clarke and General Harris strolled in. The timing couldn't have been more critical. Perhaps they would be receptive to our newfound purpose, which could be the turning point we needed.

With a surge of hope and determination, we delved into the details of our three loci of dissonance mission. We explained our vision for positive change, both for ourselves and humanity as a whole. But as we made our plea, skepticism hung heavy in the air. The room seemed to buzz with questions about our unusual source: an oracle from the spirit world. What did we honestly expect to happen if, by some stretch, we succeeded with all three loci?

Senator Clarke, though intrigued, couldn't hide her skepticism. "This is certainly unique," she began cautiously. "But I must admit, I find it hard to believe that an oracle from the spirit world can guide you in such a concrete mission. What if this mission of yours fails? Have you considered the repercussions?"

Gus nodded, understanding the concerns. "Senator, we share your doubts, but what we've witnessed so far gives us hope. It's not about blind belief; it's about recognizing the potential for change. And as for the consequences of failure, we're prepared to take responsibility and face whatever comes."

"While I admire your determination," the senator began, "I have to wonder about the practicality of it all. The Taliban and The Vanguard are powerful forces. Are you prepared for the potential backlash if things don't go as planned?"

I responded, "Senator, we've considered the risks. But we believe that if we don't try, who will? And if we succeed, we can inspire others to follow our lead."

General Harris, the most skeptical of all, folded his arms and grumbled, "I'm not sold on the idea that some oracle in heaven can dictate our actions. And even if you succeed with all three loci, what's the endgame? What do you expect to achieve?"

Gus leaned forward, his eyes meeting the general's with unwavering determination. "We don't expect an oracle to dictate our actions, but it has provided us with guidance we couldn't have found elsewhere. As for the endgame, we hope to set a precedent for peaceful resolutions worldwide by resolving these three major conflicts. It's a lofty goal, but isn't that what humanity needs?"

The room fell into a contemplative silence as they grappled with the unconventional nature of our mission. It was a tense moment, with the world's weight seemingly hanging in the balance. Finally, General Harris let out a reluctant sigh and nodded. "Fine, you have my cautious support. But remember one misstep, and I'll hold all three of you accountable."

With that, we had secured the endorsement of those in positions of authority, although their skepticism lingered. It marked the initial stride in our journey to reshape the world through compassion and understanding, but the road ahead remained uncertain.

Chapter 43
Trek through Afghanistan

The journey to Kabul was an odyssey of grit and perseverance, a path that wound through Pakistan's rugged and unforgiving terrain and into the heart of Afghanistan—known as the graveyard of empires, where once the British Empire, then the Soviet Union, and most recently, the United States all tried to conquer but failed miserably. Accompanied by a seasoned guide named Ahmed, a local whose deeply etched lines and sunbaked skin bore witness to countless trials endured in this unforgiving landscape, I embarked on the expedition.

Navigating a labyrinth of treacherous trails, our sturdy and resilient steeds proved to be trusty companions. Their hooves echoed with rhythmic certainty as they clambered over uneven terrain, navigating rocky paths with the surefootedness of creatures born to these mountains. The elements offered no mercy; the sun's relentless scorching by day and the biting cold of Afghan nights chilling me to the bone. Yet, my determination remained unyielding, driven by the profound knowledge that my purpose was to make an extraordinary difference in the lives of Kabul's women and girls.

Amid the challenge, my own trepidation loomed large; the towering beasts beneath me were as daunting as the mission I'd undertaken. Each stride of the horse required a silent mantra of courage, a constant mental push to overcome the fear that clenched with icy fingers around my heart. This journey was not just across the unforgiving landscape of Afghanistan but also through the valleys of my anxieties, a personal pilgrimage toward the strength I knew I possessed.

As Ahmed led me deeper into Afghanistan, the towering peaks of the Hindu Kush Mountains loomed overhead, their jagged silhouettes a stark reminder of the land's turbulent history. The landscape's rugged beauty concealed the deep scars etched into the earth by decades of military conflict.

Amidst the trials and tribulations of this arduous journey, my mind couldn't help but drift back to my life's extraordinary path. Just a few short months ago, I was a university student, my daily existence characterized by lectures, exams, and the familiar rhythms of academic life. Never in my wildest dreams did I envision myself traversing treacherous terrain in a remote and dangerous land, embarking on a mission to safeguard humanity from venomous ethereal entities.

The pivotal moment in my life had come with my encounter with Gus, a connection that defied conventional understanding and reasoning. Gus wasn't just an eternal soulmate; he was my partner in a quest that transcended the boundaries of the known world. As I journeyed through the Afghan landscape, I couldn't help but marvel at the intricate tapestry of events that had led me to this point. My life had radically transformed, shifting from the mundane to the extraordinary. It was a path illuminated by love, purpose, and an unwavering belief in the power of unlikely individuals to serve as catalysts for change in a world shrouded in shadows.

The risks ahead were substantial, but I drew strength from knowing I was far from alone on this voyage. Monica had emerged as my guiding light, armed with her profound expertise in dreams and a newfound understanding of the interplay between the human spirit and the soul world. Her influence had also played a pivotal role in redirecting the Covenant's mission, steering it away from confrontation and toward our newfound approach of wielding love and compassion as weapons against the Asuras' hostile intent.

As the majestic mountains loomed closer, their presence a testament to the resilience of the Afghan people, I felt a profound sense of purpose. My life had been irrevocably altered, and I was ready to embrace the extraordinary path that fate had set before me.

Each step brought me closer to my destination, heightening my awareness of the weight of my mission. The lives of countless women and girls rested on my shoulders, their hopes and dreams intertwined with mine. Yes, the path was fraught with danger. But I could not be deterred. I was resolute in my purpose, unwavering in my commitment to effect change for those who had suffered for far too long.

Our journey through Afghanistan's rugged terrain was filled with breathtaking landscapes and unexpected challenges. We traveled through many remote villages, each nestled among the imposing mountains. The Afghan people, resilient and resourceful, welcomed us with cautious curiosity. They were initially surprised to see an American woman traversing their rugged terrain, but their innate hospitality prevailed. As we approached a village, I noticed a group of local children had gathered. Their eyes sparkled with curiosity and a hint of shyness as they watched our arrival. With a warm smile, I knelt and extended my hand in greeting. It didn't take long for their initial shyness to melt away. Soon, we were engaged in an impromptu game of tag, laughter echoing through the village's narrow alleys. The children's energy and enthusiasm were infectious, and I couldn't help but be swept up in the joy of the moment. Despite the language barrier, we communicated through smiles, gestures, and simple games, forming a good connection.

In another village further along our journey, we had the privilege of meeting a group of wise elders who had gathered in the shade of a centuries-old tree. They sat in a circle, their faces etched with the lines of time and wisdom. With a few words from Ahmed, they welcomed us with gracious nods and warm smiles. The elders shared stories of their ancestors, tales that stretched back generations and were woven into the very fabric of their culture. They spoke of ancient traditions passed down through the ages that had sustained their way of life. Each story was a precious thread in the tapestry of their history, and I listened with rapt attention.

As the sun dipped below the horizon, the elders extended an invitation to join them for the evening meal. They had prepared a feast of traditional cuisine, a rich mosaic of flavors and aromas.

We sat cross-legged on the floor and shared the communal experience of savoring these time-honored dishes. Around us, the village came alive with laughter and conversation, the air filled with the fragrant scents of spices. It was a moment of connection as we broke bread together and celebrated the richness of a culture steeped in history.

These stories from my journey through Afghanistan's remote villages testify to the power of human connection. Amid unfamiliar surroundings and language barriers, we discovered that the universal language of laughter, smiles, and shared experiences can bridge even the widest of cultural gaps. Each encounter left an indelible mark on my heart, reminding me of the resilience and warmth of the Afghan people.

Yet, our journey was not without its challenges. The terrain demanded every ounce of my physical strength and mental resilience. Ahmed continued navigating us through treacherous mountain paths that seemed to defy gravity. The unpredictable weather tested my endurance, with sudden storms and biting cold.

But as we pushed onward, the landscape transformed, revealing a city scarred by conflict and adversity—Kabul. Its labyrinthine streets and war-scarred buildings were a stark reminder of the challenges ahead. Here I would seek out Mahbouba Seraj, a renowned human rights activist and advocate for women's empowerment in Afghanistan, whose determination and compassion shone as a beacon of hope.

I hoped that the adventures and encounters on the road had prepared me for the trials awaiting me in Kabul. The weight of my mission had grown heavier, but my spirit remained light. With the stories and experiences of the Afghan people as my guide, I stood on the precipice of a profound endeavor, ready to make a difference in the lives of those who had known both hardship and hope. The path to change may have been treacherous, but I walked it with unwavering determination, fueled by the memories of the remarkable people I had met.

Chapter 44
Taliban

The sprawling labyrinth of Kabul's streets stretched before me as I approached, a place I had only dreamed of visiting in my wildest, most ambitious moments. The journey had been arduous, fraught with challenges and dangers at every turn, but I was driven by a purpose that transcended fear. I'd come to Kabul to make a difference, to bring hope to the women who had endured unimaginable hardships.

As I neared the city's heart, the cacophony of life in Kabul washed over me. The streets were alive with the hustle and bustle of people going about their daily lives, their voices creating a symphony of languages and dialects that spoke of the city's rich tapestry of cultures and histories. The buildings, scarred by years of conflict, bore witness to the resilience of its inhabitants.

My reverie was shattered when, without warning, three shadowy figures materialized from the bustling crowd. Their faces were obscured by coverings, leaving only their intense eyes visible, and their actions were swift and forceful. Strong hands gripped my arms, their fingers like vices, and before I could utter a word, I was unceremoniously shoved into a beat-up, windowless Ford van. The rusty door slammed shut behind me.

Fear gripped me like a vice in the dimly lit confines. My heart pounded in my chest; each beat a drumming reminder of my vulnerability. Questions tumbled through my mind like a turbulent river. Who were these men? What were their intentions? The oppressive uncertainty was suffocating, and the distant echoes of Kabul's chaotic streets outside starkly contrasted with the darkness that enveloped me within.

Minutes stretched into an eternity as the van navigated the winding streets, its engine growling like a restless beast. The air inside grew close, and I stole furtive glances at my captors. Intense and unrelenting eyes bore into me, their intentions shrouded in mystery. It was as if they were trying to decipher the enigma of the young American woman who had dared to traverse the perilous trails to Kabul.

The van abruptly stopped, and the doors swung open with a creak. As I stepped out onto the uneven cobblestones, I stood before the Arg, the presidential palace of Afghanistan. Since the abolition of the presidency by the Taliban, it had served as the meeting place of the Cabinet of Afghanistan. The imposing structure, now eerily silent, spoke volumes about the tumultuous history of this war-torn nation.

Though weathered by time and conflict, the palace's exterior still retained an air of majesty. Its architecture told the story of a bygone era, with intricately carved details adorning the façade. The grandeur I had anticipated had survived, at least partly, despite the ravages of war. As I gazed up at the ornate columns and towering archways, it was as if I could hear the echoes of a past era, a time when this place had been a symbol of power and prestige.

However, my awe at the palace's exterior gave way to a different reality as I entered its halls. The opulent trappings I'd imagined were conspicuously absent. The once-luxurious interiors had been stripped to their bare walls, leaving a stark emptiness behind. The walls that had once witnessed history now echoed with the haunting whispers of a nation in turmoil.

Despite the absence of opulence, the architecture remained a testament to the wonders of the recent past, a reminder of what endured beneath the scars of conflict. The grandeur may have faded within these walls, but the enduring spirit of the Afghan people persevered, waiting to shape the course of events in the years to come.

I was led up a wide stone staircase, the steps worn and weathered by countless footsteps. The long, vast halls stretched before me, their faded grandeur hinting at a time when this palace was a hub of activity and power. As I walked through the echoing corridors, a wave of nervousness washed over me, its tendrils tightening around my heart. Men gathered along the walls, their eyes fixed upon me with a palpable intensity. In a land where burkas were the common attire for women, I couldn't help but feel conspicuous. The absence of at least a headscarf to conceal my hair made me acutely aware of their scrutiny. Each step I took seemed to amplify the weight of their gaze, and my heart quickened in response to the unfamiliar and unsettling attention.

Every footfall echoed in the vast, cavernous halls, and each sound reminded me of my vulnerability in this unfamiliar territory. The stark contrast between my Western attire and the traditional dress of the few women who studied me added to the tension that coiled within. Their whispers and hushed conversations intensified my unease. I couldn't understand their Pashto words, but the tone carried a mixture of curiosity and suspicion. The air seemed to crackle with an unspoken question: Who was this foreign woman, and what was she doing here?

As I made my way toward the presidential office, I felt the weight of history pressing upon me. Once filled with the bustling activity of a government in power, the corridors now held an eerie silence. The grandeur of the past had been stripped away, leaving a haunting reminder of the nation's turbulent journey.

Finally, I was led into the sparse presidential offices, where a group of men had gathered, their eyes fixated on me. Their presence heightened my anxiety, and I couldn't help but wonder about their intentions. I was acutely aware of my vulnerability.

As I stood, feeling the weight of their collective gaze, one of them stepped forward. He was a middle-aged, bearded individual with a calm demeanor that contrasted the tense atmosphere. The man wore long, loose-fitting garments like a robe and baggy pants. His outfit had earthy, muted colors, blending in with the surroundings. A cloth headdress wrapped his head, which gave him a traditional and unassuming appearance. "American woman," he began, "you are here to meet our spiritual leader—Mullah Hibatullah Akhundzada. You should be honored."

I blinked, my heart pounding in my chest. The name was unfamiliar to me, but the seriousness of the situation was unmistakable. I had heard of the Taliban and their presence in Afghanistan, but I had never expected to come face-to-face with a Mullah. Before I could process this revelation fully, the man gestured for me to follow him. My steps were hesitant as I trailed behind him, the weight of uncertainty heavy upon my shoulders. I had embarked on this journey with a mission, but now I found myself facing a meeting I could never have anticipated.

Then there he was. The moment our eyes met, a shiver ran down my spine. The air in the room seemed charged with an unspoken tension, and I couldn't shake the feeling that my life had taken an unforeseen and perilous turn. The Mullah's eyes held a depth of knowledge and experience; at that moment, I understood I was in the presence of a powerful and enigmatic figure. I couldn't help but wonder what destiny had in store for me in this place of power and intrigue.

I couldn't conceal my confusion any longer, and my voice trembled slightly as I responded, "Sir, I don't understand why you've brought me here."

He regarded me with a faint, enigmatic smile. "You see, Emma, unexpected occurrences can be significant in these tumultuous times. Though fraught with danger, your journey speaks of a determination and courage uncommon among those from your part of the world."

Pleased that he spoke English so well, I hesitated momentarily before finding my voice again. "Your English is good."

Mullah Akhundzada nodded slowly, his gaze unwavering. "Indeed, it is. It is a valuable skill in a world as interconnected as ours."

As his unexpected command of the language hung in the air, I found myself momentarily stunned, grappling with the revelation that this man, the enigmatic leader of the Taliban, was not only aware of my presence and my name but could communicate fluently in a language I had assumed would be foreign to him. It was a reminder of the complex world I had entered, where expectations and assumptions could be upended instantly.

Mullah Akhundzada leaned forward slightly, his eyes locked onto mine. "You might be wondering, young lady," he began, his voice steady and measured, "how you managed to arrive here in Kabul so easily despite the treacherous journey."

I shrugged.

"You've been watched."

"I have?" I asked, my voice trembling with a mix of curiosity and fear.

The Mullah leaned back in his chair, his gaze never leaving mine. "Yes," he replied, his tone calm and unwavering. "We've been aware of your progress since your journey began in Pakistan."

I couldn't believe what I was hearing. My heart raced as I tried to process the implications of his words. Every step I had taken, every challenge I had faced, had been scrutinized by unseen eyes. It was a level of surveillance that sent shivers down my spine and left me feeling exposed and vulnerable.

"But why?" I managed to ask, my voice barely above a whisper.

The Mullah's expression remained impassive as he replied, "We're curious about your intentions, your purpose in coming here."

The room seemed to close in as I grappled with the enormity of what he was saying. My mission, my purpose, had been under constant observation. I couldn't help but wonder how much they knew, how much they had uncovered about my true intentions in Kabul. The air in the room remained thick, but a flicker of understanding dawned on me. "You want to know why I'm here; what drives me to undertake this journey?"

Chapter 45
Prison

Standing before the Mullah, my heart pounded like a caged bird desperate for freedom. It was a chance to plead my case to advocate for the voiceless women and girls suffering under the oppressive rule of the Taliban. My challenging journey, spanning thousands of miles, had a singular purpose—to meet Mahbouba Seraj, the fierce advocate for Afghan women's rights.

I began, my voice steady but laced with urgency, "I've come a great distance, enduring countless hardships, to speak with Mahbouba Seraj. I understand she's the beacon of hope, advocating for dialogue between the Taliban and women who have endured unspeakable suffering. I believe that together, we can shed light on the atrocities committed against Afghan women and bring their stories to the world's attention."

The Mullah, a middle-aged man with a beard that flowed like a river of gray, listened intently. Though carrying the weight of many years, his eyes seemed to betray a hint of curiosity. For a brief moment, it felt like my words had found their mark, that the wall between us was cracking, understanding within reach.

I delved into my experiences, recounting the tales of resilient women and girls I had encountered on my journey. Their stories were etched in my memory, and as I shared them, I hoped to convey their strength, dreams, and indomitable spirit.

"Take Amina, for instance," I continued, my voice filled with conviction. "She's a young girl I met from a remote village who looked at me with the hope that one day she would have a chance for a better life. She deserves justice, equality, and the chance to build a better future. They yearn for the world to know their struggles, dreams, and determination to overcome adversity."

The Mullah's gaze was unwavering, and his occasional nods seemed to signal agreement with my words. It was a fragile hope but felt like a ray of light piercing the darkness. I understood that our conversation was drawing to a close as the Mullah's countenance changed subtly. The warmth in his eyes faded, replaced by a mysterious mask. He rose from his seat with a curt nod, signaling to the guards to intervene.

My heart sank as I was led away from the Mullah's office. Instead of heading toward the path of diplomacy and dialogue I had hoped for, I found myself guided down a foreboding staircase, the air growing colder with each step. The guards opened a heavy door, revealing a nightmarish realm—a Taliban prison cell chock full of dozens of young women, faces etched with fear and suffering. The conditions were appalling, with overcrowded cells and meager rations. Despair hung in the air like a suffocating fog.

As I entered the dimly lit prison, I was met with a sea of faces marked by shock and disbelief. These women had been left behind when the United States evacuated their armed forces from Afghanistan. Their expressions told a story of betrayal and abandonment. The cramped, squalid conditions amplified the sense of hopelessness.

I approached a group of women near the entrance. Their expressions held curiosity and resentment as they engaged in hushed Pashto conversations, their voices laden with bitterness. Pointing in my direction, they mouthed a single recognizable word, "American," revealing a complex array of emotions and buried memories. As I tried to engage with them, one woman, her eyes filled with anger and sorrow, stepped forward. She appeared to be a leader, her voice carrying the weight of their collective frustration.

"Why are you here? What do you want from us?" she demanded, her voice laced with skepticism.

"I've come to help," I said and immediately regretted the words as they escaped my mouth.

The woman scoffed. "You Americans abandoned us when we needed you the most. Our hopes were crushed when your troops left, and now you come here to help? What could you do?” she said with a grimace.

I pleaded my case, explaining that I had journeyed to Kabul to meet Mahbouba Seraj, the courageous advocate for Afghan women’s rights. I hoped that my association with her would lend credibility to my presence, but instead, I was met with mocking laughter.

“Mahbouba Seraj?” the leader scoffed. “You truly believe she’s the savior who can change our fate? You Americans are so naïve. She may speak of dialogue and change, but the reality”—she paused to sweep an arm—“is far different.” Though most didn’t understand our words, they got the gist and nodded in agreement, their faces etched with resignation. They had witnessed the fleeting promises of change, only to see their hopes dashed again.

I felt a crushing weight settle over me as I realized the depth of their disillusionment. It was a stark reminder of the complex web of geopolitics and suffering that had brought me here and the enormity of the task ahead. With a heavy heart, I settled against the mold-infested rock wall, surrounded by the silent cries of women who had endured far more than anyone should have to bear. I could only wonder what lay ahead in this harrowing chapter of my mission.

*

As the hours dragged on in that wretched cell, my despair deepened. The overcrowded conditions were suffocating, and the oppressive air was heavy with the pungent stench of sickness and desperation. Some of the women appeared so frail and lifeless that it seemed death had already claimed them. The stench-filled wooden waste buckets in the corners served as a constant reminder of our confinement and the deplorable conditions.

I huddled, my knees pulled to my chest, and couldn’t help but shiver, not from cold but from the fear gnawing at my insides like a relentless beast, threatening to consume what little hope remained. The dim light was filtered through a small, barred window high above, casting eerie shadows on the faces of my fellow captives. The sounds of coughing and stifled sobs filled the air.

The meager meal of watered-down stew was a tasteless reminder of our helplessness. I barely picked at it, my appetite diminished by the bleakness of our circumstances. The murmurs of the women around me were filled with resignation, their voices slightly rising above a whisper. In the suffocating confines of our dimly lit cell, a woman, her eyes reflecting a weariness that seemed to extend beyond the prison's walls, cautiously settled beside me. We exchanged glances, two souls bound by the cruel twist of fate that had brought us together in this wretched place. After a moment of silence, she leaned in closer, her voice trembling with trepidation and trust.

"I'm…" She hesitated, her voice barely more than a whisper, as if revealing her name was an act of vulnerability. Finally, she continued, "I'm Fatima."

I nodded, grateful for this small act of trust. "I'm Emma," I replied softly, my voice betraying the blend of fear and curiosity that churned within me. "How old are you, Fatima?"

Fatima's eyes welled up with tears as she recounted her story. "I'm thirty-two," she said, her voice quivering. "I was in university before the Americans left. Back then, things were different. Women could study and pursue their dreams. That's where I learned English. But now…" She trailed off, her gaze drifting to our crowded cell's dark, damp corner. "It's illegal for women to get an education. I protested in a rally, and they took me prisoner along with others," she said, gesturing to those around us. Each syllable carried the weight of her suffering and oppression. I felt an overwhelming surge of empathy for Fatima, and tears welled in my eyes.

"I can't imagine what you've been through," I whispered, my voice choked with emotion. "To have your dreams shattered like that, to endure this for so long…" I couldn't find the words to express the sorrow that welled up within me.

Fatima gave me a sad smile, a glimmer of resilience in her eyes. "We all have stories, Emma. We're survivors in our way. But I fear there's little hope for us here."

"But what about Mahbouba Seraj?" I said, grasping her frail hand. "Have you heard of her?"

Fatima's eyes welled with a mix of admiration and hope. "Heard of her? Mahbouba Seraj," she began, her voice filled with reverence, "she's our only hope, Emma. When the Taliban seized power, many women's rights activists fled, fearing the reprisals that were sure to come. But not Mahbouba Seraj. She refused to leave, even though she holds an American passport."

I leaned in closer, my curiosity piqued by this woman who had become a symbol of resistance against the dark forces that had descended upon Afghanistan.

"She's been relentless," Fatima continued, her eyes reflecting both admiration and sadness. "Despite the Taliban's intimidation, she's continued to advocate for the rights of women and girls. She runs a network of shelters for those fleeing domestic abuse, providing a lifeline to the most vulnerable among us. During the last sixteen months," Fatima continued, "the Taliban has imposed severe restrictions on women—how we dress, our freedom of movement, our right to work, and education. They've waged a brutal crackdown on dissent, targeting human rights defenders, women activists, journalists, and intellectuals. Even peaceful protests by women demanding their basic rights have been met with violence."

I listened intently, my heart sinking with each word. The challenges faced by women in this worn-torn country seemed insurmountable, but the resilience of people like Mahbouba Seraj gave me hope.

"Seraj's work and courage were recognized," Fatima said, her voice tinged with pride. "She was nominated for the Nobel Peace Prize." As the night enveloped us in its darkness, I couldn't help but ponder the immense challenges that loomed ahead. Mahbouba Seraj, a last cry for hope, continued her tireless struggle for a brighter future against all odds.

With these thoughts swirling in my mind, I decided as I drifted into sleep that night—a decision born of determination and a sense of purpose—if I couldn't reach the leading women's advocate in the waking world, perhaps I could connect with her in the realm of dreams. I settled onto the cold, stone floor with newfound resolve. Tonight, I would go lucid and seek out this remarkable woman, even if she remained unaware of my presence.

Chapter 46
Dreams of Mahbouba

Determined, I closed my eyes within the dank cell and shut out the oppressive reality surrounding me, embracing the dream world. With exhaustion already consuming me, sleep came quickly, allowing me to embark on a journey into the depths of my consciousness. My awareness sharpened amidst surreal landscapes and swirling mists. I could sense this realm's fluidity and the limitless possibilities it offered. As before, I became fully aware of my presence in this ethereal domain.

My thoughts were clear, and my purpose was unwavering. I reached out, not with physical hands, but with the very essence of my being. "Mahbouba," I called out, echoing through the dreamscapes. "I need you. I must find you."

The dream world responded, revealing its enigmas like the petals of a cosmic flower. My quest to reach Mahbouba in my dreams would lead me through surreal and profound landscapes, guided by the indomitable strength of my spirit. My determination to find this remarkable woman remained unwavering as I navigated the ethereal landscapes. Each step I took felt like a leap into the unknown, but I was fueled by a profound sense of purpose.

Finally, amidst the shifting dreamscapes, I spotted a figure in the distance. There she was—Mahbouba, an elderly woman with silver hair that cascaded gracefully around her shoulders and large brown eyes that held the wisdom of a thousand lifetimes. Unlike previous encounters with those in the dream world, she was seemingly lost and confused, her presence flickering like a distant star.

She was dressed in a white linen gown that flowed with ethereal grace, its purity contrasting beautifully with the vivid brown sash she wore, pulled tight at her waist. Her appearance exuded a sense of serenity and strength, and I knew I had found the woman I sought.

This was my chance. I extended my ethereal hand toward her, hoping to bridge the gap between our consciousnesses. But as my spectral fingers brushed against her, Mahbouba recoiled, her expression contorted in fear. To her, my presence must have felt like a haunting nightmare, an intrusion into her sleep. Panic washed over her, and she began to back away.

"No, wait! I only want to speak with you," I cried, echoing like a distant whisper. But to Mahbouba, I was an enigma, a source of terror in the surreal landscape of her dreams. Realization dawned on me. Attempting to reach Mahbouba in this state while she was not lucid was futile. My presence was perceived as a nightmare, causing her distress. With a heavy heart, I retreated, allowing the dream world to fold back upon itself. As I awakened in my prison cell, frustration gnawed at me. I had come so close, yet Mahbouba remained elusive.

Desperation now fueled my thoughts, birthing a new idea. I needed guidance, someone well-versed in the intricacies of navigating the dream world. My mind turned to Gus. But I wondered about the time difference between Kabul and Boston. *What hour was it back home?* Calculating a nine-hour gap, I realized it must be mid-morning, making it impossible for us to connect in the dream world.

My desperation reached its zenith. Day by agonizing day, I grappled with my confinement's futility. My attempts to reach Mahbouba through the ethereal realm had yielded naught but frustration, leaving me haunted by the knowledge that she remained oblivious to my presence. Then, amidst the shadows of despair, a daring and audacious plan began to take shape.

As the moon cast its pallid glow upon the prison, I embarked on a journey deep into the labyrinth of my subconscious. Armed with the arcane knowledge of lucid dreaming, I melded my determination with my new knowledge of the metaphysical, crafting an intricate spell to bridge the gaping chasm separating the Mullah and me. In the ethereal realm, I wove a tapestry of gossamer threads, each a shimmering conduit connecting our dreamscapes.

My essence ascended, a fleeting wisp of consciousness traversing the enigmatic boundaries of the Mullah's dream world. There, I found myself immersed in a surreal landscape, a nightmarish realm distorted and perverted by the Asuric influence that gripped the Mullah's psyche. Undeterred, I ventured deeper into this surreal dreamscape, my senses assailed by grotesque visions that mirrored the twisted nature of the Mullah's subconscious.

Within this tumultuous realm, I searched for the source of the devilish force that bound the Mullah in its thrall. It did not take long to locate the shadowy entity—a grotesque Asura lurking in the darkest recesses of his consciousness. With unwavering resolve, I launched my ethereal assault, summoning the innermost reserves of my strength—a beacon of luminous defiance against the shroud of darkness.

The battle raged on, a cosmic clash of spiritual forces, each vying for dominance over the Mullah's vulnerable soul. The Mullah stirred uneasily in his physical slumber, a furrow of confusion marring his brow.

My spell wove its intricate tapestry of magic, systematically unraveling the Asura's vicious grip on the Mullah's psyche. Gradually, but with relentless determination, I chipped away at the grotesque influence, banishing it from the Mullah's dreamscape. The Asura howled in defiant protest, yet the brilliance of my ethereal light remained undiminished.

As the Asura's influence waned, I seized the opportunity to communicate with the Mullah on a subconscious level. It was not a conventional conversation but rather the planting of an idea, a seed of transformation. In the depths of his dream, I conveyed the urgent need to change the Taliban's oppressive treatment of women and to grant me safe passage out of the country with my fellow prisoners. The Mullah's mind absorbed the message, and a glimmer of understanding flickered in his dreamlike state.

In that ethereal realm, where the boundaries of reality blurred, the Mullah's inner turmoil manifested as a fierce storm. The conflicting forces of his beliefs and the newfound awareness wrestled for dominance. It was a tumultuous struggle, and I watched, my ethereal presence a beacon of hope amidst the chaos.

Slowly but surely, the Mullah's dream began to shift. The oppressive darkness that had shrouded him started to dissipate, replaced by a dawning realization of the need for change. The Asura's cries grew fainter as the Mullah's inner light grew more assertive. It was a delicate dance of transformation, played out in the hidden recesses of his subconscious.

And then, like a phoenix rising from the ashes, there was a subtle change in the atmosphere of his dream. A spark of compassion and understanding flickered in his subconscious like a distant star in the night sky. The dream showed him a path forward that hinted at equality and justice, but it remained enigmatic, just beyond his complete comprehension. No conscious vow declaration or concrete plan formed in that dreamlike state. Instead, it was as if the Mullah's soul held the potential for change.

As the first rays of dawn broke in the waking world, the Mullah's physical form stirred. Unbeknownst to him, his dream had been a battleground. The cosmic clash of spiritual forces had left an indelible mark on his subconscious, setting the stage for a future awakening.

I, the ethereal warrior in this clandestine battle, watched with a sense of fulfillment. While the Mullah had not made any conscious decisions in his dream, the seeds of transformation had been sown in the most unlikely of places, and the journey toward enlightenment and change had begun, even if it remained hidden for now.

Chapter 47
Mullah Miracle

As the first rays of dawn gently bathed the prison cell in a soft, golden glow, I awoke, filled with a sense of unease mingled with curiosity. The abruptness of my awakening, coupled with the unfamiliarity of the situation, left me disoriented. "Where are you taking me?" I questioned in a sleepy haze, my voice trembling with a touch of fear and the remnants of slumber.

The guards responded with stern commands in their native Pashto. Their words were incomprehensible to me, yet the urgency in their gestures left no room for questions. I had to maintain silence and comply with their instructions. Amidst the shuffle of my departure, my fellow prisoners spoke in hushed voices, their expressions a blend of concern and intrigue. Their eyes mirrored the uncertainty of my release, creating an unspoken connection among us. I couldn't help but wonder about the fate that awaited me beyond these prison walls.

As the guards led me through the now-familiar corridors and up a staircase to the main floor of the presidential palace, my disheveled appearance became acutely apparent. My hair was tangled and unruly, my clothes bore the stains and wrinkles of my imprisonment, and the urgency of a full bladder added to my discomfort.

Upon arriving outside the Mullah's office, a woman approached me with a quick, assessing glance. She gestured toward a nearby bathroom, granting me a much-needed respite.

As I stood in that private space, the surreal nature of my journey weighed heavily on my mind. Memories from the dream world, where the Mullah and I had shared an unexplainable connection, resurfaced with vivid clarity. I couldn't help but contemplate the significance of this unexpected encounter and the mysterious forces at play.

Returning to the Mullah's office, I held my head high, concealing the inner turmoil. A mix of anticipation and apprehension coursed through me as I awaited the explanation for the purpose of our meeting. Standing at the precipice of the unknown, I braced myself for the revelations that lay ahead.

The kind woman made a sweeping gesture, indicating that I should enter the Mullah's office. Stepping inside, I was immediately taken aback by the profound transformation I witnessed in him. The darkness that had once clouded his gaze had lifted, replaced by a clarity and wisdom that seemed almost miraculous. It was as if I had broken the vice-like grip of the Asuras' influence, and a glimmer of hope began to shine through the cracks of uncertainty.

"Hello, Emma," the Mullah greeted me, his tone carrying a warmth that contrasted our initial meeting. I struggled to find my voice in response to his unexpected welcome.

His gaze bore into mine as he continued, "I've been pondering your presence here and the risks you've taken." I nodded in acknowledgment, still taken aback by the shift in his demeanor.

"What if I were to offer you a chance to leave this place and return home?" he proposed, his words hanging like an elusive promise.

"Go back home?" I repeated, my disbelief evident in my voice. "You mean, just leave?"

A gentle smile graced the Mullah's lips as he gestured toward a nearby table and chairs, and we took our seats. He leaned forward, locked his eyes on mine, and dropped the bombshell.

"More than that," he clarified, his tone thick with significance. "Leave with the women from your cell."

The words hit me like a thunderbolt, and I felt like I might tumble out of my chair. "Are you serious?" I stammered, my voice trembling with disbelief.

The Mullah extended his hands in a placating gesture and raised his shoulders in a nonchalant shrug. "Do I not impress you as a serious man?"

I nodded fervently, my heart racing as I hung on to the tantalizing possibility of freedom.

With an air of anticipation, the Mullah prepared to reveal the origins of his decision. "It was a dream," he confessed, his tone laden with significance, and I leaned in, eager to hear the story behind this remarkable turn of events. "I found myself standing in a vast, glorious garden. Its beauty was beyond earthly description, with flowers of every hue, their fragrances mingling in the air. I walked through this paradise, the soft grass beneath my feet and the gentle breeze whispering secrets to the leaves."

He paused, his eyes glistening with unshed tears, allowing the image to settle in our minds. "And then," he continued, his voice quivering with emotion, "a radiant light descended from the heavens. It bathed the garden in a luminous glow, and I felt an overwhelming sense of peace and serenity." His words painted a vivid picture of the dream, and I listened with bated breath, captivated.

"Amid this divine radiance," he continued, his voice trembling, "an angel descended. His presence was awe-inspiring, his wings glistening like purest silver. He introduced himself as Jibril, a messenger of Allah."

I couldn't help but gasp at the mention of the angel Jibril.

The Mullah's voice took on a respectful tone, and a tear rolled down his cheek. "Jibril spoke to me," he whispered, his words echoing with divine authority. "He told me it was my duty to follow a path of compassion and understanding and seek peace and reconciliation. He instructed me to release the women, ensure their safety, and guide them back with you to your homeland."

My heart swelled with astonishment and gratitude. Jibril's visitation had set in motion events that held the promise of freedom and redemption.

The Mullah wiped away a tear and composed himself, continuing, "I will allow the women to accompany you with a secure escort back to Pakistan. From there, arrangements will be made for their safe passage to America. I have been entrusted to follow a path of peace and compassion, and I believe it is the right course of action."

I nodded in awe and deep appreciation for the Mullah's decision; his newfound purpose, inspired by the angel Jibril's visit, could change our lives and the lives of the women who had suffered in that prison cell. With profound gratitude and hope, I looked at the Mullah, knowing that forces beyond our understanding had guided these events and that the journey toward freedom and redemption had just taken an unexpected and miraculous turn.

*

Word of the Mullah's remarkable transformation spread through the prison like wildfire, leaving guards and staff in shock and disbelief. I couldn't understand their words, but their expressions and gestures conveyed vehement protest against his sudden change of heart and the orders to release the women. It seemed as though the very foundations of their allegiance had been shaken to the core. Despite the dissent swirling around him, the Mullah remained resolute in his decision. He summoned armed guards to ensure the safe transportation of the forty-two women to Pakistan, where, according to the Mullah, arrangements would be made for their flight to America. It was a logistical and emotional whirlwind, events that would forever alter the course of our journey.

As the news of our impending release and journey to America reached the ears of my fellow prisoners, unparalleled excitement and joy enveloped our shared cell. Tears of relief and gratitude flowed freely, and laughter echoed off the prison walls. The weight of suffering seemed to lift instantly, replaced by the soaring hope of freedom and opportunity. The indomitable strength of the human spirit shone brightly, and the power of redemption and reconciliation became tangible realities. As we prepared for the next chapter of our odyssey, I couldn't help but think that the influence I had wielded in the dream world had pierced through the Asuras' defenses, bringing about a miracle that would resonate through the annals of history—an extraordinary story of hope, resilience,

233

and the unwavering capacity of the human spirit to conquer even the darkest of nightmares.

Chapter 48
A Detour

The anticipation in the air was palpable as I stood on the tarmac, surrounded by reporters and news organizations. The response to Emma's incredible achievement had been overwhelming, and now it was my turn to play my part. Just the day before, during an all-staff meeting, I had proposed a radical shift in The Vanguard's mission, and as expected, it shocked everyone, causing me to wonder if I would control power long enough to see it through.

But for now, the media and the world were in a frenzy, awaiting Emma's triumphant return. However, my phone buzzed before I could fully absorb the moment. It was Derek, and he sounded urgent. I slipped away, hoping that whatever had come up wouldn't overshadow the day's significance. Standing in a dark alleyway, far from the mob scene, I held my phone to my ear as Derek informed me of a problem requiring immediate attention. As I hurriedly conferred with him, I couldn't help but feel frustration. This was the moment I had been waiting for, the opportunity to embrace our new mission publicly, but it seemed that fate had other plans.

As I concluded the call, two imposing figures suddenly appeared at my side, their faces masked by stern determination. Without a word, they grabbed my arms and forcibly shoved me into a car that had pulled up alongside us. Panic coursed through me as the vehicle sped away from the tarmac, leaving behind the media and the historical moment that had been within my grasp.

My mind raced with questions and uncertainty. What was happening? Who were these men, and where were they taking me? The car's windows offered no glimpse of the outside world, and I was left with a sinking feeling that the path ahead was shrouded in darkness.

The journey seemed endless as we sped toward the far end of the airport, leaving behind the world of reporters, cameras, and Emma's historical return. Finally, the car drove into an empty hangar. As it came to a stop, one of the men demanded that I get out. Standing alongside the car, I saw a single office in the corner where some light spilled from the open doorway. A sharp push against my back urged me forward. Upon reaching the door, I hesitated a moment. But another push encouraged me through.

Once inside, I was met by the imposing figure of a man in an army uniform. His muscular build and the captain's epaulets on his shoulders spoke of authority and power. He pulled up a chair and sat across from me, his stern gaze fixed on mine. His first question cut through the tension like a knife. "What's your relationship with Emma Zigler?"

I hesitated momentarily, choosing my words carefully. "Umm, Emma and I are colleagues," I replied evenly, sounding innocent.

The captain's expression remained inscrutable, and he pressed on. "Your girlfriend has become an international sensation and a major problem for the president."

My heart sank as I considered the implications of my sudden vulnerability.

The captain's voice lowered to a chilling whisper. "Monica Taylor, General Harris, and Senator Clarke have all been arrested as enemies of the state, charged with treason. Your involvement, and Emma's, is well— undeniable."

"Am I under arrest?" I asked as dread washed over me.

The captain smiled and said, "That depends."

I exhaled and asked, "On what?"

The captain stood up and took a few steps before turning to look at me. "We're very interested in your abilities to enter the spirit world."

I swallowed hard, wondering if they tortured Monica to pry out the information. "If you agree to assist the administration with its important work by taking us into…"

"The dream world?" I concluded.

The captain shook his head with a smile. "No, Gus. We want to go further."

I rubbed the back of my neck, wondering how much they knew. "But what about Emma?" I said, pointing outwards. "She's an international hero. You can't expect her to comply."

"As long as you provide what we ask for, we won't need her," he said, returning to the chair across from me.

I nodded, absorbing the threat. "What do you want me to do?"

"Oh, that's not for me to say. There's a plane waiting," he said, pointing toward the tarmac.

"Where are you taking me?"

"No need to worry about that."

With swift efficiency, I was led out of the room. As I walked, I wondered about Emma, her fate entwined with mine, yet uncertain. What would become of her after my abrupt disappearance?

We emerged into the cool night air, and I stood on the tarmac again. But this time, there was no media frenzy, no cameras or cheering crowds. Instead, an unmarked jet stood before us, its engines humming with quiet power. I was guided up the jet's steps into a plush, private cabin. The captain followed, his expression unreadable. As the cabin door closed behind us, I had a sense of finality.

The engines roared to life, and the jet taxied down the runway. The destination remained unknown, the path ahead uncertain. I could only hope that whatever lay ahead still offered me a chance to make a difference, to shape a future where compassion and empathy prevailed, but, truthfully, it seemed that fascism still gripped my reality.

Chapter 49
Emma Returns

As I boarded the plane, flanked by forty-two young women whose lives were on the cusp of transformation, a surge of emotions coursed through me like a tidal wave. Gratitude and excitement hung in the air, infused with the palpable sense of embarking on a journey toward a land of hope and boundless opportunity. The cabin seemed alive, filled with the resonating hum of chatter and the joyful symphony of laughter. These brave souls, survivors of trials, were now bound for America—a land where dreams could take root and flourish. However, the recent rise in fascism threatened to cast a shadow over the ideals of hope and opportunity, making our journey more poignant and vital than ever.

Amidst the jubilant commotion that engulfed us, Fatima, her eyes glistening with newfound hope, approached me. Her voice quivered with emotion as she spoke, her words laden with the weight of our collective journey. "Emma, you've given us a chance at a new life. Because of you, we're heading toward a future with hope." Her tears flowed freely, a poignant testament to the profound gratitude that surged within her and reverberated throughout the cabin. Yet, beneath her tears lay an unspoken question, a curiosity that demanded satisfaction. Leaning closer, she lowered her voice, glancing cautiously to ensure our conversation remained private. "Can I ask you a question?"

I furrowed my brow in response to her whispered inquiry and replied, my voice tinged with solemnity and pride, "What's on your mind?"

With a subtle smile that bore both wisdom and innocence, Fatima asked the question that I assumed lingered in the minds of many. "What did you say to convince the Mullah to release us?"

Inhaling a deep breath, I contemplated conveying the essence of that pivotal moment. "Well," I began, choosing my words carefully, "let's just say I reached deep within his soul."

Fatima's smile widened, her eyes reflecting a profound understanding of the situation. "You certainly did."

I nodded, a chuckle escaping me as I appreciated the accuracy of Fatima's assessment, tinged with the knowledge of the extraordinary connection that had facilitated our freedom.

Throughout the long flight, emotions flowed as abundantly as the tears we could have filled buckets with. I looked around at these resilient individuals, each a testament to the indomitable human spirit. Their stories, etched into their faces, their dreams articulated in their words, and their hopes whispered in their laughter, formed a tapestry of shared experiences that transcended language and culture.

With Fatima translating, I addressed the women in a moment of profound connection, my voice brimming with warmth and encouragement. "You all possess incredible strength. This is just the beginning of your journey, and I have no doubt you'll achieve remarkable things in America." The unity and purpose that enveloped us in that cabin were undeniable, and my heart swelled with pride, knowing that my actions had set these remarkable lives on a new and promising trajectory.

Later on, settled into my seat with the Atlantic Ocean sprawled below, my mind rewound to that surreal moment in the prison cell that had ushered in the women's release. At first, my declaration had hung like an impossible dream, a notion too fantastical to believe. The women's initial skepticism had been tangible as they exchanged uncertain glances. Yet, as if guided by fate, the guards, under the Mullah's newfound awakening, had ordered them to their feet and led us out of the dim cellar. The journey that followed, spanning six hours from Kabul to Islamabad, was a trek that bridged the gaping chasm between captivity and freedom. The Islamabad airport greeted us with the reassuring sight of a chartered US government plane—a beacon of hope and deliverance, its wings poised to carry us toward a new beginning.

Amidst the jubilation of our release, I couldn't help but ponder the intricate political maneuvers that had orchestrated our freedom. It appeared plausible that the Taliban government had reached out to the president, who I assumed was eager to seize credit for the liberation of these women as an astute public relations move on the global stage. Yet, a shroud of uncertainty enfolded me. How would I be dealt with? Would I be permitted to openly share my role, or would I be silenced to align with the administration's narrative? The latter seemed more plausible. My thoughts meandered to Gus, my steadfast partner in the shared mission of transformation. The question of his success in reshaping The Vanguard, molding it into an organization steeped in compassion and dedicated to positive change, gnawed at my thoughts. I longed to see his face, hear his voice's cadence, and exchange the tales of our respective journeys—a yearning that held me in its grip.

As the plane continued over the boundless Atlantic, drawing us closer to our destination, my thoughts swirled in hope, uncertainty, and anticipation. Yet, in the whirlwind of emotions and queries, one question blazed in the recesses of my mind—would Gus be at the airport, ready to welcome the dawn of our next chapter? The answer remained shrouded in mystery, an enigma awaiting unraveling as our journey carried us forward.

Hours passed, and the plane soared steadily. Finally, as we descended, excitement and anticipation swelled within the cabin. The moment of reunion with Gus, the embrace of our intertwined destinies, was tantalizingly close. Yet, the outcome remained uncertain.

As the plane wheels kissed the tarmac, I braced myself for the momentous reunion, my heart pounding with trepidation and exhilaration.

Chapter 50
Removed

A wave of excitement rippled through the cabin as the plane touched down. The women, now filled with anticipation and dreams of a new life in America, chatted animatedly, their faces radiant with hope. The atmosphere was electric, charged with the energy of transformation.

But the entrance of two imposing men disrupted the celebratory mood. Their arrival was abrupt and unexpected, sending a hush through the cabin. Conversations faltered as the passengers exchanged puzzled glances. The men, dressed in dark suits, exuded an air of authority that demanded attention.

With a sense of trepidation gnawing at my gut, I watched as one of the men approached a flight staff member. Their exchange was brief before he pointed at me. My heart sank as I understood. As they closed the distance between us, anxiety and defiance welled up. I couldn't help but wonder what this meant for my journey and my mission. They stopped before me, and their stern expressions betrayed no hint of their intentions.

"Remain seated while the Afghan women disembark," one of them instructed, his voice unwavering.

A chill ran down my spine as the realization washed over me. They intended to keep me hidden from the media, away from prying eyes. But why? Would they whisk me away, make me disappear? The uncertainty gnawed at me. I nodded in reluctant compliance, my mind racing. The women began to disembark, their smiles and anticipation contrasting sharply with the shadow of uncertainty that now enveloped me. As each one passed, I exchanged reassuring glances and offered words of encouragement, though my heart was heavy.

The cabin gradually emptied, leaving me alone with the two enigmatic men. The minutes ticked by, each stretching into an eternity as

I waited for the truth behind their actions to unfold. The plane, once filled with hope and dreams, now felt like a cocoon of secrets and uncertainty.

I braced myself for whatever lay ahead, determined to face this unexpected twist in my journey with courage and resilience. But deep down, a nagging fear lingered—would I emerge from this ordeal unscathed, or would I truly disappear into the shadows, erased from the world I had fought so hard to change?

I remained seated, my eyes fixed on the empty seats before me. It felt like an eternity, surrounded by the eerie silence of an otherwise jubilant arrival. The men who had singled me out ensured I didn't even have the liberty to open the window shades and catch a glimpse of the reception below. Their vigilance was unnerving, as if they were determined to keep me hidden from the prying eyes of the media and the world.

The muted celebrations outside saddened me deeply. I longed to join in the joy and relief of the Afghan women as they stepped onto American soil, but I was trapped in this cocoon of secrecy and uncertainty. The threat these men posed hung over me like a dark cloud, casting a shadow over what should have been a triumphant moment. Desperation compelled me to speak with them, to demand answers, but my inquiries were met with stubborn silence. They seemed resolute in their mission, whatever it might be, and their stoic demeanor only fueled my anxiety.

Time dragged on. Over an hour later, when the tarmac had finally cleared of the media frenzy and the Afghan women had been safely transported to their next destination, I was escorted off the plane. The moment felt surreal, like a clandestine operation conducted under the cover of darkness.

They led me to a waiting car, its windows tinted. As I stepped inside, the door closed with a resounding thud, sealing me within this world of uncertainty. The engine roared to life, and the car began to move, carrying me further into the unknown.

What was going to happen to me? What had I stumbled into, and how would it shape my destiny? The road ahead was shrouded in darkness, and I couldn't help but wonder if I was heading toward a fate from which there was no return.

*

The night held an air of secrecy as I approached a nondescript office building. Shadows danced across the cold, concrete facade, and the city's bustling streets seemed oblivious to my fate. I slipped through the quiet side entrance, unnoticed by the few late-night stragglers who lingered nearby. Two figures met me, their faces concealed by the shadows. Neither uttered a word as they guided me into a service elevator. The metallic doors slid shut, and I felt trepidation coursing through my veins.

The tension grew palpable, and I couldn't help but cast wary glances at the two men who flanked me. The silence was stifling, broken only by the soft hum of the elevator's descent. Finally, the elevator doors whispered open, revealing a dimly lit corridor. I was given a gentle nudge, directing me toward a nondescript steel door. My heart raced as I approached it.

One of the men rapped his knuckles against the unyielding door. A series of tumblers engaged with a soft click, and the portal swung open, revealing a scene I could scarcely believe. There, standing amidst an array of intricate equipment, was Monica. My astonishment spilled out in a shocked exclamation of her name, "Monica!" She turned to face me, her expression a mix of surprise and relief. I hurried toward her.

She stood beside a lounger, surrounded by the apparatus that had once monitored my journeys into the dream world and beyond. A flood of memories washed over me, and I couldn't help but inquire about Gus, the missing link in this surreal puzzle.

Before Monica could respond, a figure emerged from the shadows, his presence commanding our immediate attention. He introduced himself as Derek, a name that held a certain weight in my mind, linked to The Vanguard and the shadowy figures that pulled the strings of power. Derek wasted no time in dispelling any illusions. "Gus is no longer a concern," he stated firmly, a sense of finality in his words, "nor are your partners in your treasonous plot—Senator Clarke and General Harris."

My heart pounded as I faced Derek. Dread settled like a heavy shroud over me, and I couldn't shake the sinking feeling that something terrible had befallen Gus.

"What have you done to them? Where's Gus?" My voice trembled with fear and anger as I took a hesitant step closer to Derek, my hand clenched into a tight fist.

His words hung like a dark omen, casting a pall of uncertainty over us. The implication was clear—enemies of the state were tried for treason, and in the current political climate, the consequences could be dire, swift and fatal. I couldn't bear the thought of Gus facing such a fate. Unable to contain my anxiety, I stammered, "What do you want from me?" I braced myself for the unsettling truth that loomed on the horizon.

Derek's response was chilling in its simplicity. Thanks to the data gleaned from Monica's dream equipment at Harvard, he claimed to know everything about our ventures into the spirit world. "We want to see this for ourselves," he declared, his eyes harboring secrets yet to be unveiled. Our destinies converged in an unexpected alliance in that dimly lit room, shrouded in mystery and foreboding. The boundaries of reality and the metaphysical blurred, and our journey into the unknown was far from over.

Chapter 51
Put Under

As Monica meticulously fine-tuned the intricate dream equipment, I found my mind wandering to the profound encounter Gus and I had with the oracle. In that otherworldly moment, we were given a sacred mission, a cosmic duty that transcended the boundaries of the earthly and the spiritual realms. It was a quest that carried the weight of destiny.

The oracle had entrusted us with three earthly tasks and three spiritual quests, each intertwined in the intricate dance of cosmic significance. These earthly tasks were designated as the "loci of dissonance," specific places or situations where the absence of empathy had birthed suffering in its myriad forms.

I chose to embark on a mission that resonated deeply within my soul—to extend a helping hand to the women of this world, to be their advocate in a faraway realm. It led me to the war-torn streets of Kabul, where the plight of Afghan women was a harsh testament to the absence of empathy. It was a journey that had cost me much, but I knew my locus had been achieved.

Gus was responsible for catalyzing a transformation within The Vanguard of Purity, an organization that had long embraced an agenda of hostility and intolerance. His mission was to shift it toward a benevolent path, a formidable task that seemed to teeter on the brink of failure. If we couldn't alter The Vanguard's trajectory, our entire endeavor risked crumbling into dust.

The ultimate challenge loomed on the horizon—the third loci of dissonance. It was a call to initiate a transformation within one of the right-wing networks, turning their hatred rhetoric into a chorus of acceptance, love, and understanding. Yet, at this juncture, that goal appeared to be a distant star in the night sky, far beyond our reach.

This quest wasn't confined to the earthly realm alone. Even if, by some miraculous twist of fate, we succeeded in reshaping these loci of dissonance—these crucibles of suffering that held the potential for change—we would have to venture back into the ethereal realm, where the waters of destiny flowed in the form of three Rivers of Essence.

The oracle had unveiled these mystic rivers to us—the River of Sorrow, the River of Joy, and the River of Tranquility. These sacred waters held the collective emotions of all sentient beings, an ocean of raw, unfiltered sentiment that coursed through the cosmos.

We would require a vessel of unparalleled empathy to navigate these tumultuous waters. We could only gain the power to disarm the Asuras, the vicious guardians of the soul we sought to redeem, by immersing ourselves in these rivers' profound lessons. These Asuras had woven intricate defenses around their charges, and only by absorbing the wisdom of the three rivers could we hope to penetrate their labyrinthine fortifications.

As Derek loomed in the shadowy background, his presence a foreboding omen, I couldn't help but feel the weight of our cosmic destiny pressing down upon me. The journey ahead was fraught with peril, but I was bound by a sacred purpose, a mission to ignite the sparks of empathy and transformation in a world marred by dissonance. But with the fate of Gus now in the balance, I had no idea if my quest had come to its unfulfilled conclusion.

"It's time," she declared, her tone carrying the weight of a thousand mysteries. In response, I reluctantly nodded and settled into the sumptuous lounger. Monica, the maestro of this surreal symphony, moved with a graceful finesse, her fingers deftly attaching the intricate sensors to my head and arms. Each connection felt like a tether to the unknown, drawing me closer to the impending odyssey. Amid her meticulous adjustments, she leaned in, her voice a whisper saturated with enigma. "Look for Gus." Her words caressed my ear, carrying a hidden significance that sent a shiver down my spine. "He's waiting for you."

Derek, the ever-watchful guardian of our expedition, remained steadfast in his vigil, his attention locked onto the multitude of monitors that adorned the room. Monica's cryptic message seemed to pass him by, but a seed of concern sprouted in the depths of my being. I couldn't help but wonder about the profound layers of meaning concealed within her enigmatic directive as my heart quickened in anticipation of what lay ahead.

No longer tethered to the concerns of being observed by Derek and the nefarious envoys he represented, I steeled myself for the impending slumber. The urgency of my mission loomed large, a pressing weight upon my heart. My sole purpose was to locate Gus, unravel the threads of destiny, and reclaim our purpose's course, steering it away from the grasp of the Asuras that had ensnared humanity.

As the world around me faded into darkness, the ethereal strains of Mozart's "A Little Night Music" gently cradled my consciousness, lulling me into the realm of dreams. In an instant, I found myself standing upon the precipice of the spirit world, but this encounter held an aura of uniqueness that set it apart from my previous journeys. I stood amidst a cosmic panorama, the celestial bodies of distant planets illuminating the boundless starlit expanse before me. It was a surreal tableau that hinted at the profound revelations awaiting me.

A celestial being, radiant as a star in the midnight sky, approached with serene wisdom. Its presence exuded an otherworldly grace as it beckoned me closer. I ventured to inquire, trembling with awe and trepidation, "Am I departed from the realm of the living? Have I crossed into the threshold of the afterlife?"

A soft, ethereal laughter echoed like celestial chimes, and the angelic guide replied, "No, dear traveler, not you. It is Gus who has traversed the boundary. He stood accused of treason, his fate swiftly sealed by your enemies. There, revenge has wielded its unforgiving blade, pronouncing him guilty and condemning him to the inevitable embrace of the death penalty."

The weight of those words bore down upon me, and I grappled with the enormity of the revelation. Gus, my steadfast comrade, my eternal soulmate, had ventured into the abyss of uncertainty, ensnared by the tendrils of treachery and deceit. The spirit world had woven a tapestry of sorrow and foreboding. As the angelic guide extended a luminous hand, I knew the path ahead would be fraught with challenges, mysteries, and the relentless pursuit of truth.

"Gus!" I cried out. "Bring me to him."

My impassioned plea reverberated through the very bedrock of the ethereal terrain, causing the earth to tremble in response. A tumultuous whirlwind of dust spiraled around me, a mesmerizing prelude to a cosmic performance of profound import. A figure materialized from within the heart of this swirling tempest, and it was none other than Gus himself. Yet, he no longer bore the visage of his earthly form; instead, an ethereal presence enveloped him, an embodiment of transcendence and light.

Gus's voice, a melody woven from the fabric of the cosmos, resonated through the cosmic expanse. "Emma," he said, "I am sorry for my departure and for leaving you behind in the realm of the living. My time in the earthly realm has drawn close, but yours has not yet reached its final stanza. You must forge ahead, continue our sacred quest, and fulfill fate's purpose for us."

Tears welled in my eyes, their luminous essence mirroring the celestial realm surrounding us. "What has happened to you? Who did this?"

"After a mock trial for treason, I was found guilty and immediately sentenced to death by lethal injection."

As I gazed upon him, my voice trembled with sorrow, the essence of our ethereal surroundings tinged with melancholy. "Oh, Gus, my beloved," I murmured, my outstretched hand reaching toward him, longing to grasp the ungraspable.

"It was an act of desperation," Gus continued, "orchestrated by the Asurian forces at work with their minions on Earth." As the truth unfolded, the celestial realm seemed to hold its breath, the cosmic tapestry quivering in response to the injustice that had befallen Gus.

"But I cannot fathom this journey without you by my side," I confessed, my voice trembling with the weight of our separation.

Gus's ethereal presence, radiant with otherworldly light, offered a reassuring smile. "There is no need," he assured me, his words imbued with profound wisdom. "Your earthly requirements are done. The three loci of dissonance have been achieved."

I shook my head, my eyes pleading with him. "This is not so," I protested, gesturing behind me as if pointing to the unfinished path we had traveled. "You were to transform The Vanguard, then the two of us were meant to remake the RightView News service a balanced, truthful carrier to the masses. There's still much to accomplish, but without you, it's impossible."

Gus extended his hand toward me, a gesture of solace and understanding. "Oh, it has been accomplished; let me show you."

I reached out and took his hand, the connection sparking a profound transformation. In an instant, we stood before a grand assembly hall, which had once been the heart of The Vanguard's operations.

"But how is this possible? I entered the dream world moments ago. Your right-hand man Derek had me taken off the plane and brought to a secret place with Monica to observe my abilities in the dream world."

"Time here is not linear, so what you remember happened a while ago. Let me show you what's occurred since."

Then, within the blink of an eye, I witnessed an assembly of members of what was once The Vanguard of Purity but is now called *The Harmony Seekers*, a new organization—transformed by the very same people who ran it but were released from the grasp of the Asuras. I observed a new mission dedicated to spreading the word of the profound connection between the earthly realm and the spirit world. The name Harmony Seekers resonated with the very essence of their mission, encapsulating their unwavering commitment to fostering unity, empathy, and understanding among humanity.

They embarked on a journey transcending ordinary existence's boundaries with their hearts aligned with the cosmic symphony. They sought to harmonize the dissonant chords of the world, weaving a tapestry of compassion and enlightenment that would resonate through the ages. Gus, his presence now ethereal and radiant, offered a serene smile as he explained, "You set it all in motion by your act in Kabul, my dear Emma. You knocked over the first domino, and the ripples of that choice have cascaded through the tapestry of existence."

My curiosity burned brightly, and I leaned in, eager for more insights. "But what about the third locus—the transformation of RightView News?"

With a graceful sweep of his arm, Gus conjured an awe-inspiring vision. It was as if the fabric of reality had shifted to reveal a digital sanctuary known as "The Pulse." This news service beckoned people worldwide to share the rich tapestry of their lives, stories, and insights. It evolved into a vast reservoir of human experiences, a luminous reflection of our collective soul.

Gus's words became a symphony of images, weaving together the narrative of the fastest-growing news service in the world—a beacon of truth and unity that transcended the limitations of language and borders. Its popularity stretched to the farthest reaches of the earth, a testament to the harmonious ideals that had taken root in every facet of its existence.

I saw celestial beings' craftsmanship in this divine tapestry as if angels had personally woven it. Translated into hundreds of languages, it traversed the globe, promising enlightenment and unity. Every detail bore the mark of the divine, from the profound stories it shared to the harmonious voices that came together to deliver its messages.

This vision revealed how "The Pulse" had become a symbol of hope and transformation, an emblem of humanity's capacity for compassion and understanding. It stood as a powerful tribute to the profound change that had washed over the world's collective consciousness, all thanks to the choices Gus and I had made.

As I beheld this breathtaking tapestry, I was overwhelmed by pride and purpose. Our journey had borne fruit, and the world had blossomed into a better place because of it.

"Does this mean our work is done?" I asked, my voice trembling with a mixture of relief and uncertainty.

Gus replied with serene wisdom, "The earthly work is completed, Emma. Now, we can fulfill our tasks here in the spirit world before I embark on my journey toward rebirth."

I furrowed my brow, seeking clarity in this enigmatic transition. "What do you mean?"

Gus's gaze held the weight of ages as he reminded me, "Don't you remember what the oracle told us?"

The memory of the oracle's words washed over me like a gentle tide, carrying the weight of destiny. "Once you've completed your tasks on Earth," the oracle's ethereal voice echoed, "you will return to the ethereal realm, where you must journey through the three Rivers of Essence: the River of Sorrow, the River of Joy, and the River of Tranquility. These rivers hold the collective emotions of all sentient beings. By navigating them, you will learn to embrace emotional complexity in its purest form. Your vessel for this perilous journey will be none other than the *Sphere of Empathy*. Only when you have absorbed the lessons of these rivers can your Sphere be powerful enough to disarm the Asuras and penetrate the labyrinthine defenses around the soul you seek to redeem."

The gravity of these words settled upon me like a sacred mantle, and I realized that our journey was a path that would lead us through the depths of human emotion, a journey of profound transformation that awaited us in the ethereal realm.

Chapter 52
The Three Rivers

Gus began to speak. His voice carried the gentle cadence of someone who had traversed the realms of existence, bridging the living and the ethereal. "Emma, life is perceived as an unending odyssey of spiritual evolution, a tapestry woven across the earthly, spiritual, and ethereal dimensions. When I spoke of my journey toward rebirth, I referred to the cyclical nature of souls, much akin to the Earth's changing seasons."

His words settled like seeds in fertile soil, each carrying the weight of profound truth. "Here, birth and death are not mere endpoints but transitions within the grand symphony of existence. When our earthly tasks are fulfilled, as mine have been, we move into the spiritual realm to further our growth and enlightenment. It's akin to returning to a spiritual school, where we dive deeper into the profound mysteries of existence and gather wisdom that will illuminate our future earthly incarnations."

Gus's gaze acknowledged my unique vantage point; I served as a bridge between realms, allowing me to understand the interconnectedness of our spiritual experiences.

"During this journey toward birth," he continued, "we can refine our spiritual essence, shedding any impurities or limitations acquired during our earthly sojourn. It's a period of introspection, contemplation, and communion with higher spiritual entities. We become like seeds, nurtured in the fertile soil of the spiritual realm, ready to sprout anew in the earthly realm when the cosmic timing aligns." His gentle touch on my hand conveyed the depth of our connection and the wisdom he wished to impart.

"So, while my days upon the earth have paused for now," Gus whispered, "this journey toward birth continues my spiritual evolution. It's a phase of growth and transformation that aligns with the belief in the interconnectedness of our spiritual experiences across different planes of existence. And as we soon will navigate the three Rivers of Essence, we shall carry with us the lessons and wisdom gained from this journey, enriching our souls for the cycles that await us in the ever-unfolding tapestry of existence."

Moved by his words, I spoke with a longing voice. "That's wonderful, Gus. If we can navigate through the three Rivers of Essence, can we still approach the Asuras and breach their defenses?"

Gus nodded, his ethereal presence exuding a sense of assurance. "As long as you can continue to enter the spirit realm through the dream world, I see no reason why not. However, I am still learning my abilities as a soul. It's quite different from having a physical body."

A determined resolve filled me as I looked at the celestial world around us. "Well," I declared, "let's get this done so you can move on."

"And don't forget our quest to save humanity."

*

Gus and I stood at the edge of the River of Sorrow, its waters shimmering with a mournful, silvery light that seemed to weep with the collective grief of all sentient beings. Gus's voice carried reverence as he spoke. "This is where we begin, Emma. The River of Sorrow holds all sentient beings' collective grief, pain, and sadness. It's a river that will immerse us in profound sorrow and empathy."

I nodded, bracing myself for the emotional journey that lay ahead. Before us, a boat of translucent light materialized, its form ethereal yet solid. Without hesitation, we stepped onto it, and with otherworldly grace, it glided effortlessly into the sorrowful waters of the river.

The currents of the River of Sorrow carried us deeper into a world of shared human suffering, and as we journeyed, the haunting faces of countless souls began to emerge from the depths. These were not ordinary faces; they were visages etched with raw and unfiltered expressions of anguish. Each countenance bore the weight of its unique sorrows, manifested in many horrifying forms.

Some faces were twisted in perpetual agony, their features contorted as if trapped in an eternal moment of torment. These souls had endured unimaginable pain during their earthly lives, and their anguish now manifested as grotesque masks of suffering. The deep lines of despair marked other faces, their eyes hollow and vacant, staring into the abyss of their sorrow. These souls had known profound loss and heartache; their stories were etched into the very lines of their existence.

In the cold, mournful light of the River of Sorrow, we heard their voices, a cacophony of lamentations that filled the air. They spoke of shattered dreams, unfulfilled hopes, and the relentless ache of unhealed wounds. Their stories of pain and heartache echoed around us, weaving a tapestry of despair that seemed to stretch into infinity.

We were surrounded by the cries of those who had suffered, their voices a haunting chorus reverberating through our souls' depths. It was a symphony of sorrow, a testament to the depth of human suffering that touched every corner of existence. As we drifted among these tormented faces, we could feel their pain seeping into our very beings. It was an overwhelming experience, as if we had been submerged in an ocean of despair. But we did not turn away; instead, we embraced the suffering of others, allowing it to wash over us.

In that surreal and heartbreaking moment, we understood the interconnectedness of all living beings. The faces in the River of Sorrow were not strangers; they were reflections of our shared humanity, a stark reminder of the fragility of the human experience. As we drifted, we listened to their tales, felt their anguish, and shared their grief. It was as if we had been submerged in an ocean of tears, drowning in the sorrows of humanity. But we held fast to each other, our hands intertwined, drawing strength from our connection.

The stories were heart-wrenching, the pain palpable, but we didn't shy away. Instead, we embraced the suffering of others, allowing it to seep into our souls. With every passing moment, our empathy deepened, and we came to understand the importance of connecting with the struggles and hardships of others.

We forged a bond with the shared human experience, our hearts becoming vessels for the collective grief of the world. The River of Sorrow had demanded compassion, and we had willingly surrendered to its currents. Along the way, we encountered countless stories of struggles and hardships, each a lesson in resilience and the indomitable human spirit.

As we reached the end of this sorrowful journey, a profound transformation occurred within us. We had learned the healing power of empathy, and our hearts had grown more compassionate. The River of Sorrow had been a crucible of emotions, and we emerged from its waters with a newfound understanding of human suffering. The stories of those we had met along the way lingered in our hearts, a constant reminder of the strength and courage displayed by individuals facing unimaginable challenges.

Our lessons were about the universality of pain and the incredible capacity for hope and perseverance that resided within each person. We realized empathy was not a passive emotion but a catalyst for positive change. Armed with this newfound understanding, we vowed to carry the lessons of the River of Sorrow with us, using them to make a difference in the lives of others and to inspire compassion wherever we went.

*

The River of Joy beckoned us with its vibrant and effervescent cascade of colors, each hue reflecting happiness and jubilation. As we stepped onto another boat, its form made of translucent light, we were immediately enveloped in waves of unbridled joy. The air resonated with laughter, and a symphony of pleasure echoed around us.

This river was a celebration of life itself, a testament to the beauty of existence and the boundless capacity for joy within the human spirit. The waters sparkled with a kaleidoscope of colors, each hue representing a different facet of human happiness. It was as if the essence of joy had been distilled into this shimmering river. As our boat glided effortlessly downstream, we became one with the river's currents, and it was as though we were dancing on the surface of happiness itself. Laughter

255

echoed in the air, a chorus of joyous voices that celebrated the collective moments of love, laughter, and ecstasy that had graced humanity.

We watched as scenes of jubilation unfolded around us. Couples in love shared tender moments, children echoed with infectious laughter, and people from all walks of life celebrated their triumphs. The River of Joy was a living tapestry of happiness, a vivid reminder of the beauty that could be found in even the simplest moments.

Gus and I couldn't help but join in the celebration. We laughed and danced with the river's currents, our hearts filled with gratitude and love. It was an experience that transcended the boundaries of the earthly and spiritual realms. As we swayed to the rhythm of the river's joyful currents, we felt an undeniable connection to the essence of life itself.

Amid this joyous journey, we understood the importance of cherishing the moments of happiness and embracing the interconnectedness of all living beings. The River of Joy taught us the wisdom of love and the transformative power of gratitude. As we continued down its vibrant waters, our souls were enriched by the boundless joy surrounding us, and we carried that radiant light within us as we prepared to face the final river on our quest.

*

On approaching the River of Tranquility, a profound serenity enveloped me like a soft, comforting embrace. This ethereal waterway mirrored the tranquil stillness of a moonlit night, its surface a reflection of the heavens above. Its waters held within them the collective serenity, wisdom, and moments of profound clarity experienced by all sentient beings. Unlike our previous journeys, there was no boat to carry us along this river's gentle currents. Instead, we consciously submerged ourselves into its chilled waters, allowing them to envelop us in their soothing embrace. As we did so, a sense of inner peace washed over us like a balm for the soul. The river cradled us, its currents guiding us with a gentle touch.

This was unlike anything we had encountered before. It was not a river of action and movement but of utter stillness. Here, the very essence of serenity seemed to permeate the air, calming the turbulence of our thoughts and emotions. It was a river that offered solace from the relentless ebb and flow of existence, a respite from the challenges and trials of the earthly realm. As we floated upon its surface, our senses were heightened, and our awareness deepened. It was as though the river itself whispered ancient secrets of inner peace and harmony. We learned the value of mindfulness, the art of being fully present in the moment, and the transformative power of meditation.

In the River of Tranquility, we discovered the profound wisdom that arises from inner stillness, the clarity that comes when the ripples of the mind settle into calm waters. This river prepared us for the ultimate task that lay ahead—to disarm the Asuras and penetrate the labyrinthine defenses surrounding the souls we sought to redeem. The river bestowed upon us the gift of tranquility, and we carried it within us as we approached the culmination of our quest.

A profound realization struck me as our journey through the three Rivers of Essence neared its conclusion. Gus, now a soul traversing the ethereal realms, and I, firmly anchored among the living, locked eyes in a silent exchange that transcended the boundaries of our existence. Our connection bridged the earthly and spiritual kingdoms, and in that shared gaze, our souls spoke a wordless language of understanding. The wisdom of ages was etched in our eyes, a testament to our transformation—one a soul on a cosmic journey, the other a mortal with a mission to fulfill.

The River of Sorrow had immersed us in the depths of human suffering, forging within us a wellspring of compassion that ran as deep as the river. The River of Joy celebrated the beauty of existence, filling our hearts with boundless love and gratitude for the interconnectedness of all living beings. The River of Tranquility had granted us inner peace and clarity, preparing us for the ultimate task.

Now, as we stood on the threshold of the next phase of our quest, we were no longer the same souls who had embarked on this journey. We had been renewed through the experiences of the three Rivers of Essence, and we were ready to face the challenges ahead with a newfound sense of purpose and understanding.

Our quest to bring about a shift in human consciousness and align it with the wisdom of the oracle was no longer a distant dream but a tangible reality that beckoned us forward. Our determination grew more robust with each passing moment, and our bond deepened. We were not alone in this endeavor, for we carried with us the collective wisdom of the rivers and the guidance of the spiritual realm.

As we stood on the threshold of the unknown, we were filled with a profound sense of hope and purpose. The wisdom of the ages flowed within us, and we were ready to share it with the world to bring about a transformation that would ripple through the tapestry of human existence.

Chapter 53
The Sun Demon

Remaining in the spirit world, Gus and I drew closer to the sub-earthly realm where the Asuras dwelled. Here, their malignant presence tainted the very essence of the place, and within their dark influence, the soul of the president was trapped. What was once a core of innocence and goodness was nearly extinguished, a mere flicker beneath the oppressive weight of the Asuras' grip. Still, we held onto the belief that somewhere deep within, a spark of his true self remained, struggling to break free.

The venom emanating from the Asuras intensified as we approached this foreboding realm. It surrounded us like a suffocating shroud, attempting to stop our advance. But we had been granted a newfound power, a reward for completing our earthly and spiritual quests. This strength allowed us to pierce through the barriers erected by the Asuras, leaving the tortured soul exposed and vulnerable.

The Asuras, aware of our intrusion, materialized before us, their forms grotesque and twisted, their eyes gleaming with sinister intelligence. Their voices resonated with a dissonant harmony that sent shivers down my spine when they spoke. "You dare to intrude upon our domain?" one of them hissed, its voice a cacophonous symphony.

I stepped forward, my resolve unshaken. "We seek to free this man's soul from your grasp," I declared, my voice carrying the weight of our purpose.

Gus's radiant form by my side added, "We've journeyed through the three Rivers of Essence, armed with the wisdom and power to confront the darkness that has ensnared him."

The Asuras recoiled, their grotesque features contorting with rage. They lashed out with tendrils of dark energy, attempting to thwart our progress, but Gus and I stood firm. Our inner light blazed brighter with each step toward the president's imprisoned soul. The air was tense as we pressed on, determined to face the forces that held him captive. The Asuras, sensing our threat, summoned their hideous powers desperately to protect their prize.

But we were unyielding, our determination unwavering. The battle between light and darkness unfolded in a whirlwind of ethereal energy and malevolent fury. The very fabric of the sub-earthly realm quaked with the intensity of our clash. As we reached the president, I could see the faint glimmer of goodness that still clung to him, like a fragile ember amid a storm. I extended my hand, my touch radiating warmth and compassion.

"Sir," I called out, my voice filled with kindness, "we are here to free you from the darkness surrounding you. You are not beyond redemption."

The soul trembled as if awakening from a long and harrowing nightmare. Once clouded with malice, his eyes met mine, and for a fleeting moment, I saw a glimmer of recognition and hope. The Asuras howled in fury, their power waning in the face of our unwavering determination and compassion. The battle between light and darkness raged on, but Gus and I knew we carried the essence of transformation— the power to redeem a soul lost to the abyss.

A sudden ominous presence loomed on the horizon. In the distance, a swarm of Asuras materialized, their numbers stretching beyond counting. Thousands of humanoid figures with grotesque features and wings buzzed like insects, their collective malevolence palpable.

With a synchronized, chilling unity, they launched a tremendous assault, their dark forms descending upon us like locusts. Their wings beat with an unsettling cadence, creating an eerie symphony. Gus and I braced ourselves as the swarm engulfed us. The Asuras' onslaught was unrelenting, their wicked intent evident in their many attacks. They struck with tendrils of dark energy, attempting to overwhelm us with their sheer numbers and venomous power. Their twisted figures rippled and writhed with malice. Gus and I extended our arms, and beams of luminous energy streamed from our outstretched hands, forming protective barriers that stopped the encroaching darkness.

Gus and I countered the attacks with a serene resolve, our minds attuned to the harmony we discovered through the three Rivers of Essence. With each thought of compassion, understanding, and unity, we radiated waves of positive energy that repelled the Asuras. Gus and I drew from the depths of our purpose, our connection to the mission of empathy and compassion. In their twisted existence, the Asuras carried the weight of their suffering, and some among them, touched by the light of our determination, wavered in their evil intent.

Gus and I knew that this battle was not just about defeating the Asuras; it was about offering them a path toward release from their darkness. Amidst their shared pain and desolation, I detected a glimmer of conflict, a yearning to be free from the obscurity that shackled them.

As we battled, I reached out, attempting to touch the fractured souls of the Asuras. Their malignancy was powerful and infectious, but within even the darkest of beings, there is a spark of potential for transformation. Gus's presence by my side bolstered my resolve. Together, we became a beacon of light within the swirling abyss of the Asuras' attack. We fought for the president and the redemption of others who had fallen.

As the battle raged on, I caught glimpses of the imprisoned soul, its flickering ember of goodness growing brighter. The Asuras, once united in their assault, began to falter as doubt and conflict rippled through their ranks. Some hesitated, their dark wings slowing. A fragile balance hung in the air—between redemption and damnation, between light that seeks to pierce the darkness and darkness that seeks to extinguish the light. As we began to think we had defeated the Asuras, dread encircled us. The air grew heavy, and an ominous, blackish-blue light flickered in the distance, beckoning for our attention. Gus and I exchanged wary glances as we slowly drifted backward, separating ourselves from this mysterious apparition.

As the presence drew nearer, its form began to take shape, emerging from the shadows with an eerie, evil grace. It stood before us as if forged from the depths of despair. Its wings, veined and twisted like the gnarled branches of a cursed tree, were the hue of charred charcoal, hinting at the hostility that emanated from within. This being possessed a sculpted torso, its muscular legs exuding raw, unsettling power. Its head was crowned with two ribbed horns that spiraled backward, like the grotesque adornments of a demonic monarch. Instead of a mouth, it had a hollow abyss that seemed to devour the very essence of sound.

Then, as if to defy the laws of reality, it spoke. Its voice echoed in our minds, a sinister presence that sent shivers down our spines. "I am the Sun Demon known as Sorath," it proclaimed, resonating with an otherworldly authority. The very air trembled in response, and the darkness intensified as if drawing all light and hope into its shadowy grasp. Its eyes, cold and reptilian, fixated upon us with a predatory intensity, penetrating the soul, stripping away the facade of our spiritual forms to reveal our innermost fears and vulnerabilities.

Sorath's voice reverberated through the sub-earthly realm as he continued to fix his gaze upon us. "Why have you intruded upon my domain?" His words chilled the echoing void. "What purpose could you, mere mortals and ethereal wanderers, possibly have that would lead you to defy my work?"

Gus and I exchanged a determined glance, our resolve unshaken by the Sun Demon's presence. I found my voice and spoke with conviction. "We are here to bring balance and harmony to the earthly realm," I declared. "Your influence has brought nothing but discord and darkness, and we cannot allow it to continue."

Gus added, his voice carrying the weight of centuries of wisdom, "We seek to free this soul from your evil grasp. Your corruption has nurtured him for too long, and it is time for him to find his path toward redemption."

Sorath responded with sinister, echoing laughter that sent shivers through our very essence. "Impressive," he hissed, his eyes narrowing with intent. "Your efforts, while commendable for earthly beings, one who has crossed into the spirit world, are ultimately futile. This human is mine, bound to me since his previous incarnations. His time has come, and the Asuras are ready to claim dominion over the earthly realm."

Gus and I stood our ground, unwavering. "You underestimate the power of redemption and the resilience of the human spirit," I countered. "We will not allow you to continue your maleficent reign."

Sorath's horned head tilted slightly, an eerie semblance of curiosity in his eyeless gaze. "Very well," he conceded, his voice dripping with condescension. "Let us see if your determination can withstand the might of the Sun Demon's wrath."

Chapter 54
Emma's Soul

Sorath, the Sun Demon, unfurled its massive, black wings, its veil-like membrane casting an ominous shadow that enshrouded me. It was like a palpable darkness descended upon my ethereal form, an inescapable cloak of hostility. Its voice, a sinister whisper that resonated within the depths of my consciousness, declared, "This is how I consume souls. Gus is already dead; he's useless to me, but you," it said, pausing to lean in, "you have potential. I'll take control of your essence here."

Fear gripped me, paralyzing my will as I realized the full extent of Sorath's power. It was a power beyond anything I had encountered, and the idea of resisting seemed futile. "Why, Sorath?" I pleaded, my voice quivering. "Why continue down this path of darkness and corruption? There is another way, a path toward redemption and healing."

Sorath's reptilian gaze bore down, an unsettling intensity that seemed to strip away my defenses. "You made it very easy by delivering yourself to me," it hissed, a cruel smile forming on its featureless visage. "When you return to the earthly realm, you will continue the work I've spent my eternity building upon."

I felt helpless in the weight of the Sun Demon's presence. Doubts gnawed at my soul, and the fear of becoming a pawn in its malignant schemes loomed large. I worried that my essence would be corrupted and I would spend an eternity under Sorath's grasp. With a sinking heart, I glanced at Gus, desperate for a lifeline, a glimmer of hope. But as the being's influence grew more robust, I feared that this might be when darkness prevailed, and its malefic grasp irrevocably ensnared my soul.

A chilling dread settled in the pit of my being as I realized the magnitude of the peril I faced. The very essence of wickedness had descended upon me, its insidious tendrils penetrating every crevice of my spiritual form. I quivered with fear, my heart pounding in a rhythm of terror I had never known. Slowly, inevitably, I felt Sorath enveloping me in an inescapable shroud of darkness. It was suffocating, like being submerged in an abyss of despair, and each passing moment seemed to tighten the vice-like grip, squeezing the life and light out of me.

Desperation welled within as I attempted to scream, to break free from his relentless grip, but it was as if my voice had been stolen, silenced by an unseen force. A sinister intrusion slithered down my throat, causing me to choke and gag, the sensation of violation intensifying my fear.

The world around me became a blur of shifting shadows and grotesque forms. It was a surreal and horrifying descent into the unknown, a journey into the heart of darkness that threatened to consume me whole. As the influence of Sorath continued to spread, my very essence underwent a grotesque transformation. I could feel corruption seeping into my soul, twisting and distorting my core. The sensation was excruciating and strangely alluring, a perverse pleasure amidst the encroaching horror.

I was overwhelmed by a fear unlike any I had ever known, a terror that gripped my soul and threatened to drag me into an eternity of darkness and despair. It was a moment of profound vulnerability, a stark realization that I had ventured too far and met my match in the sinister Sun Demon Sorath. A strange and unsettling sensation overtook me. It was as if a twisted force had seized control, and the once-clear boundaries of right and wrong blurred into a sinister gray. I felt myself slipping away from the perspective of the collective good, and a newfound selfishness began to dominate my thoughts. It was a perversion of pleasure that reveled in pursuing power and control over others. The idea of manipulating people to do my bidding became an intoxicating obsession, a debased thrill that sent shivers down my spine.

My perception of beauty took on a sinister allure, and I envisioned using it as a weapon to draw in those who could satisfy my dark desires. It was a vision of decadence and indulgence, a world where I could have everything I desired, regardless of the consequences.

The presence of the Sun Demon filled me with a twisted sense of empowerment. It whispered promises of boundless potential and limitless possibilities, all tainted by a perverse hunger for dominance. With its corrupting influence coursing through my veins, I believed I could ascend to unparalleled power and dominion.

Suddenly, a glimmer of hope emerged. Like a distant star, a faint white light began to shine, casting a feeble glow upon the shadows that enveloped me. This light felt different, purer, and filled with an invincible force. The distant glow grew, gradually encroaching upon the darkness that threatened to devour me, as if a divine beacon drew closer, pushing back the evil shadows that sought to claim my soul.

Then, in a breathtaking crescendo of brilliance, the radiance overwhelmed and surrounded me. A voice, resonant and commanding, rang out, shaking the foundations of the sub-earthly domain. "Sun Demon, you will release Emma. Your work here is done."

The words carried the weight of cosmic authority, and their sound reverberated through my very being. As the light intensified, I had to shade my eyes, for its brilliance was blinding. And there, emerging from the heart of the luminous radiance, stood an immense, majestic angel. Its form was glorious, with wings that stretched so far that their tips disappeared into the boundless expanse of the spiritual realm. The angel wielded a golden sword adorned with colorful jewels that sparkled like stars in the night sky.

I felt a sense of protection and liberation, as if the very heavens themselves had intervened to rescue me from the clutches of the Sun Demon. The angel exerted his divine authority with a majestic sweep of his open palm. The very gesture seemed to carry the weight of the cosmos as it pushed aside the Sun Demon, casting the baneful entity aside like a shadow in the presence of pure light.

"I am the Archangel Michael." His voice resounded with power and grace, a declaration of his celestial status that sent tremors through the spiritual realm. The Sun Demon, confronted by the presence of the great

Archangel, recoiled in fear, its menacing form slithering away into the shadows, vanquished by the radiance of the divine presence.

Stunned, I felt the poison that had threatened to consume me leave my being, as if Michael's presence had the power to cleanse the taint of my disease.

"You've done much," Michael said, his voice harmoniously blending compassion and admonition. "But you've gone too far, Emma. Forcing me to enter a forbidden place."

I felt a pang of regret and deep humility as I faced the Archangel, recognizing the gravity of my actions. "I am sorry," I confessed, my voice trembling with remorse, "but I needed to get to the president. I hope I haven't done you harm."

Michael's gaze softened, and he extended a hand toward me, the golden light of his touch infused with compassion. "A noble purpose guided your intentions, but you ventured into perilous realms. It is not for the living to meddle in the affairs of the sub-earthly. Some boundaries must not be crossed for the sake of both realms."

I smiled with gratitude and relief, for I had been rescued from the brink of spiritual corruption by the very embodiment of divine protection. The Archangel's hand reached out, and as he touched my head, a surge of pure, radiant energy coursed through me. In that moment, the boundaries between the spirit world and the earthly realm dissolved, and I felt myself being pulled through a shimmering portal of light. With a sudden and profound shift, I returned to the earthly realm; though unfamiliar, the surroundings enveloped me like a comforting embrace. I was alone, the ethereal realm and its tumultuous encounters now a distant memory.

The room was bathed in the soft glow of dawn, and peace and serenity washed over me. It was as if the Archangel lingered in the air with an essence of divine protection and guidance.

I took a deep breath, feeling the weight of my otherworldly journey slowly lifting from my shoulders. While I had ventured into the depths of the spirit world and faced the evil Sun Demon, I had also been touched by the grace of the Archangel, a guardian of light and purity. As I reflected on the experiences of that night, I knew that my path had been forever altered. I had glimpsed the realms beyond the earthly, encountered darkness and divine radiance, and emerged with a newfound understanding of the interconnectedness of all existence. I embraced the dawning day, ready to carry the lessons of my extraordinary journey into the world of the living, forever changed by the encounter with the spiritual realms and the beings that inhabited them.

Chapter 55
Mother

For what felt like an eternity, I had battled lethal forces and encountered divine beings. Time had lost meaning, and the boundaries between reality and the ethereal had blurred into a surreal tapestry of experiences. Then, as abruptly as my journey had begun, I found myself back in the earthly realm. I blinked in the soft light of a hospital room, the sterile scent of antiseptic washing over me. It was as if I had been torn from one world and thrust back into another, the transition jarring and disorienting.

As my senses slowly adjusted to the familiar surroundings, I became aware of a warm presence by my bedside. Mother's eyes filled with tears of relief and joy, and her hand reached out to touch mine. "Emmashka," she whispered, her voice trembling with emotion. "You're awake."

Emotions flooded my heart, and I struggled to form words. With a weak smile, I managed to whisper, "Mamashka." In an exuberant embrace, we held each other, our tears mingling in a profound connection. It was a reunion that transcended the physical boundaries, a testament to the enduring bond between a mother and her child. As I regained my strength and my ability to communicate, I felt an overwhelming need to share my experiences with her.

But as I tried to articulate my journey, I realized my words sounded like fragments of a dream, disjointed and surreal. How could I explain the inexplicable, the realms beyond human comprehension? "Mamashka," I began, my voice wavering, "I… I need to tell you something. I… I went to another place. A place beyond this world."

Mother's eyes widened with concern, and she held my hand even tighter. "Emma, you've been in a coma for six months. Your mind's playing tricks on you."

I nodded, understanding the skepticism my words might elicit. It all felt so real and vivid, yet I couldn't deny the possibility that it had been a product of my subconscious mind during my coma. But one truth remained undeniable, piercing my heart like a dagger. "Mamashka," I whispered, my voice breaking, "Gus… Gus was with me."

Her expression softened, and she squeezed my hand gently. "Emma, Gus…" Her voice trembled as she continued, "Gus is dead. He… he passed while you were in a coma."

I knew Gus had died, but the weight of those words bore down on me like a heavy stone. Gus, my soulmate and companion, had journeyed with me until the end. His fate had been sealed by the same enigmatic forces that had touched my life. Tears welled up, and I closed my eyes for a moment, remembering the radiant presence of Gus, his unwavering support, and the sacrifices he had made.

As I opened my eyes again, I met her gaze, and at that moment, I knew that Gus might have left the earthly realm, but the lessons and wisdom he imparted would continue to guide my path. Determined, I whispered, "I have much to share with you. About Gus, about the spirit world, about everything." And as we sat there, mother and daughter, bound by love and the experiences that had touched our lives, I began to weave the tale of my incredible journey, knowing that the mysteries of the spirit world were now a part of my earthly existence, forever shaping the course of my destiny.

*

The next day, I eagerly awaited Monica's arrival in my hospital room as the soft morning light filtered through the blinds. When she entered, her warm smile and sparkling eyes conveyed relief and affection as we embraced, momentarily dispelling the weight of our shared experiences and the world's uncertainties. "Emma," Monica said tenderly, "I can't believe you're finally awake. We've all been so worried about you."

Tears welled in my eyes as I clung to Monica, grateful for her unwavering support and comforting presence. "I missed you, Monica. It feels like an eternity."

Monica shifted her expression, a mix of curiosity and awe. "Emma, you look different. There's something about your eyes."

I nodded, realizing that my journey in the spirit world had left its mark on me, even in the physical realm. "Monica, there's so much I need to tell you." As we settled in a quiet corner of the room, I recounted the extraordinary events from the spirit world, including my encounters with Sorath the Sun Demon, and the Archangel Michael and the many lessons I had learned.

Monica listened with amazement and wonder, her belief in the inexplicable growing stronger with each word. "Emma, this is incredible. It's like something out of a fantasy novel. But I know it's real."

"Oh, it's real," I affirmed. "And there's more, but first, I want to hear about Gus."

Monica's expression grew somber as she recounted the events during my coma. "It was a chaotic time. Do you remember right before you fell into a coma, the Covenant was exposed? We're still unsure how, but it led to the capture and the eventual execution of Gus, General Harris, and Senator Clarke for treason."

"I do remember," I said, reaching to clutch Monica's hand. "But what about me? Why wasn't I—"

"You were spared," Monica interjected quietly. "Spared because you were in a coma. With your fame, Derek and his cohorts decided it was better to let you lie there, untouched, like a living monument to their supposed mercy. A vegetable, they presumed, with no chance of awakening. They never expected you to come out of the coma."

"Oh my," Emma murmured.

"They kept me around to operate the dream lab," Monica explained. "It was seen as a powerful weapon to exploit."

I shook my head slowly, trying to absorb the weight of her words. I imagined how the dream lab, a weapon in their hands, would contribute exponentially to the chaos that had enveloped America. The realization was a bitter pill to swallow. Monica continued her account of the world's transformation, and as she spoke, I felt a growing sense of disbelief and fascination. "America descended into madness," Monica began, her voice carrying the weight of the world's turmoil. "It resembled the darkest days of Nazi Germany. The president's power seemed insurmountable, his authoritarian rule casting a long shadow over the nation."

I listened intently, my mind struggling to reconcile the image of the ruthless leader.

"But then," Monica continued, her words filled with wonder and reverence, "as if he underwent a profound transformation by divine intervention, a veil lifted from the president's soul. He became a different person—a compassionate leader, driven by a genuine desire to foster unity and heal the nation's wounds." As Monica spoke, the room seemed to hush as if the air held its breath in awe of the extraordinary change she described. I leaned in, captivated by the magnitude of this transformation, my curiosity burning like a relentless fire.

The image of the president, once a symbol of ruthless authority, morphing into a sympathetic figure who sought to unite and heal, was beyond comprehension. It was a narrative that defied reason and logic. But from the perspective of the soul world, it made perfect sense. "It seems I was able to reach within and release him from the grip of the Asuras."

She nodded, her eyes reflecting the same sense of wonder that had gripped me. "It truly does, Emma."

Monica leaned in as she began to explain the changes that had taken place. "Emma, you won't believe the transformation," she began, her voice filled with enthusiasm. "He initiated bipartisan dialogues, reformed immigration, prioritized renewable energy, and enhanced health care. And that's just the beginning!"

As Monica continued, I was drawn into her description of this remarkable world. "He pushed to reinstate a woman's right to choose, pursued diplomacy for international peace, and promoted social justice," she said. "The improvements in education and how they addressed income inequality have been nothing short of astounding."

Listening to Monica, it became clear that these changes mirrored the democratic principles that defined this society. It was a world where voices resonated freely, and freedom of expression was a sacred right. Human rights were at the core, safeguarding each citizen's life, liberty, and dignity. Civil liberties were held in high regard, and diversity was celebrated. Transparency and accountability were the pillars of this society, and the judiciary stood as a beacon of justice. Even in the marketplace, a careful balance was struck between liberty and regulation, ensuring fairness. Environmental stewardship was paramount, protecting the planet for future generations and all cherished freedom of movement.

I couldn't help but feel a sense of hope and inspiration as Monica concluded her description. The journey toward a brighter tomorrow paved with the principles of democracy led this world out of the darkness of authoritarianism. It was a powerful reminder of what could be achieved when people came together to uphold the values of justice, equality, and freedom. The astonishing shift left me in awe. "All these changes in such a short time?"

"Yes," Monica replied, "your journey into the spirit world seems to have had a decisive impact, promoting unity and progressive policies."

I nodded. "Yes, Monica. It seems our encounters affected both the president and the world."

Monica absorbed the gravity of my words. "It's a testament to the power of the spiritual realm and our interconnected actions."

I felt mixed emotions as we contemplated our role in reshaping the world. The path ahead remained uncertain, but with Monica by my side and the enduring bonds of our shared experiences, there was hope that we could navigate the extraordinary and inexplicable, guiding our destinies in the ever-changing tapestry of existence.

Chapter 56
Searching for Gus

The transition from the dream world to the spirit world was seamless, a journey guided by the threads of destiny. As I emerged into clarity, I felt the familiar embrace of ethereal mists, signaling my arrival in the realm of boundless possibilities. In the spirit world, I soared among the celestial spheres, each one a tapestry of cosmic energies and wisdom. My quest was to reunite with Gus, who had embarked on a remarkable odyssey through these transcendent realms. It was a journey of self-discovery and karmic reckoning, and I was eager to share his afterlife experiences.

My feet carried me to the crimson expanse of Mars, a world bathed in an otherworldly radiance. On the Martian landscapes, I witnessed the dance of the Spirits of Motion. These beings shimmered like ethereal mirages, their forms fluid and graceful as they moved in harmony with the cosmic rhythms of the universe. But as I watched this cosmic ballet, my thoughts turned to Gus and our shared past and the time when I had ventured into the darkest depths of the dream world, where the Asuras held him captive.

Gus stood at the heart of this ballet, his presence a light in the Martian twilight. He conversed with the elusive spirits, their words carrying the weight of heavenly wisdom. As I approached, I marveled at the transformation that had taken place within him. When Gus turned to face me, his eyes held a radiant warmth that mirrored the love that had bound our souls through countless lifetimes. Our embrace was a fusion of ethereal forms, a testament to the timeless connection that defined our existence.

"Emma," Gus whispered, his voice a melody that resonated with the very essence of our souls. "I've missed you."

Tears of joy welled in my eyes as I held him close. "I've missed you too, Gus. Your journey has been extraordinary."

Gus nodded, his eyes aglow with the wisdom he had gained. "The Spirits of Motion have taught me the dance of karma, the intricate steps of cause and effect that shape our destinies. It's a dance that we all must master."

I listened with reverence as Gus shared the cosmic insights he had acquired on his celestial odyssey. The universe unfolded before us, a tapestry of interconnected destinies and cosmic forces, each step of the dance a profound revelation. Gus made a promise that resonated with the eternal nature of our bond. "Emma, no matter where our souls may wander in the vast expanse of existence, I will wait for you. Our connection is timeless, and we will find each other once more in each incarnation."

I nodded, my heart overflowing with love and gratitude. "I will always find my way to you, Gus, just as you will find your way to me."

With that, we shared a final embrace, our forms merging in a luminous clutch of souls. In that timeless moment, we knew our love would endure through the ever-unfolding tapestry of existence.

Gus returned to the Spirits of Motion as the figures took on shapes closer to recognizable human forms and began moving in an ethereal dance punctuated by energetic gestures, an interpretation of a living body in motion. First, they moved in geometric unison, then the dancers split into groups. Some formed wide circles, while others glided in straight lines.

It was as if I were witnessing the essence of life itself, a symphony of movements that transcended the boundaries of the physical realm. Each graceful gesture and fluid motion emanated a sense of harmony and vitality.

It was clear that the dance represented the living body's role as a conduit for vital energies, orchestrating the forces that sustained and animated the physical organism. I continued to observe the mesmerizing dance, captivated by the intricate interplay of the ethereal beings. They moved in perfect synchrony, their forms shifting and merging in a graceful display of cosmic choreography. I was peering into the very heart of existence.

As I prepared to return to the physical world, I carried a newfound understanding of the interconnectedness of all things and the beauty of the dance that sustained life itself. Our accomplishments in defeating the Asuras and ushering in a new era for humanity had been remarkable. Yet, I was aware that the Sun Demon would forever seek to return to challenge the harmony we had achieved.

My journey was far from over, and the cosmic dance of light and darkness would continue. But with love as my guide and the wisdom of the spirit world as my ally, I was ready to face the challenges ahead, protect the fragile balance of existence, and ensure that the flame of compassion and understanding would burn eternally bright.

THE END

About the Novelist

Neil Perry Gordon burst onto the literary scene with a flourish, his name synonymous with the riveting realms of historical and metaphysical fiction. With an impressive roster of twelve novels, his storytelling genius shines brilliantly in his latest opus: *The Asuras: A Dream World Odyssey*. Critics from Kirkus to the Midwest Book Review have lauded his narrative artistry, while a legion of fans on Amazon and Goodreads have festooned his works with glowing accolades.

An alumnus of the Green Meadow Waldorf School, Neil's fervor for storytelling was kindled and nurtured amidst an atmosphere that celebrated the arts not as mere disciplines, but as vital, living experiences to be wholeheartedly imbibed.

Regarding the craft of writing, Neil is a maestro conducting an orchestra of characters and plots, preferring to let inspiration lead in an organic symphony of creation. This approach has birthed tales replete with unexpected turns and thrilling escapades that keep readers on the edge of their seats. His narratives deftly weave intricate character development with heart-pounding action, striking a tempo that resonates with his audience.

Neil Perry Gordon's unwavering commitment to the written word and his flair for conjuring vivid narrative tapestries have cemented his status as a master of his genres. With every new title released, he continues to enchant and enlighten, offering sumptuous literary feasts that celebrate the profound tapestry of the human condition.